Is Life Fate or

A Novel

A. J. Bushy

Writers Club Press
San Jose New York Lincoln Shanghai

Is Life Fate or Destiny?
A Novel

Writers Club Press
an imprint of iUniverse, Inc.

For information address:
iUniverse, Inc.
5220 S. 16th St., Suite 200
Lincoln, NE 68512
www.iuniverse.com

ISBN: 0-595-24653-2

Printed in the United States of America

I dedicate this book to my late wife Sue

Acknowledgements

I would like to thank the new lady in my life, Cindy, who has given so much help, encouragement and understanding in the writing of this book.

Prologue

Gibraltar 1985

Entering the Mediterranean from the Atlantic, the Rock of Gibraltar looks majestic sitting just off the Spanish coast. As you pass through the straight of Gibraltar and further into the Mediterranean, the outline of the Rock changes. The man-made side of the Rock comes into view. Just like a winter sky-slope, the Rock reservoir makes the Rock look like something out of a Disney theme park.

The Rock is so important to the British Government. The military secrets she holds within its honeycomb interior are known to only a few.

The local residents can only guess or make up stories regarding the Rock's secrets.

The Spanish Government knows how important the Rock is. They still want the rock returned to them, because of its importance. They know it would be beyond their wildest dream for the British Government to give in and return such a valuable military outpost. It would be a miracle.

Some of the state of the art equipment includes a satellite tracking system that can pinpoint any ship in the Northern Hemisphere. There are the submarine pens that can keep up to six submarines hidden at any one time.

The underwater tracking network keeps a track on any underwater movement anywhere in the Mediterranean. The complex radio listen-

ing station could be the most valuable. It covers the whole Arab world, every radio conversation taped and analysed by British intelligence.

Inside the Rock, among the maze of corridors and offices, is the office of Brigadier Robin Baxter, commander in chief of British forces on the Rock and Mediterranean.

He was a small thin man with a weasel looking face.

Fresh out of Sandhurst, he had joined Field Marshall Montgomery as a junior officer. He distinguished himself in the North Africa campaign and later by crossing the Rhine into Germany.

Since then he patterned himself on his great hero Field Marshall Montgomery; like him, the army had become his life.

Brigadier Baxter was from the old school where discipline ruled the army. He hated the modern army—young soldiers running home to their mothers and fathers, complaining of their treatment! He was glad he was just weeks away from retirement.

He sat at his desk reading the daily newspapers. Every newspaper had headlines covering yesterday's events—the unthinkable shoot-out that turned the main square of Gibraltar into a battlefield. He picked up the London Telegraph. The headlines made him cringe: "Massacre on the Rock!"

The knock on the door interrupted his reading.

"Come!" he bellowed.

The Rock's adjutant Major David Oakley-Smith (his recent bride refused to be called Smith so they spliced in and hyphenated her maiden name, Oakley) was smart in appearance, but looked older than his thirty-seven years: black greased hair, parted in the middle, his complexion dark with a small but well-groomed moustache. The Brigadier was concerned. The Major was just a pen pusher: he had never seen action.

"What a bloody mess," the Brigadier said before the Major had a chance to say anything.

"Good morning Sir," the Major responded, ignoring the Brigadier's comments.

The Brigadier, aware of his rudeness, apologised and offered the Major a seat. "Well, what have you got for me?" he asked, modulating the tone of his voice.

"Well it seems the IRA had plans of disrupting the visit of H.M.S. Invincible and Prince Andrew. We don't know exactly what they were trying to do." The Major opened his briefcase and extracted some notes. "The problem is the moment M16 are involved they hush everything up. It's hard to get any information from them, but with the help from the local police I've been able to put two and two together." He referred to the notes he had in front of him. "The SAS had inside information and had the IRA under surveillance from the time they entered Britain in Holyhead. We can only assume the IRA realised they were cornered. So, they decided to go out in a blaze of glory—with as much publicity as possible."

The Brigadier interrupted: "What happened to the SAS survivor?"

"M16 put him on a military flight back to the UK last night. He's most likely being de-briefed at this moment." The Major returned to his notes in front of him. "In the last hour I've had a telex from London. It says there will be a press statement via the Foreign Office at noon today. A copy has been sent to the Rock's Governor."

The Brigadier sat there, his right hand rubbing his chin as if he were checking for stubble. His thoughts were interrupted by three sharp knocks at the door. "Come in!" This time the Brigadier spoke in a polite manner.

The door opened. Major Kenneth Kyle, a doctor in the Royal Army Medical Corps, entered the office and greeted the Brigadier with a "Good morning." The Brigadier liked and admired the doctor who was six feet tall with fair hair and was considered good looking: with his fair skin that was clean-shaven, his boyish looks made him look a lot younger than his forty-one years. He had the reputation of being quite a character and was a 'hero' amongst the solders. Besides his many tours of Northern Ireland, he had performed surgery while under attack from the Argentines during the Falklands war, for which he received the George Medal.

"Please sit down Major," the Brigadier said, indicating the chair next to the adjutant. "Do you have your report on yesterday's killings?" The Brigadier hoped it was straightforward.

"M16 wanted to see it first, but I came straight to you. It makes good reading." The doctor opened the green file, checking that the eight-page document was inside before handing the file to the Brigadier.

"I'll read it later. Just give me a run down on what you've found." The Brigadier laid the file on the desk in front of him. He looked at the doctor and waited for him to continue.

"Well, there were eight people shot; seven were killed outright and one is in intensive care. There were three IRA terrorists and two SAS men killed in an exchange of gunfire. Meanwhile stray bullets killed two civilians and wounded one man—that's our man in intensive care." The doctor paused for a response. Nothing came from the Brigadier or from the adjutant, so he continued, "Everything was straightforward. The two civilians killed were ordinary people who were in the wrong place at the wrong time. There was a young New Zealand radio officer, a crewmember on the British cable-laying ship 'The Essex.' The ship only came to Gibraltar for repairs. He'd only been married four weeks, the worst of it being his new wife was with him when he died."

Still no response from the two officers. "Our man in intensive care was travelling with a work colleague. Both were cabin crewmembers with British Worldwide Airways and were on holiday together. The young lady was killed outright."

The expression on the doctor's face changed to bewilderment. "As I said, everything 'was' straightforward. I took blood samples to analyse. That's when things became complicated."

He finally had the full attention of the Brigadier. "What do you mean, complicated?" The Brigadier picked up the file from the desk and shuffled through the papers.

The doctor pointed at the file. "If you turn to the last page—my findings are there."

The Brigadier turned to the last page and read to himself. When he had finished he looked directly at the doctor, at the same time handing the document to the adjutant. "Surely this can't be right?" he said to the doctor.

The doctor replied, "I'm not a pathologist, but the tests I have performed give me the results you have there. I've sent them to the military hospital at Woolwich to double-check. I should have the results confirmed within a week."

The Brigadier looked bemused. "So, what you're saying is, our man in intensive care fathered four of the dead, including one of the IRA members?"

"Yes sir," replied the doctor.

CHAPTER 1

1985

Corporal Paul Quinley put the gearstick into drive, released the handbrake and slowly eased his foot onto the throttle. The black Mercedes moved slowly through the ship's hull and up the ramp. The quayside at Harwich had not changed. He passed customs and moved out of the dock through the town. He followed the signs for Manningtree. From there, he would cross the country to Coventry.

Paul had been in the army for seventeen years. Only three years to go and he will have completed his twenty years service. He had spent the years as a driver with the Royal Corp of Transport.

The last three years he had been a driver with the diplomatic staff in the Western section of Berlin. He was one of the few army personnel with clearance to drive through the Brandenburg Gate into East Berlin. His duties consisted of driving western diplomats on inspection tours of the eastern sector—though on some occasions the so-called diplomats were clearly a part of British intelligence.

After every excursion into East Berlin Paul was debriefed by British intelligence, in case he had noticed changes within the sector. He never realised just how important some of the information he brought back was to British Intelligence.

MI6 and Special Branch were impressed with Paul's knowledge of the eastern sector and, in particular, his relationship he had established with many of the East German guards. These factors had MI6 and Special Branch pull a few strings to keep him in Western Berlin. He enjoyed the easy life so much he never realised the secret services were using him.

He liked the job he was doing; it was certainly far removed from the normal routine of army life.

The three years he had spent in the sector had taken its toll, however. Lack of exercise had affected his six-foot frame; he had gone from his normal fourteen stone in weight to sixteen stone. His hair was long, going grey and scruffy, and the large handlebar moustache, also going grey, would have looked better on a sergeant on horse guard parade.

Occasionally the normal routine was broken, and this was such an occasion. His orders were to drive the left-hand drive black Mercedes from Western Berlin to the Hook of Holland. He was booked on the overnight ferry to Harwich. From there he would complete the early morning drive to Coventry and the small back street garage.

Paul had done the trip on four previous occasions. Consequently he knew the route and routine. The mechanics would take the car and hand him a replacement. The modification to the Mercedes would take between ten to fourteen days. He would then collect the car and drive back to Western Germany. There it would mysteriously disappear.

He knew Special Branch will have taken it and handed it over to the SAS who would then use it for undercover work in the Eastern Sector.

Since leaving his quarters he had an uneasy feeling—a feeling of apprehension, and things were clearly not going to be straightforward.

He arrived at the garage just after midday and the garage owner handed him the keys to a Mark 2 Ford Escort, telling him to telephone the garage in ten days. This was the usual procedure, but he still felt uneasy and wished he knew why.

He had planned to stay with his parents until the Mercedes was ready for collection. The small farm was near the village of Meriden, about halfway between Coventry and Birmingham.

He hated the farm life and everything that went with it. It was one big struggle to make ends meet. He could never work out how his parents survived year after year. He never liked to visit them for it made him feel guilty.

The truth is he had joined the army to escape the farm. His father was so disappointed it took several years before he would speak to Paul. The last two years had been easier, for at least they were on speaking terms once again.

His mother was proud of him in army uniform. She knew he would never settle down to farm life. However, his father always prayed that one day his son would take over the running of the farm.

The quietness of the farm made a pleasant change to the hustle and bustle of Berlin. For the first time in his life he enjoyed helping his father. The fine weather encouraged him to rise early in the morning and do the morning milking.

The tens days passed by quickly. Paul had worked hard but had been pleased with the home life. For the first time in years he was able to communicate with his father. Even so, he was glad when the time came to telephone the garage.

He dialed the garage number. After two rings someone answered: "Tykes garage, John speaking." Paul hesitated. He was not expecting anybody to answer so quickly. "Paul here," he said. "I'm ringing regarding the Mercedes."

"The car is ready." It was John, the owner of the garage. "You need to pick it up today. By the way, you have new orders."

Before Paul had a chance to ask any questions John had hung up. The uneasiness returned. New orders—where were they sending him? He felt vulnerable.

He packed his bag, said his goodbyes to his parents and promised not to leave it long before the next visit. For the first time in nearly twenty years his father gave him a hug.

He made his way to Coventry and the small back street garage. He parked just to the left of the locked double doors and rang the bell. He knew from past experience you couldn't hear the bell from where you are. It rings in the back office so it takes several minutes for anybody to respond. It was two minutes before there was the sound of keys, followed by the sound of a bolt being pulled back.

Steve, a forty-five-year-old mechanic, stood at the door. "Oh it's you—John's in the back office. Have you locked the Escort?" He spoke with a strong Birmingham accent.

"Yes, here's the keys."

Paul handed the keys to Steve, entered the garage and made his way to the rear office. The black Mercedes gleamed under the garage lighting where it had its own parking space in front of the office. At a glance, the car didn't look any different.

John, the garage owner, was seated behind his desk. He was a tall, thin man, the skin on his face pale and scarred with pot marks. His mouth was sunk, giving the affect of being toothless, though he had all his teeth that were brown stained from years of smoking. This did not stop him from being smart, however, for he was dressed in a freshly pressed white shirt, blue tie and spotlessly clean red overalls. He was a man of few words.

He signed a cheque which he sealed in an envelope and placed in a tray marked 'OUT TRAY' before looking up at Paul. "Ah, there you are," he said, opening the top draw to his desk. "I was beginning to think you weren't coming." He removed a set of keys and an envelope. He handed both items to Paul. "The envelope contains new orders—you can read it here. The car is all ready. It has a fall tank of petrol. The tank's been modified—it holds fifty gallons. Anything else you need to know I'm sure your superiors will keep you informed."

Paul took the keys, placed them in his pocket, and opened the envelope. On the slip of paper inside were a set of numbers and the words 'Ring this number from a public call box.' Paul looked at John. "Is that all?"

"I'm afraid so," John smiled with a shrug. "Well, I need to get on, so if you don't want anything else I'll say goodbye and good luck to you."

Paul made himself comfortable behind the steering wheel. It didn't feel any different, but he knew from experience the work on the Mercedes would have run into thousands of pounds.

Steve had opened both garage doors; he stood at the entrance waiting to guide Paul and the Mercedes out of the garage. Paul turned the key to the ignition and backed the Mercedes towards the street. Steve gave him the all clear and Paul pressed the button to the electric window. "Thanks Steve, where's the nearest phone box?"

"Down to the end of the road, turn right. Fifty yards on the left there's two."

Paul waved a thank you and drove off. He stopped the Mercedes beside the two telephone boxes that were situated in front of a row of twelve shops.

He entered the first box and picked up the receiver, checking the dial tone. To his surprise it was working. He reached inside his pocket, took out the piece of paper with a telephone number, and dialed.

A woman's voice answered within two rings: "Yes?" The harshness in her voice made Paul hesitate.

"My name is Paul Quinley. I've been told to ring this number."

"Hold the line," she replied, and after a few minutes she came back on the line. "What's your pay number?"

He told her.

"Where are you now?" she asked.

"Coventry," he replied.

"Right, you are to make your way to Stirling Lines barracks in Hereford. They will expect you some time this afternoon. Report to the guardroom. Do you understand?" Paul tried to digest what she was saying. The woman became inpatient. "Do you understand?" she repeated.

"Well—yes," Paul finally managed to say.

She replied with a good luck and hung up. Paul was surprised by the abruptness of the call and why everybody was wishing him good luck. He made his way back to the car. His stomach had knotted up.

Stirling Line barracks—that was the SAS base. He wondered what they wanted from him. He was thirty-four years of age and until now he had kept well away from trouble. He had never had to put his life on the line for his country. Now, suddenly, he was wanted by the SAS!

His thoughts were interrupted by a policeman telling him to move on. The car was parked on double yellow lines.

He drove off, heading for the M6 motorway and Birmingham. He stopped fifteen minutes later for a late breakfast at one of the motorway cafes.

While he waited for his order of an 'all-day breakfast' he planned his route. He decided to take the A38 from Birmingham and join the M5 motorway at junction 4 until junction 8, then join the M50 motorway till the end; that would take him to the A49 straight into Hereford.

Just over three hours later he arrived. To his surprise the camp was in the middle of a housing estate. He drove directly to the guardroom. An armed corporal of the paratroops regiments walked round the back of the car and came to the left-hand drive side. Paul had already pressed the button to lower the electric window. The paratrooper, who held an automatic rifle and wore a red beret with a winged cap badge, glanced through the open window, keeping his distance. Paul saw that his badge had been painted black and thought he must have just returned from a tour of Northern Ireland where the cap badge was darkened so as not to reflect any light for the benefit of a would be sniper. The man was clean-shaven, about 5ft 10ins tall, with muscles on muscles.

"Can I help you, sir?" the paratrooper asked in a London accent.

Paul liked being called sir. "Yes, I'm corporal Quinley. I've been told to report to the guard room."

"Have you got your army I.D?" the paratrooper asked.

Paul took out his wallet. Next to his cash card was his I.D. which he handed to the guard. The guard proceeded back round the car and into to the guardhouse.

Paul was wondering what a corporal in the paratroops regiment was doing guarding the SAS. Thinking about it, he would most probably be on an SAS induction course. Many paras were fed up of throwing themselves out of planes. They wanted to be heroes and storm embassies. If that were the case he would have to take his turn on guard duty. Suddenly a sergeant with the cream beret and badge of the SAS appeared. He walked to the passenger side of the Mercedes and tried to open the door. Paul released the lock and the sergeant opened the door at the second attempt, got in and shut the door. The barrier separating the car from the barracks opened and the sergeant gave directions. After a few minutes Paul parked the Mercedes. The sergeant looked at Paul. "You can leave your gear in the car. However, you'd better lock it—you can't trust anybody around here." Paul couldn't make out his accent; might be the West Country, he thought.

He followed the sergeant to a small office with a sign reading 'Warfare wing.' Through the main door they came to a hallway with three uncomfortable looking chairs. The sergeant walked towards a door directly in front of them and knocked. An educated voice came from inside: "Come in!" The sergeant opened the door and indicated to Paul to enter and followed him in to the desk, handing Paul's I.D. to a man wearing the insignia of a Colonel.

"Corporal Quinley, sir."

"Thank you sergeant," the Colonel said and casually dismissed him: "You can leave us." The sergeant left the room with no formalities.

Paul stood at attention, too frightened to move. The man in front of him was clean-shaven but scruffy, his shirt a size too big and badly ironed. The knot of his tie was not tied in the manner one would expect from a Colonel. Paul felt disappointed, expecting the commander of the world famous SAS regiment to be immaculate. It would help, too, if the man combed his hair, he thought.

What Paul didn't know was that the man in front of him was a military genius. He had master minded the SAS operations on the Falklands and South Georgia. He was also involved with many operations in Ireland, north and south of the border.

He looked up at Paul. "Stand at ease," he said as if they where old friends. "Well, you're not the best specimen I've seen—but you'll have to do." He leaned back in his chair twiddling a pencil between his fingers. "Do you know why you're here?"

"No sir," Paul replied.

There was an unexpected knock at the door.

"Come in," the Colonel said in a manner that was so casual Paul was surprised the man had even bothered to call out.

The door opened and two men in civilian clothes entered. The first man was about 5ft 10ins tall, fit, tanned, and looked far too healthy. His dark brown wavy hair and his brown eyes went well with his tanned skin. The wide mouth with thin lips gave him the rugged look that most women find irresistible. He wore black casual shoes, blue denim jeans and a blue sloppy shirt. "Afternoon sir!" the man said with a Geordie accent. Paul suppressed a twinge of jealousy.

The second man had long hair with a nanny-goat beard and fawn-coloured jeans. The white granddad shirt went with the white socks and brown sandals. He nodded his head towards the Colonel without speaking. It was hard for Paul to believe this man was a member of the elite fighting unit.

"Right, gentlemen—now we are all here I would like you to be seated." The colonel pointed to the chairs arranged in front of his desk. "This is corporal Paul Quinley who I briefed you both on this morning." He pointed to Paul, then pointed his pencil at himself. "My name is Colonel Brown and this is Kevin." He nodded towards the good-looking brown haired soldier. "This is Ian, better known as Pickle." He directed the pencil towards the hippie look-alike. Colonel Brown opened a green file in front of him. "Well Paul, we have an urgent job on our hands and we need you as our driver." He turned a page in the file. "A quick bit of research and a bit of skullduggery on my part put your name in the frame. Special Branch and MI6 have a file on you and speak highly of the work you've done in Berlin."

Paul's expression registered total shock. "But sir, I…I only drive," he stammered.

"Well, that may be, but you must do it well for Special Branch and MI6 to sit up and take notice." The Colonel turned another page. "Anyway, you've been assigned to me until this operation is over." He looked directly at Paul. "I know you will have a lot of questions. Kevin will go into the details when he brief's you. Don't worry—you're in good hands. These boys will look after you."

He closed the file in front of him and looked at Kevin. "Right Kevin, I will leave it to you to brief Paul." He turned to look at Paul. "Paul, whatever happens, you stay close to Kevin and Pickle until this operation is over, understand?" He waited for a reply.

"Yes sir," Paul answered.

"Right, let's get on with it and good luck."

The three men stood and left the room.

Paul had felt at ease until the Colonel wished them good luck. He was the third person to do so today. He hoped he was not going to need it.

Kevin was a twenty-six year old orphan. He had never known home life. The only life he new before the army was the orphanage just north of Newcastle. He had worked hard to become part of the

SAS. Since he joined the regiment it had become his whole life. He lived and breathed the regiment.

He looked Paul up and down and smiled. "Let's go and look at what they've done to the Mercedes. Do you know anything?"

"No, I just deliver the car to your compound in Berlin," Paul explained. "There you boys take over, drive them to the Eastern sector never to be seen again."

"That sounds about right," Kevin said with a wide grin on his face.

Meanwhile Pickle excused himself and disappeared to the washroom. Kevin and Paul crossed the road to the Mercedes.

Kevin indicated to Paul to get in the driver's side and made his way to the front passenger door, opened it and got in. He leaned across and pressed a button under the steering wheel. Paul couldn't believe he'd never noticed the button before. The panel just below the gearstick opened, revealing a selection of eight switches. Kevin pushed down the first switch and a monitor appeared from just below the glove box. The second switch brought the monitor to life: the screen flickered, then revealed a map. Kevin looked at Paul. "Do you recognise the map?" he asked with humour in his voice.

"Is it the local area?" Paul asked with pride.

"Yes, very good. The built-in tracking device has a radius of fifty miles; as long as we have a bug on what we're following, we can't go wrong."

The third switch controlled the front door panels, and the fourth the rear door panels. The panels dropped: neatly packed in each door was a browning automatic pistol and a submachine gun. Kevin pushed the fifth switch and the middle of the steering wheel opened, revealing another browning automatic.

"Have you ever used a Browning?" Kevin asked, taking the gun and checking the safety catch was on.

"Only on the firing range," Paul replied.

Kevin returned the gun to the steering wheel compartment. "If we come up against any trouble, that's yours—only use it if I tell you to, understand?"

The sixth switch blanked the monitor screen and returned it to its hiding place. The seventh and eighth switches controlled the two-way radio situated in the rear of the car, neatly placed in the armrest.

Kevin explained that all the windows on the Mercedes were bullet proof. The fifty-gallon petrol tank took up most of the rear of the car. Kevin made his final check of the car, then told Paul to drive him and the car to the armory.

Pickle was already at the armory, checking and priming four stun grenades. He looked at Paul and smiled. "Ready for business?"

Paul was surprised to hear the excitement in Pickle's Welsh voice. He wondered why he was called Pickle.

In the meantime Kevin had drawn the ammunition for the fire-arms in the car. Both SAS men armed the weapons in the car and made them safe. Kevin turned to Paul.

"Right, let's go to my billet and I'll put you in the picture."

Pickle interrupted. "You don't need me for this briefing, do you?"

"Not really," Kevin answered.

"Right, drop me off at the NAAFI and I'll meet you in there later."

They dropped Pickle off and made their way to Kevin's billet. The room was small but comfortable. A T.V., Video and Hi Fi—all set on a sideboard to the left of the door. Facing the sideboard in the middle of the room was a settee, large enough for three people. Kevin beck-oned Paul to sit, then, going to the refrigerator in the corner of the room, took out two John Smiths cans of beer. Without saying a word he gave a can to Paul who accepted the can and pulled the ring. The look on his face showed it tasted good. He made himself comfortable and waited for Kevin to begin.

Kevin sat on a small coffee table facing Paul. He explained that an SAS colleague had infiltrated a part of the IRA in Dublin. He had been able to inform headquarters that an IRA cell was on the move.

They were booked on the Dublin to Holyhead ferry and would be arriving the next morning Friday 6th June. The man had managed to plant a tracking device on the Range Rover they were using. Kevin's orders were to locate the vehicle and follow at a safe distance.

Kevin finished his drink. "Would you like another beer?" he asked Paul.

"Yes please—that one went down well."

Kevin returned from the refrigerator with two more beers, handed one to Paul, then sat back on the coffee table and continued his briefing.

"What we need to know is what's their target, and when they intend to hit. When we have found out that information, we pass everything over to Special Branch. They will take it from there; they don't like us getting involved on the mainland. There's too many questions from the press." Kevin smiled "It's as easy as that."

Paul let out a sigh of relief. "Sounds pretty straightforward. When do we start?" For the first time he felt more confident and it showed in his voice.

"First of all, I'll see about a temporary billet for you." Kevin consulted his watch and looked back at Paul. "It's 1800 now, so we'll go for dinner in the mess, have a couple of beers and then bed. I'll arrange a call for 0300 hours; we can be on the road by 0400 hours, which will give us plenty of time." He added as an afterthought: "Oh, I'll expect you to plan the route to Holyhead."

The rest of the evening went as planned, supper followed by two pints in the sergeants' mess. At nine o'clock Paul retired to his temporary billet and lay on his cot-like bed and mulled over the day's events. Kevin had made the whole thing sound easy—so why did he still feel uneasy?

Kevin had certainly impressed him. He liked the man. He was sure he could rely on him. The only problem Paul had was that Kevin's mind seemed to drift occasionally, as if he had something else on his mind. Paul relegated the idea to the back of his mind. These boys knew what they were doing. Nevertheless his thoughts would not shut down and drifted back to the evening and he had to concede there were times when Kevin's mind seemed to be on other matters, but he hoped he was wrong. He remembered Pickle and the smile—was it the smile of a psychopath? Paul fell asleep hoping and praying all this was a dream. He would wake up in the morning in his nice safe bed in West Berlin. But no such luck.

The sergeant of the guardroom called them at 0300 hours. The three men were in the Mercedes and on the road by 0400 hours. The 155-mile journey took just under three hours. They had an hour to wait for the ferry to dock. They put the hour to good use, calling at the dock's transport café that served up three full English breakfasts with generous supplies of bread and butter, washed down with three large mugs of tea. "You can't beat a good breakfast—it sets you up for the day," Pickle observed with a broad grin.

Shortly before eight o'clock Kevin instructed Paul to drive to the ferry terminal. Kevin studied the road leaving the ferry. He worked out where to park so that no vehicle could leave the dock area without passing them. They parked and waited.

The ferry moored alongside the quay at ten minutes passed eight, its bow facing the exit ramp. The large bow lifted to reveal the watertight hydraulic doors; within seconds they opened and vehicles started the short journey along the ramp. It was five minutes before the Range Rover appeared—the vehicle was new but dirty. The original metallic green had become a rust colour with all the mud it had collected over the months. It passed the black Mercedes and headed towards the A5. Kevin was sitting in the rear seat. Pickle was in the front passenger seat next to Paul.

Kevin leaned forward with his head between Paul and Pickle. "Right, Paul, let's have the monitor on."

Paul pressed the button on the steering column and the panel opened. He pushed down the first two switches. The monitor appeared and the screen mapped out the local area.

"We'll give them 10 miles, then we'll follow," Kevin said as an order.

Paul suddenly thought of all the James Bond movies he had seen. Was it *Goldfinger* where Bond followed the Rolls Royce across the Swiss Alps with a tracking device? One thing Paul was not was a James Bond! Any action he would have to leave to the experts.

The monitor's screen showed the Range Rover ten miles ahead of them. Paul started the Mercedes, put the gearstick into drive and headed for the A5. It became a bore, mile after mile following a little bleep. The Range Rover only stopped once for six minutes, just before Shrewsbury, probably for petrol.

Pickle seemed to be mesmerized by the monitor, his eyes never leaving the screen. He was a man possessed.

Kevin sat in the rear of the car studying a map and trying to anticipate the IRA's next move.

Paul smiled to himself. Nothing seemed to be real. It was as if he had a front seat in a theatre watching everything from the outside. This could not be happening to him.

The uneasy feeling returned.

The Range Rover carried on through Shrewsbury to Wellington. There it joined the M54. Kevin said aloud, "I reckon they're heading for Birmingham. How's the petrol situation, Paul?"

Paul looked at the gauge. "We should get about 1,000 miles out of the modified tank; we've done 335 miles. The gauge will not kick in until the original 25-gallon tank comes into service. That should come into effect in another 165 miles. So there's no problem at the moment."

The Range Rover left the M54 and joined the M6.

"Birmingham or London, it looks to me," Pickle said without taking his eyes from the screen.

Within minutes the Range Rover left the M6 and joined the M5. Kevin glanced back at the map.

"It must be the West Country they're heading for," Kevin said, not meaning to sound surprised. He wondered what was so important for the IRA to bring out a cell in the open and put them at risk. This whole operation was unusual.

"It's the 6th of June. Can either of you think of anything going on in or around the West Country that might interest our friends?" Kevin knew he wasn't going to get an answer. Both Paul and Pickle shook their heads without answering. Kevin sat back in the seat and thought. "Right, this is what we're going to do—we'll increase speed and pass the Range Rover. Get as far ahead of them as possible. That will give us time to stop at the next Motorway service station. In the meantime I'll radio on to Brown—see if he can come up with anything." Kevin folded the map, disappointed he hadn't come up with any ideas. He had hoped to have had some idea what the IRA were up to by now.

The Mercedes increased speed. It didn't take long to catch and pass the Range Rover. Fifteen miles latter the Mercedes took the slip road to the motorway service station. Paul filled the Mercedes with petrol while Pickle visited the toilet and the shop.

Kevin sat staring out at the green fields waiting for the reply from Colonel Brown.

Paul paid for the petrol with money Kevin had given him minutes earlier. Pickle returned from the shop with a half dozen Mars bars. He handed one to Paul and Kevin. "Well," he said to Kevin, "has Brown been back to us yet?" Kevin shook his head as he tore the wrapper from the Mars bar.

To everyone's surprise the Range Rover entered the service station and stopped at the pumps next to the Mercedes. The Mercedes pulled away from the petrol pumps and parked in the Restaurants car park. Kevin produced a miniature camera and began taking pictures of the suspected IRA men.

The three men who occupied the Range Rover climbed out. The driver looked about fifty years of age with ginger hair on either side of a bald head. Two days of unshaven ginger hair covered his face. His dark green corduroy trousers were held up by brown clip-on bracers. A very large stomach, the result of years of drinking draught beer, hid the waistband of the trousers. His white shirt was wet with sweat under the armpits and down the back. The tail of the shirt had become free and hung loose outside his trousers.

He made his way to the rear of the Range Rover, unscrewed the petrol cap and started to fill the vehicle with diesel.

The man, who had been in the front passenger seat, stretched his thin body. He had long black greasy hair that rested on his shoulders. He was small and young—in his twenties—and dressed in black trousers with a shine that had come from years of wear. They were kept in place with a thick leather belt with a large brass buckle. The red checked shirt was a size too big. He made his way to the toilet, walking with a cocky sway. The black pointed cowboy boots with two-inch heels made him look feminine. Anybody who knew him would know not to tell him this—for he wouldn't hesitate to produce his colt revolver and blow a man's head off if he dared bring the fact to his notice.

The third man had dark brown hair, brown eyes and a dark complexion that made him look out of place as an IRA terrorist. He had class and it showed, for his clothes were not from any of the high street stores but designer clothes made to measure. Every movement suggested a man of authority.

The man reminded Paul of someone—and it took him several minutes before he realized the man was Kevin's double: they could be brothers.

Five minutes later all three returned to the Range Rover. The car moved off and joined the motorway.

Paul broke the silence. "If they needed fuel, I wonder why they stopped for six minutes on the A5? It wouldn't have been for petrol—or diesel."

"True, but I don't think we need worry about that at the moment," Kevin replied. "Give them the ten miles and we'll follow." He put his camera away.

As soon as the Range Rover had reached the ten-mile range, they followed, both vehicles travelling at a steady 70 miles an hour. Colonel Brown had been on the radio; there was nothing within the region they could find that could be of possible interest to the IRA.

Suddenly at junction fifteen the Range Rover left the M5 and joined the M4 heading east. Kevin grabbed the map and wondered what they were up to. Eight minutes later they pulled off the M4 at junction eighteen and joined the A46. They by-passed Bath and then joined the A36. Kevin put down the map. "It looks like they're heading for Wiltshire. Plenty of army bases to choose from there." He thought for a moment. "I think we'll close the gap to five miles." Paul responded and the needle went from forty to fifty miles an hour.

The Range Rover kept going, passed Salisbury down towards Southampton where it joined the M27 at junction two. It by-passed Southampton and headed east. Pickle, never taking his eyes from the monitor, pointed out that they had left the motorway and were heading towards Portsmouth.

Ten minutes passed before Pickle leaned forward and adjusted the monitor. He looked back at Kevin. "They've stopped. It looks to me like the ferry terminal."

Kevin thought for a moment. He told Paul to drive as close as possible to the terminal but out of sight of the Range Rover. Paul did just that.

Kevin told Pickle to have a scout around and try and find out what the IRA cell was up to. In the meantime he would radio through to Brown.

Kevin finished his call to Captain Brown. "We're to wait and see what Pickle comes up with, then radio back."

Paul couldn't stand it any more. "Why do they call him *Pickle*?"

Kevin smiled. "Well, the story goes like this: while on tour in Saudi Arabia training the king's personal guard, while on desert manoeuvres, one of the guards produced hashish. It wasn't long before everyone was stoned out of their mind. Pickle was a bit worse for wear—he drifted from the main camp and passed out. When he came to, local bandits had picked him up. All night they tortured him." Kevin took a slug of water and passed the plastic bottle to Paul before continuing. "Nobody knows what they actually did to him. Anyway, the next morning he escaped. But before leaving he cut off the balls of his torturer, put them in a container and urinated on them. The acid in the urine preserved them until he was able to return to base. There he put them in a jar and pickled them. As far as we know they're still in the back of his locker."

Paul laughed. He realised there was more to the scruffy long-haired hippie and made a firm decision never to cross him.

Twenty minutes passed before Pickle returned to the car. He sat in the front seat, turned and spoke to Kevin. "It looks like the end of the road for us—they're booked on the ten o'clock ferry to the Spanish port of Bilbao."

Kevin radioed the information back to Brown who in turn told them to stand by. A few minutes passed. Captain Brown was back on the radio. It could be the IRA cell was making its way to Gibraltar.

In two days' time HMS *Invincible* was making a three-day official visit to Gibraltar. Prince Andrew would be a serving crewmember on board the ship. They all agreed this was the most likely target for the IRA.

Colonel Brown was already pulling strings and having the Mercedes and the three men booked on the Bilbao ferry.

The new information had suddenly brought life to the SAS men—the monotonous surveillance work could now turn into a major operation. Kevin had new orders: no matter what happened, they must not lose the Range Rover. If the IRA cell crossed the border on to the Rock of Gibraltar, they were to detain them and hand them over to the local authority. Special Branch would take it from there.

Kevin consulted his watch. "It's 15:10—you two stay here. I'm going to check on the state of play." He opened the rear door and moved towards the terminal. He returned within minutes. "The Range Rover has taken up position on the grid ready for embarkation. I think we should do the same. Then perhaps we can find a place to eat."

Paul drove the Mercedes to the embarkation grid.

The marshals in bright orange tabard guided them into lane four. The Range Rover had taken up position in lane one between a Ford transit and a mini bus. Paul and his two companions locked the Mercedes and headed towards the nearest eating-house.

They returned to the Mercedes just before seven that evening. To their surprise most of the parking lanes had filled up. Three juggernaut lorries occupied the first lane, while four modern coaches, all from the same company, took up the next lane. The next two lanes were full with cars and their caravans, while the rest of the lanes had been taken up with about fifty assorted cars. Paul looked at Kevin, then at the ferry, *The Patricia*, then back at Kevin. "I can't believe this lot will get on board tonight," he said.

"Yeah, it doesn't look good," Kevin agreed. "Give me your passports. I'll check with the terminal." He took the passports from Paul and Pickle and headed for the terminal. He returned twenty-five minutes later. "Well, our tickets were there—we're on deck 5, cabin 5103, sharing, I'm afraid." He grinned and added: "Oh, by the way, the ship will take all these vehicles and more if need be."

The marshals started to allow the vehicles on board at 8:30 p.m. The Mercedes was on board by 9 p.m. The marshals had positioned the car amidships. From where they were they could not see the Range Rover. Paul and Pickle made their way to the cabin.

Kevin went looking for the Range Rover. He found it one deck lower in the bow section.

The four-berth cabin was small for the three of them. Paul folded one of the top bunks away into a recess. This still did not free much room. To the left of the main door was a smaller door that led to the shower and toilet. The cramped cabin was only large enough for one person at a time to shower and change—not that anyone wanted to share the shower.

The crossing took thirty hours, arriving off Bilbao at 4 a.m. Sunday morning. The ship was alongside at 5 a.m. Spanish regulations did not allow vehicles and passengers to disembark until 7 a.m. It was more like 8 a.m. before the Mercedes had cleared customs and the dock area.

Bilbao is a very large and busy town. The transmitter became more of a problem than an aid within the back streets of the dock area. Pickle took charge of navigation and followed the inconsistent road signs. It took them over an hour to reach the main E5 going south. In that time they had not been able to pick up any signal from the Range Rover. Kevin produced a local map he had obtained from the ship's duty-free shop.

After several miles they were still unable to pick up the signal from the Range Rover. "Is it possible the Range Rover is more than the fifty miles ahead of us?" Kevin asked, again not expecting an answer.

"It's also possible we're barking up the wrong tree," Pickle volunteered. "The IRA does have ties with the Basque Separatist movement. They work from northern Spain."

They all agreed to give it an hour and see what happens.

Within forty-five minutes they picked up the bleep from the Range Rover. Kevin studied the map. "I wonder if they'll head straight for the border or do it in two legs?" He folded the map in a way that would make it easy to consult at any time.

Allowing for a stop for petrol and food, Pickle reckoned they could reach the border around nine that evening. Kevin shook his head. "No, I think they'll do it in two legs."

It took just over three hours for the Mercedes to bypass Madrid on the E5 ring road. Paul was careful to keep the ten-mile distance between the Mercedes and the Range Rover. Paul made a mental note of the motorway signs. The last one had stated Cordoba 404km.

Four hours later they passed Cordoba.

Paul came off the motorway down the slip road and joined the N331, the main road to Malaga. The Range Rover had completed the same manoeuvre ten minutes earlier. A few minutes later the monitor indicated the Range Rover had stopped.

"So, they're having a night on the town in Malaga," Kevin said, leaning forward to study the monitor.

"What we need to do now is find somewhere to eat and hold up for the night." They came to a little village just north of Malaga.

The Range Rover had still not moved. "Let's hope they stay where they are for the evening," Kevin said, indicating to Paul to stop. The village tavern supplied them with steak, chips and salad, washed down with a bottle of local red wine. Kevin checked the monitor twice—so far so good.

The wine relaxed all three of them and soon they were back in the car heading for Malaga. Paul drove back onto the N331.

Two miles further Kevin suddenly said, "Turn right here!" They turned onto a small dirt road. Fifty yards along the dusty track they came to an olive grove. "Park here," Kevin instructed. "We'll stay put here till they're on the move again." He pulled out a coin, flicked it in the air, caught it and placed it on the back of his hand. "Paul, what do you want—heads or tails?"

"Tails," Paul said, not caring one way or the other.

Kevin took his hand away. "Tails it is—first, second or third watch?"

"I'll take the third." (He knew he would have two hours sleep; he felt tied and lifeless.)

Kevin took the first watch, each person doing an hour followed by two hours' sleep.

Paul began to feel uneasy again. He wondered what tomorrow would bring. The driving had tired him. He wanted to sleep, but sleep never came. When he finely fell asleep Kevin disturbed them.

"Quick! They're on the move."

Paul woke in a panic. He had trouble adjusting his seat. He checked the time—6 a.m. He started the engine, engaged first gear and they were on their away. Kevin had worked out they were about two hours away from Gibraltar, so they needed to be right on the Range Rover's tail before crossing the border. Kevin instructed Paul to make up the distance between them. They caught up with the Range Rover in just over an hour. For the final run into Gibraltar they kept the Range Rover in sight.

They reached the town of La Linea just after 8 a.m. There were fifteen cars and vans waiting at the crossing, each vehicle taking about six minutes to clear. A Fiat van had placed itself between the Range Rover and the Mercedes.

An hour and ten minutes later the Spanish guards had cleared the Range Rover. Fifty yards ahead of them was the Gibraltar immigration post, manned by men in the unmistakable uniform of the British bobby. This time the Range Rover and its passengers were cleared and released within ten minutes.

Lucky for the Mercedes and its crew, the driver of the Fiat was a Spanish national, late for work on the Rock, and the Spanish police let him pass with just a quick check of his papers.

Paul drove forward a few feet. A Spanish policeman put his head through the open window with the greeting: "*Buenos Dias*?"

"*Buenos Dias*!" responded Pickle who struck up a conversion in Spanish with the policeman.

The policeman was impressed by the way he joked and laughed. Pickle turned to Kevin and Paul, indicating the policeman wanted their passports. He in turn passed them to the outstretched hand of the policeman who checked them while another policeman at the rear of the car indicated he wanted the boot opened. Paul released the catch from inside the Mercedes. Pickle in the meantime had got out and was speaking to both policemen. They checked the boot and the passports were handed back to Pickle who replied, "*Gracias!*" and got back in the car.

"Right, we're all clear to go," he said. The barrier in front of the Mercedes slowly lifted. Paul eased the large black car slowly towards the Immigration post. As he approached the barrier the red stoplight turned to green, the barrier lifted and a policeman dressed in black trousers, white shirt and the typical British helmet waved the Mercedes through.

Traffic lights controlled all movement across the main Military and civil runway that separated the Rock from the mainland.

Again, the red light turned to green, giving the Mercedes right of way. Colonel Brown had cleared a path for them.

"Switch the monitor on, Paul—let's see where they are." Pickle tapped the monitor as if he were checking whether it was working or not. "It looks as if they're parked up in the main square." He turned towards Kevin in the rear seat.

"Right, let's see what they're up to," Kevin said. Pickle, who knew the Rock well, guided Paul and the Range Rover to the main square.

As the Mercedes turned into the square, the Range Rover pulled in front of them side on. The only person in the vehicle was the fifty-year-old driver. The Mercedes stopped fifteen feet short of the Range Rover.

Without warning the young man with long greasy hair appeared leaning on the bonnet of the Range Rover, a 9 mm submachine gun directed at them. Paul instantly released both switches controlling the door panels. Everything seemed to go into slow motion while in reality his action had been quick thinking and impressed both Pickle and Kevin. Paul crouched down, making himself as small as possible under the steering wheel.

The young man squeezed the trigger of the submachine gun.

The bullet-proof windscreen shattered but did its job—not one bullet penetrated the interior.

Pickle took the submachine gun from its hiding place, opened the door and stepped out, using the door as protection. The young terrorist fired again. Twelve rounds penetrated Pickle's ankles and lower legs. The pain was unbearable...

The pain he had endured in the Saudi Arabian desert was unbearable. The smiling toothless Arab torturer and four accomplices held him down with his legs spread-eagled like a woman giving birth. His torturer used a hot poker to burn his penis and testicles, and as if that wasn't enough they finished off their evil work on his anus. And they performed this unspeakable deed just for the fun of it. His penis and testicles were so badly burned that sex had become impossible. He hated having bowel movements which brought immense pain. Nevertheless, the memory brought a smile to his face...his torturer, wherever he was, was minus his penis and balls. They were safe in his locker—in the pickle jar.

The pain in his feet and lower legs was so intense his legs were unable to support him and he crumpled to the ground. The terrorist, seeing Pickle on the ground, fired another burst, this time hitting him in the chest, neck and head. Pickle died without having returned a single shot.

Kevin had taken his favourite weapon, the 9 mm browning, from the Mercedes' rear door panel. The young terrorists had been so busy concentrating on Pickle that he hadn't noticed Kevin who climbed out of the back door, taking cover at the rear of the Mercedes. When the firing stopped, Kevin took aim and fired once. The bullet hit the youngster between the eyes, killing him instantly. The driver of the

Range Rover appeared from nowhere, grabbed the young man's machine-gun and tried to aim and fire. But the rage within him made him unsteady.

Kevin adjusted his position and squeezed the trigger twice. The first bullet hit the man in the throat. The man tried in vain to yell abuse. Before he realised he couldn't speak the second bullet took his right eye out and blew the back of his skull away.

Twenty feet behind Kevin, hidden in a doorway, stood the figure of the third terrorist. The elegant man in the designer clothes moved forward and raised the Usi German automatic machine pistol.

The gun was not accurate at a distance, but at ten rounds a second it was deadly at close range. He moved three paces forward and fired a short burst. Ten out of the fifteen rounds hit Kevin in the back, giving him no chance to return fire. It was the second bullet that killed him, ricocheting off his spine into his heart.

Paul had watched Pickle die. He heard Kevin open the rear door, then the sound of a single gunshot, a short lapse, then two gunshots in quick succession. From his position kneeling under the car's dashboard he could just see out of the rear door. The sight of Kevin lying face down, his back a mass of blood, spurred him into action.

He reached for the selection of buttons, pressed down the fifth switch, and the inner part of the steering wheel opened to reveal the Browning automatic pistol. He made sure the safety catch was off and crawled out of the car through the passenger door over Pickle and to the rear of the Mercedes. Kneeling behind the wheel, he heard footsteps approaching the car. He stood up quickly, pointing the gun in the direction of the footsteps. The terrorist's face registered complete surprise—he didn't expect to see anyone alive.

Paul squeezed the trigger, again and again, until the gun was empty.

The terrorist fell. As he died his trigger finger set off the Uzi machine pistol that spat bullets around the square until the magazine was empty. All went quiet. Then a scream—then another—and another.

CHAPTER 2

Terry 1958

Terry Gibbons took his suitcase from the taxi's front fender, leaned across and gave the driver seven shillings and sixpence and told him to keep the change. He tended to over tip, knowing there are certain jobs that rely on tips—like his own job.

He stood and looked up in admiration. The ship looked magnificent. The white hull and white superstructure blended in nicely with the beige funnel. The twenty thousand-ton liner overshadowed the large cargo sheds of King George the Fifth dock. S.S. *Argentine*, flagship to the British-owned South Atlantic line, was one of the largest liners to enter the London Royal Docks.

In 1953 the ship had been launched at Belfast shipyard, built especially for the beef trade. Five hundred thousand cubic feet of refrigerated cargo space made it one of the largest ships to import beef from Argentine. Besides the cargo space it could accommodate one hundred first-class passengers with all the pomp and luxury a first-class passenger would expect. Below decks there was accommodation for four hundred tourist passengers, usually emigrants from Spain and Portugal preparing for a new life in Brazil or Argentine.

Terry made his way to the gangway. He was returning to the ship after ten days leave. Ten days was quite enough—he couldn't wait to get back into the swing of things. The Merchant Navy had been his life since leaving school at fifteen. He had joined the S.S. *Argentine* as a pageboy six years earlier and was now a senior steward in charge of the first-class lounge.

Terry stood five feet ten inches tall. The healthy bronze tan went well with his dark brown wavy hair, a result of years of taking advantage of the South Atlantic sun. His thin lips and generous mouth gave him his natural good looks. Besides this, he had been gifted with dark brown sexy eyes that seemed to captivate women. He never needed to invite women to his bed—his eyes did it for him. He looked good in his navy blue blazer and grey trousers. He was always well dressed and took great care regarding personal hygiene.

At the top of the gangway he had his identity card checked by the shore side quartermaster who informed him the door to the crew quarters was locked due to the main working alleyway being painted. For the time being crewmembers were to use the passenger alleyway on C deck, then make their way to amidships and enter crew quarters from there. He walked the alleyway to amidships where there were two watertight doors. He knew from experience that the left-hand door led to the stewardesses' quarters—twelve single cabins. For the first time in ages he thought of Carol and wondered what had become of her. Behind the right-hand door was a stairway leading to the crew cabins.

He opened the right-hand door and made his way down the stairway, turning left at the bottom; three doors along he dropped his case and produced a key. He entered the cabin that was just as he and his cabin mate, John Long, had left it—spotless.

John, a large round-faced Yorkshireman from Harrogate, would take the night sleeper from Leeds and arrive back at the ship the following morning.

Terry put his case on the bottom bunk and started to unpack. Strangely, his mind went back to his first voyage and the first encounter with Carol. He would never forget that voyage.

* * *

His first time on a ship, the fifteen-year-old 'East-end'-wise boy felt vulnerable amongst the three hundred older crewmembers. He felt silly in his pageboy uniform with its pillbox hat, maroon jacket and white gloves. He may have felt silly, but he looked smart. It wasn't long before he found out he could use the uniform to his advantage. The older lady passengers loved to mother him and use him for any type of errand. This led to the ladies trying to gain his favours by over tipping him.

Terry loved the attention and played the passengers against one another, making him more money then he had ever seen before.

The duties of a pageboy depended on the roster for the day. The day Carol entered his life the roster had assigned him to the Purser's office as a messenger. He had finished his morning duties, eaten lunch, and had decided to go on deck to sunbathe. The sun felt good. He closed his eyes and dozed. He woke with embarrassment—the erection he had was forcing his penis outside his swimming trunks! He looked around and gave a sigh of relief—nobody had noticed his predicament. He decided on a shower before starting work and picked up his towel and pillow and sensed someone was watching. He looked up to see a stewardess in her white uniform. She looked down at Terry, licked her lips and grinned. He blushed and made a hasty retreat to his cabin.

He showered, dressed for duty, and at 4 p.m. reported for duty at the purser's office. His first task was the to deliver the daily newssheet which had the next day's entertainment information. These newssheets had to be delivered to all first-class passenger cabins that afternoon. This became the bedroom stewards' and stewardesses' responsibility. It was Terry's job to make sure all stewards and stewardesses had the correct quantity.

He started his round on 'A' deck. He knocked on the door of the steward's pantry and walked in. His face reddened. The lady in the white uniform was sitting on a stool drinking a cup of tea. He knew her as Carol, an 'A'-deck stewardess. He walked to the workbench.

"Hi, how many newssheets do you require?" He tried to hide his embarrassment and, to make it worse, his erection returned. Carol, turning to the sink and rinsing her cup, replied, "All cabins are taken. If you give me thirty-three—eleven for me, eleven for Tom and the same for Robin..." He counted out thirty-three newssheets. When he turned to leave she was standing between him and the door. She locked the door and placed the key down her brassier, smiling. "I think we should do something about your problem, don't you?" she said sweetly, moving towards him and kissing him.

Though Terry was a virgin he thought of himself as experienced when it came to kissing. He hadn't realised he had moved up a class. Her tongue was down his throat, her lips acting like a plunger, sucking his breath from his lungs. At the same time, her hands where undoing the buttons of his fly. Before he could take in what was happening his trousers where around his ankles, his underpants around his knees. He had an erection that beat all erections—so hard and urgent he felt proud of himself!

Carol looked down. "Ooh, you *are* a big boy." She dropped to her knees, her mouth enveloping his penis. It wasn't long before beads of sweat appeared on his forehead. His legs went weak and his penis erupted like a volcano. She sucked, milking him with her lips till there was nothing left. Then she stood up and looked at him. His embarrassment turned to joy, for he had never experienced anything like this in his life. She reached into her brassier, produced the key and unlocked the door. Terry hadn't finished dressing. She turned and looked at him, her eyelashes fluttering as if butter wouldn't melt in her mouth. "If I knew I was going to have that for tea I wouldn't have had lunch." Terry left in a hurry, lost for words, but he would never forget the words she spoke to him.

Any excuse Terry had he made his way to the pantry on 'A'-deck, yet not once in six days did Carol acknowledge him. He began to think his inexperience had put her off. On the seventh day they passed on the main stairs. She smiled and asked him if he would like to come to her cabin for a drink after work that evening?

He finished work just before 10 p.m. He showered and put a fresh uniform on, for he would be in a lot of trouble if he were caught on the upper decks in civilian clothes. He made his way to Carol's cabin, knocked on the door that opened within seconds. He looked at her in amazement. The transformation was unbelievable. During the day her hair had been platted together, placed on top of her head in a bun that made her look plain and older than she actually was. She had now let her hair down. The long blonde hair hung just below the shoulders and swept to the left side of her face covering her left eye. The right ear had a long dangling earring. She reminded him of a film star.

She was wearing white ski pants; a red silk blouse with the corners tied around her waist made her bust more prominent. She wore a lot of makeup, but it suited her. Her two upper front teeth showed slightly under her top lip, which gave her face a smile that would melt any man's heart. Terry couldn't believe his luck—he'd never been alone with anybody who looked so sexy.

"Well, come on in, then, I won't bite!" She took his arm and, guiding him in, shut the door behind him. "Make yourself comfortable," she said, pointing to a small armchair. "What would you like to drink?" She walked sensuously to the small desk next to the bunk bed. The desk doubled as a drink trolley containing a bottle of whisky, a bottle of gin, an ice bucket and two glasses. He had only drunk beer in the past.

"Whatever you're having will be okay for me," he said, not knowing what to ask for.

He sat there studying the cabin. It was about ten feet by twelve feet. The desk where the drinks were kept faced the bunk that was fairly high off the ground, allowing room for two sets of draws. Behind him, set into a recess, was a small wardrobe with two doors.

Everything spoke of a woman's touch—the frills on the curtains that covered the small porthole, the Persian carpet that covered most of the floor.

She filled two large stemmed glasses with ice and a slice of lemon before taking the top off the Gordon's gin bottle, pouring a two-finger measure in each glass. She opened the door to the desk and removed a bottle of Tonic water, opened it and filled both glasses to the top, handing one to Terry. "Strong enough for you?" she asked, taking her glass and sitting on the bunk facing him, her feet dangling about six inches off the ground.

Terry, not knowing what to expect from his drink, took a sip, then another. He was pleasantly surprised and took to the taste as if he'd been drinking gin and tonic all his life. "It's lovely. Thank you." A lot of small talk and two drinks later she patted the bunk. "Aren't you going to join me?" It was more of a plea then a question. He wondered whether she had noticed his large erection.

He removed his shoes and jacket and sat next to her. It wasn't long before she took charge and started to undress him with skill; within minutes she had him completely naked.

He only had three items of her clothes to remove but his fingers got in the way of his thumbs and visa versa. It seemed to take an age, but in fact she was impressed and became visibly excited.

They kissed and Terry became more and more confident with every second. Her tongue moved from his mouth to his ear, then his neck. Her tongue flicked in and out like a viper's tongue, which gave Terry an unexplainable sensation. All the time she was on the move, to his nipples, further down to the belly button, bypassing his penis down the right leg to his toes. She spent several minutes sucking his toes, then up the left leg to the testicles. Her tongue massaged and kissed both testicles. Terry thought he was in heaven.

She then moved up his body, sat astride him, making sure his rock hard penis slipped into her as far as possible. She moved slowly up and down. Though he had been a virgin up until then he still felt guilty, for she was doing it all. He knew he had a lot to learn. He couldn't control himself any longer and within minutes his sexual juices flooded her vagina.

Carol took great pleasure in all that happened. "Sorry," he said, thinking he hadn't satisfied her. But he never realised her satisfaction came from having sex with young men half her age.

"Don't worry—you'll learn with experience," she smiled, getting up to pour another drink. They sat on the bunk drinking and talking, completely naked and with no inhibitions. Terry felt himself become aroused again. This time he wanted to take charge. He took her drink and put it on the table with his. "I want to make love to you this time," he whispered, and she lay back on the bunk obediently, smiling, wondering what to expect.

He copied her every move until his tongue came up her left leg. There he stopped and manoeuvred her legs so they were over his shoulders. His tongue entered her vagina and explored her silky inner flesh until he found her clitoris; there his tongue worked overtime. Her moans became louder. He stopped, moved up her body, making sure her legs stayed around his shoulders. His penis entered her and her moans turned into little pleading screams of "Yes—Oh yes!" followed by one long scream of "Ye-e-s!" Within seconds Terry's love juices spurted into her.

Carol lay there, looking at the young man next to her. He was not the usual young boy she had taken advantage of—this boy proved himself a man when it came to love making. He was born to make love and he knew he would make many women sexually happy, though he would break many hearts at the same time.

They became sexually very close for the remainder of the voyage. Terry always looked and acted a lot older then his sixteen years; indeed, he was more like a twenty-five-year-old man. He was also blessed with youthful good looks and would look twenty-five until he was in his forties.

However, by the time the voyage was nearly over, Terry was becoming increasingly bored with the situation and longed for other women. But Carol had made the big mistake of falling in love with him, though she realised nothing would come from the relationship. She doubted whether any woman would be able to control this young man. Both Terry and Carol, not knowing what the other was thinking, decided to end the relationship the day the ship docked at Tilbury.

The night before the ship docked Terry went to Carol's cabin and they made passionate love, exploring each other's bodies as if for the first time. Terry left the cabin in the early hours, deeply satisfied. It would be a generation before Carol entered his life again.

Terry's mind drifted back to the present.

He had finished unpacking. He lay on his bunk, set the alarm clock for eight o'clock that evening and fell asleep thinking of Maria.

Three hours sleep did him the world of good. He showered and dressed in his new Italian-styled suit before making his way ashore. He had plans to spend the evening touring the public houses within the dock area.

He felt good. He loved his life as a seaman.

CHAPTER 3

Carol 1953

Carol succeeded in avoiding Terry on her last day aboard the ship. She shared a taxi with her two work colleagues Tom and Robin to Waterloo station. Tom and Robin were both in time to catch the boat train home to Southampton.

Carol waited thirty minutes for her train to Bagshot. She had inherited the cottage from her mother who had died two years previously. She had been born in the cottage in the year 1919. Her father had been a professional soldier and stationed at Aldershot until the outbreak of the Second World War. Joe her father had been killed on the beaches of Dunkirk. Her mother never recovered from the shock and Carol spent the next ten years nursing her. She died on Boxing Day 1950 from a brain tumour, so the doctor said. Carol thought it was more from a prolonged broken heart. The one thing that came from her mother's death, besides the house, was freedom. Within six months she had become a stewardess in the Merchant Navy. She never realised life could be such fun. But she had one weakness—she enjoyed the thrill of young men! First, she would mother them, and then she would take them to bed and teach them the art of lovemaking. Perhaps it was all the frustration that had built up over the years nursing her demanding mother that had made her like she was.

The train journey to Bagshot was long and monotonous, stopping at all stations south. She sat staring out of the window pondering over the last fourteen weeks. She had got herself into a right mess.

She was not a bad woman, but she couldn't help herself when it came to young virgin boys—they turned her on so. This time the boy had not only turned her on, she had fallen in love with him. If that were not bad enough, the ship's doctor confirmed this morning that she was twelve weeks pregnant.

Carol's train pulled into Bagshot station at ten past three. She struggled with her case onto the platform. "Let me give you a hand, Miss Saunders," Reg offered, taking hold of her suitcase. Reg had been the station porter at Bagshot for ten years, ever since he left the sanatorium after his period of convalescing. He had nearly died in 1939 with Tuberculosis, but had been lucky, being one of the very few to come out alive. The doctors saved him by removing a damaged lung.

Reg looked a lot older then his thirty-six years. His lined, drawn face looked like a badly creased sheet that had just came out of the wash. Beside his ill health and pasty look, he was a man everybody loved; the extra attention he gave to the passengers was not for reward but for honest concern.

Reg and his wife Val had been Carol's next-door neighbours for six years. She was proud to be the Godmother to their two daughters, four-year-old Sandra and Karen, the six-year-old little madam.

"You look tired, Miss Saunders," Reg remarked with concern.

"Reg," she replied with a weak smile. "How many times do I have to tell you, my name's Carol? But I do feel tired—it's been a long day."

"The next train isn't due for another forty minutes," he said with a broad grin. "I'll carry your case home for you."

Carol wondered how he kept himself so lively and happy. Nothing seemed to get this man down—he had a good word and a smile for everybody. Suddenly she felt humble and ashamed of herself; she should be glad she was able to bring a new life into the world.

"Reg, you're a hero," she smiled, taking his arm and heading for the exit as if they were an old married couple. A hundred yards from the station down a small incline on the left stood a row of eight cottages. Carol's was the third cottage. Reg lived in the fourth. She took the keys from her bag and opened the door. "Would you like me to take the case upstairs?" Reg asked, already on the first stair.

"Yes, please Reg."

Seconds later he was back. "Val.'s been in this morning and aired the rooms," he said, making his exit.

"Tell her I'll be in later to see her and the kids—Bye."

She looked at him walking back to the station, his uniform cap pushed back on his head while he whistled am unrecognizable tune. The man was an inspiration to others. She loved the man like a brother—in fact, she loved the family. How they managed on his wages she didn't know, and the children were always smart and well fed. Carol had not offered him a tip since she knew from past experience he wouldn't accept it. So she had brought him two hundred duty-free cigarettes; even though he had had Tuberculoses, he still liked a cigarette. And a bottle of Port for Val—she loved a glass of port and lemonade.

Terry and Carol had spent the morning together in Las Palmas buying presents for her Godchildren. Terry had picked out the handmade leather camels. She was looking forward to seeing the children's faces when they unwrapped their presents; it was something she always enjoyed.

She made herself a cup of tea and then made herself comfortable in her favourite armchair. The early spring sun filtered through the open front room window, making her feel drowsy. It wasn't long before she was asleep. The wind blowing a breezy chill from the April evening woke her. She decided not to cook but walked the two hundred yards into the village and bought some Cod and Chips, then walked back home and ate them straight from the newspaper.

The unpacking of her suitcase took just a few minutes; the laundry staff had cleaned most of her clothes before she left the ship.

She lit the water heater and then turned the hot water tap on to fill the bath. The previous year she had the scullery converted into a bathroom with running hot water from a water heater—money well spent. Reg and Val, like most people in the cottages, still used the tin bath.

Carol took her time dressing, carefully applying her makeup. She always tried to look her best, even if it was for the local public house. She felt scared and lonely, yet at the same time excited about her baby. She looked at herself in the mirror. At least it didn't show at present.

The time was eight forty five. Before making her way to the local she knocked on the neighbour's door.

"Come in—it's open!" Reg shouted.

Reg and Val were sitting at their small dining table having their supper. "Carol, it's *lovely* to see you! We're having rabbit stew with dumplings—would you like some?"

Carol declined with a genuine caring tone: "No thanks—I've just had fish and chips." She added in a whisper: "I suppose the children are in bed?"

"They're in bed," Reg said in his broad Cockney accent, "but whether they're asleep or not is a different matter."

"I won't disturb them. I'll call in to see them tomorrow." Carol was pleased since she needed a drink.

She entered the empty saloon bar of the Jolly Farmer. All the noise came from the public bar. The dart team was playing at home. The bar was full, the only space being the line between the hockey and the board.

If you needed company, this was the place to be—but Carol needed to be by herself: it gave her time to think.

"Hello, Carol! Didn't know you were home—did you have a good trip?" It was the landlord's voice from behind the bar. He had been serving in the public bar and seen Carol enter, so he stopped what he was doing to give her his undivided attention. He picked up a small-stemmed glass. "The usual?"

"Yes please." She knew it was a waste of time asking for ice and lemon, for the continental ways hadn't reached Britain. "The trip was fine but very busy," she said, noticing Albert's intense look.

He was forty-two and a widower. His wife had died in the blitz during the war. He had been serving in the Royal Navy at the time and was unable to attend the funeral. He never forgave himself. The feeling of guilt had always remained with him. He stayed in the Royal Navy until 1950. With the money he had saved, and with the small pension he had coming from the Navy, he had managed to buy the Jolly Farmer public house.

He looked smart in his white shirt, dark blue tie and dark blue trousers. The blue brewers apron, oddly, didn't look out of place. Carol thought he looked like a character from one of John Mill's movies. (The trouble was she couldn't think which one.) He had poured a Gordons gin in the glass, taken the top off a tonic water and placed the drink in front of Carol.

"One and a penny," he said in an apologetic manner.

She gave him a two-shilling coin. "Have one yourself," she said as an afterthought.

"Thank you. I'll have half a bitter—that will be one and six." He took the coin, went to the till and returned with sixpence change.

Carol poured the tonic into the gin and went and sat by the log fire.

She was on her third drink when Albert came and sat next to her. "It's quietened down in the public bar. I've come to see if you're all right. You don't seem your usual self?" He looked at her with concern, though admiring her good looks.

"Well, Albert, I've got myself into a bit of mess, if you must know—and I'm the only one who can sort it out." She couldn't help feeling sorry for herself.

"Perhaps talking about it may help," he smiled, taking a chance and reaching out for her hand—a gesture she accepted. "Two heads are better than one, you know."

Carol looked into his kind face and thought for a moment—why not?

She told him everything except Terry's age. Albert listened with concern. When she had finished, he asked the obvious question: "Why won't he marry you? He must be a fool not to want you."

How could she tell him he was a sixteen-year-old boy! "Because I don't want to marry him," she sighed, downing the last of her drink. Albert took her glass, went to the optic and poured a measure of gin and knocked the top off a tonic water; he took another glass and poured himself a large rum. He returned to Carol, deep in thought.

He sat facing her, taking her hand again. She felt some reluctance, this time, but left her hand in his.

"Carol," he began nervously. He cleared his throat and began again, "Carol, I've known you since I moved here three years ago. You may not know this, but my feelings for you are special—you're never out of my mind, in fact. Many a time I've wanted to ask you out to a dance or the cinema, but because of our age different I've backed off."

Carol thought that ironic—he being worried about the eight years difference between them. She was thankful he didn't know Terry's age!

Albert cleared his throat again and continued: "I've a good business. I have six rooms upstairs, and I work hard." He took a sip from his glass. The rum warmed him and gave him the encouragement he needed. "Carol, you don't want your child to grow up without a father, do you? So marry me. I'll love your child as much as I love you. I'll give him—or her—my name; and I'll love the child as if he, or her, were my own." He smiled nervously. "Perhaps in time you may get to love me."

The look on Carol's face was complete shock. She looked into the fire, then back at Albert and burst into tears. Before he could say anything again she had run from the bar.

She arrived home, locked the door and did not step outside for a week. Val came in twice a day to check on her. Carol pretended she was having a bad week of woman's problems.

The next Thursday she bathed and took extra care with her makeup. She picked out her best frock, then walked the hundred yards to The Jolly Farmer. She entered the saloon bar. Albert, behind the bar, registered embarrassment and began to apologise.

"Albert," she interrupted him, "Before you say something we may both regret, I have come to say—I will."

Two weeks later, with a special marriage licence, they were married at Guilford registry office. Reg was proud to be best man. Val was the maiden of honour and the two children made perfect bridesmaids.

On the 10th October 1953, Carol gave birth to a beautiful 7lb 10oz baby girl, "Julie."

And it didn't take long for Carol to fall in love with Albert, a kind and caring man. Carol and Julie became his pride and joy. Everybody who knew them thought they were the perfect family and, indeed, they were. Albert brought Julie up as his own child and nobody knew any different, including Julie.

CHAPTER 4

Terry 1958

The Voyage to Argentina was uneventful. The ship left the royal docks on the evening tide and made its way to Tilbury Landing stage where she moored in the early hours. At 10 o'clock the first of the passengers started to embark. The majority being first class passengers, most of the tourist class would embark in Spain and Portugal.

At 2 p.m. that afternoon the ship left the landing stage and made its way to the Thames estuary, then into the English Channel.

Two days later the SS *Argentine* docked in to the northern Spanish port of Vigo. Two hundred and thirty five immigrants boarded and were made comfortable in the tourist-class cabins. After a night at sea the ship docked in Lisbon, the capital of Portugal. This time the ship accommodated one hundred and eighty immigrants bound for Brazil and a new life.

Across the Atlantic to the Grand Canaries islands, the ship docked at the port of Las Palmas. During the day, the ship's engineers refuelled the oil tanks and topped up the water supplies. The fresh fruit and vegetables were a welcome sight to everybody on board.

At 6 p.m. that evening the ship steamed out of the harbour and headed for the open sea. Seven days later it sailed into the beautiful Bay of Rio de Janeiro.

It's such a shame that the city is divided into two—the rich and the poor. There is the Cocacobana beach with its high-rise hotels and luxury apartments, a millionaire's paradise. Two miles across town are the slums and shantytown where poverty is so bad it has become an embarrassment to the Brazilian government.

There was an overnight stay in the great city followed by a short trip to Santos. A supply of several hundred tons of bananas for Argentine was stowed in number one hatch.

Then it was just a few miles to Uruguay and its capital Montevideo.

The last stage of the outward-bound voyage was the overnight voyage up the River Plate to Buenos Aries, the capital of Argentine.

Terry was looking foreword to returning to the capital. It was always good to see Maria again. He wandered how he was going to tell her this was going to be his last trip to Argentine. He had been on the same ship going to the same place for six years. He needed a change. He wanted to see the rest of the world—Australia, New Zealand, Canada and North America. The problem for Terry was he never knew how much she loved him.

He had met her two years previously. Their first encounter was so bizarre they were destined to become good friends—and lovers. Terry enjoyed their friendship, especially the lovemaking, but that's as far as it went.

But Maria had fallen madly in love with this good-looking Englishman and she was waiting for the time when he would propose marriage to her and take her home with him to England.

They had first met in The Zanzibar, one of the many bars in the red light district on and around the main street of Vente Cinco de Mayo. Terry had walked into the bar about 11.30 one evening. Maria greeted him and showed him to a table. She was unusual for a South American with her blonde hair reaching her shoulders. (He found out later it was her natural colour, too.) Her blue-green eyes, with a slight kink to the right eye, made her even more attractive. Her red high heel shoes made her 5ft 5ins tall. The tight red cocktail dress showed every curve of her trim but well proportioned body. Her legs looked long and shapely in her black-seamed stockings. Her good looks and magnificent body had captivated Terry. Maria, in turn, had been taken with the young man's sexy brown eyes and cheeky grin.

The job of a hostess was to encourage customers to spend. The girls made money on all the drinks that were bought for them. Marie spoke in broken English. Terry had some knowledge of Spanish so they were able to have a limited conversation.

Maria liked this young man and decided not to fleece him. She persuaded Terry not to stay—it would not be good for him. She suggested he came back at 2 a.m.when she finished work. They could go for coffee together. He looked at his watch—just after twelve. Two hours to kill. He wanted to keep a clear head for this beautiful lady.

He made his way to the centre of town and picked out one of the many restaurants on the plaza facing Cleopatra's Needle. He ordered *Bistec Completo.* He didn't have to wait long. A large oval plate arrived filled with an extra large rump steak with a fried egg on top and surrounded with French fries and a side salad. By the time he had had coffee and a brandy the time had reached 1:30 and he made his way back to Vente Cenco de Mayo. Even at this late hour the capital was buzzing, hundreds of people still drinking and eating. The weather was still very warm with men in shirt sleeves, the women in pretty coloured dresses.

He arrived back at the bar at 1.50 a.m. Maria was sitting in one of the bar's booths with what looked like a seaman who was worse for wear. Again the beautiful lady in red impressed him. She was speaking to the drunken man in his native tongue—German.

She noticed Terry and came to greet him. "I did not think you will come back," she said in her broken English.

"How could I keep away from someone as beautiful as you!" Terry said, speaking the truth.

She flashed a smile that would melt anyone's heart. "I will get rid of this man and meet you in the Blue Star bar in the next street—is open all night."

Terry found the bar without any problems. He sat on a stool at the bar and ordered a gin and tonic. There were about twelve people in the bar. He only had to wait a few minutes before she walked in with all the elegance of a lady. She had draped a red shawl over her bare shoulders and looked stunning.

She ordered a coffee for herself and asked Terry if he would like anything. He indicated the gin and tonic he had in front of him. "No thanks—I'm fine."

Maria sat next to him and smiled. "I didn't think you would come back as it was so late." She took out a packet of Chesterfield cigarettes and offered the pack to Terry. He'd never been a smoker—cigarettes gave him a headache. "No thank you," he waved his hand. She looked surprised, took one for herself, and the American zip lighter ignited first time. She took in a lungful of smoke, let it out very slowly, and took a sip of coffee.

She stared at Terry. "You're a very good looking and sexy man—do you know that?" She placed the cigarette in her mouth and inhaled, her head tilting back as she blew a smoke ring towards the ceiling. Again, she looked at Terry. "Would you like to make love to me?"

From the moment he'd set eyes on her he never wanted anything else. But he felt let down for he'd hoped she wasn't a prostitute.

"How much?" he enquired, knowing he had to make love to her no matter what the cost or circumstance. Her eyes widened and she spoke with indignation. "Just because I work in a bar, it does not make me a whore! I like you. I *want* you to make love to me!" She put her half smoked cigarette into the ashtray and crushed it until it stopped burning. Her voice modulated. "There is one problem—I cannot take you home. If you want to make love to me, it will cost you for the hotel room—nothing else, I promise."

Terry didn't care where they went; all he wanted to do was to make love to this stunning woman.

He didn't wait to finish his drink. Maria took his hand and guided him back into the street where she stopped one of the many taxis cruising the area. Five minutes later they were standing in the foyer of one of the seediest Hotel's Terry had seen. The manager, fat and lathered in sweat, took Terry's money and handed him the key to room 210. They took the lift to the second floor. The lift doors opened to reveal a large square hall with four doors; the second door they came to had the numbers 210. Terry inserted the key and opened the door. The room was very basic—a double bed against the far wall, the mattress covered with a grey sheet and a brown blanket. To the right of the bed a sink just seemed to hang from the wall, a dirty brass tap dripping into the brown-stained bowl. A wooden chair stood in front of a small window with drab orange curtains.

Maria put the main light switch on, went to the window and opened the curtains to let the streetlight shine into the room, then switched the light off. Terry had shut the door. At least with the main light out the room felt a touch more romantic. When Maria turned towards the bed Terry stepped in her way and put both arms around her waist. She smelt heavenly and he kissed her. She responded instantly and he couldn't believe his luck. His hands moved up her back to her top button that he undid with ease, then the zip. She let the dress and shawl drop to the floor. He stood back a pace and looked at her. A black brassier supported her firm breasts. Around her waist a black suspender belt was attached to the stockings that covered her amazing legs; she still wore her black pattern shoes. The combination made her look incredibly sexy.

Terry had had an erection ever since they left the Blue Star bar and he couldn't wait to get started. He led her to the bed and she began to remove her underwear. He shook his head. "No—leave them on," he whispered. "It's more exciting." Within seconds he was stripped and lying next to her.

He wanted to impress this lady. As much as he wanted to be inside her, he knew he would have to wait. First he would explore her body with his tongue, and then caress her with his hands. When she was ready he would enter her: their lovemaking would become passionate and they would come together.

His tongue moved towards her ears down to her neck. A slight fumble with her bra strap and it was off. Her breasts were round, unspeakably soft, perfectly formed. They were so perfect as she lay on her back they seemed to stand at attention, pointing to the ceiling. Terry's tongue began to lick her left nipple, his mouth engulfing as much breast as possible as he heard her suck in her breath.

There were voices outside in the corridor. His heart missed a beat at the sound of a key turning in the lock. The door opened and he froze. Two uniformed policemen stood in the doorway. One switched the light on. Terry's rock hard penis turned to jelly. Maria pushed him to one side and stood up. The policeman who had turned the light on spoke to Maria in Spanish. The only word Terry could make out was "*Vestido*!" which meant "Dress!" Maria did as they told her without saying a word.

She explained to Terry the police wanted his I.D. and that he was to stay in the room until they came for him. He reached for his trousers, found his seaman's I.D. and handed it to the nearest policeman. The other policemen took Maria by the arm and escorted her from the room. The one with the I.D. checked the photograph, left the room and locked the door behind him.

Terry, dazed and alarmed, failed to grasp what was going on. He looked at his watch—ten past three. He went to the sink, rinsed his face and looked for a towel—nothing. He dried his face on the only sheet on the bed. He dressed, lay on the bed and waited.

He must have dozed. The next thing he knew, the door was being unlocked. He looked at his watch—five past seven. Two policemen stood in the doorway. One of them beckoned to Terry with his hand—"*Arriba*!" He knew the word—"Get up!" He got off the bed and followed the policeman with the most gold braid. The younger policeman followed. The three men made their way down three flights of stairs to the entrance, out through the main doors. Waiting beside the curb was a black Morris van with the back doors open. The policeman with the braid pointed for Terry to get into the back of the Morris.

Inside, Terry was relieved to see two fellow crewmembers sitting on benches on either side of the Morris. He joined the one on the right—a man he knew as John. He knew him from the crew bar where they had played darts together. The other person Terry only knew by sight: he didn't know his name—only that the man worked on the ship as an able seaman. The doors closed and the van lurched away. It wasn't long before Terry found out they where in the same predicament as himself.

The van pulled up outside the main Buenos Aries police station. The back doors opened and all three were ushered through the main doors, past the desk to a large room that was empty except for one long bench on either side. At the far end was a large oak door.

Their footsteps echoed on the dark wooden floor. The door closed behind them, leaving the three of them alone.

They sat in silence, each worried about what was going to happen. Some of the stories Terry had heard from the older hands were frightening.

Every so often eyes peered through little spy holes around the room—an eerie feeling. It was 10:15 before anything happened. A man in grey trousers, white shirt and red tie entered by the door at the far end and pointed to John, the deckhand, speaking in clear English: "Yes please—if you will follow me." They left the room together. After five minutes the man returned alone and pointed to the other deckhand—the one Terry now knew as David: "Yes please—I would like you next." Again they left the room together.

It seemed like a lifetime before the man returned. He smiled, "Now you," his index finger indicating to Terry to come forward. He followed the man into an alleyway where the man stopped and addressed Terry: "I'm inspector Viajes. I will be taking you into an identification room. There will be twelve men. I will be expecting you to identify the hotel manager who took your money and gave you the key."

"Yes sir," Terry replied, not wanting to upset anybody.

The man opened the door, took Terry by the elbow and conducted him into the room. He spotted the manager straight away—the fourth man along. He pointed towards him and the inspector smiled, took Terry by the elbow and guided him through another door. This time the room was very large, fifty by sixty feet. There were eight desks, each screened off for privacy.

Terry was shown to one of the screened desks. As the screen was pulled back he was surprised to see Maria who jumped up from her seat and wrapped her hands around his neck, planting a big kiss on his mouth. He blushed with embarrassment. She had been sitting at the desk facing a gentleman, while next to her sat a lady wearing a black skirt and matching jacket. The white blouse she wore looked a size too small, her large breasts straining to escape.

The lady stood up and stretched her right hand towards Terry. "My name is Miss Caroline Baker—and yours?"

"Terry—Terry Gibbons," he replied, taking the lady's hand and shaking it.

Her glasses sat right on the tip of her nose. Though she was only forty her greying hair made her look older and straight-laced. She continued: "I am from the British embassy. I'm your interpreter and representative. Do you know why you are here?"

He shook his head. "Not really." He was careful not to incriminate himself. Caroline indicated the chair next to Maria and Terry sat down. She resumed her seat and at the same time started to explain the situation. "The hotel has been under surveillance for some time. The manager was taking money from the guests and keeping it for himself—in other words, thieving from his employers and defrauding the Argentine government from tax. Tax evasion is a very serious charge in Argentine. So you're a prime witness for the prosecution." She smiled. "Maria is making her statement at the moment. As soon as she has finished, we will start on you—then you can go." Caroline took a folder from the desk, opened it and took out Terry's I.D. and returned it to him. "I have informed the Purser on your ship that you have been helping the police to arrest a known villain. You may become a hero." She laughed. "I don't think so, somehow."

Terry turned and looked for the two seamen who had accompanied him "There were two deckhands brought in with me. What happened to them?"

"Oh them—I don't think they want to get involved; they couldn't or wouldn't identify the manager. It may have something to do with their compromising position. They were found in bed together."

Terry couldn't help laughing out loud. The thought of the two large deckhands having a love affair seemed incongruous.

Maria and Terry left the police station at 2:50 and went for a drink. Maria had decided not to work that evening. They arranged to meet and have dinner. They ate at the Copper Kettle, just off the main square. Maria enjoyed Terry's company. After their meal she invited Terry back to her small but clean flat. It was the first time she had invited male company back to her home.

Terry had discovered there was more to lovemaking than he realised. Carol may have taught him the skills, but Maria brought out his inner feelings. For the first time in his short life lovemaking fulfilled his needs and his appetite and he revelled in the depth of feeling he had for her.

Their relationship blossomed over the following two years. He never stopped to think he might be hurting Maria with his decision to move on and change ships, for he took it for granted she would move on to someone else. It would be much later in his life before he would find out just how much she loved him.

The ship docked in Buenos Aires at seven in the morning and all passengers had disembarked by ten.

Maria stepped from the taxi and Terry looked down from the ship's gangway and smiled. She looked lovely in her summer dress. The pre-arranged boarding pass allowed her on board. The embracing and kissing excited them both and it wasn't long before they were both on Terry's bed making passionate love. The three months apart had obviously enhanced their appetite for each other as well as bring them closer together. Both found it hard to control their emotions and before long both climaxed together in a crescendo of ecstasy.

They dressed and Maria sat on the only chair. She had so much she wanted to say and bubbled with excitement. She hoped this would be the time Terry asked her to marry him. "Terry," she said with barely suppressed excitement, "I have taken two weeks off work—is it possible for you to do the same? I want to take you to see my foster parents and their farm, perhaps spend a few days with them." She omitted the fact that she had already planned the weekend with her family.

Terry had no intentions to take his well-earned leave in Argentine, however. His mind searched for an excuse. He was fundamentally selfish and never thought of anybody but himself. But as he watched Maria and took in her bewitching smile, his heart melted and in a moment he had changed his mind. Why not, he thought? Maria's idea was a good one. Besides, since this was his last voyage to Argentine it would give him the opportunity to see more of the country and, as a bonus, he would have Marie as a companion. He left her in the cabin and went to the chief steward's office to apply for leave. To his surprise, the chief steward granted ten days leave and he packed a small bag. The smiles and enjoyment that came from Maria finally got through to him to the extent that he felt twinges of guilt.

They made their way to La Boca and Maria's apartment in a small suburb situated south of Buenos Aires. That afternoon they walked around the shops in the centre of the capital, enjoyed a light lunch and made their way back to Maria's flat. The square the flat looked down on had four restaurants. It was a pleasant place where locals met every evening, winter or summer, to discuss everything from football to world events. Terry and Maria had a pleasant evening eating and talking to the locals.

Terry had visited Argentine many times, but this was the first time he had been involved with the local community. It felt good.

In the two years they had been together, Maria had never divulged her past. That night after a long period of lovemaking she explained her past to Terry.

At twelve years of age her mother had died. She never knew who her father was. The police had picked up Maria in Buenos Aires walking the streets begging for money. She ended up being fostered by an Austrian Jew and his wife who were survivors from the German concentration camps. They had emigrated to Argentine and had set up home on the outskirts of Rosario. They had changed the tobacco farm into a stud farm, supplying horses to the Argentine pampas. The sturdy horses were needed for rounding up the world famous Argentine cattle. The couple were childless, hence were grateful when they where approached by a friend from the police department and offered Maria as a foster child.

Maria became the first of many children to pass through the farm, but she was the one they treated as their own. Over the next ten years the farm became a home to many homeless children. Sometimes there were as many as fifteen children working and studying on the farm.

Maria left for the bright lights of Buenos Aires when she was twenty-one. Her foster parents never wanted her to go and had hoped she would work the farm. She never told them the only job she could get was as a bar hostess. They would never have approved. The longer it went on, the harder it became to return, for she was headstrong and wouldn't admit she had been wrong in leaving.

Terry lay in bed half asleep listening to Maria's life story. He couldn't fathom what she was doing there when she could have had a life of contentment on the farm.

The next day they caught the bus to the capital's main train station. There they boarded the train to Rosario. When they arrived at the Rosario station they boarded an old Bedford bus to the town of Roldan. The small town only had the one street, half a mile past the town. The bus stopped at a dirt track and three-quarters of a mile along the dirt track they came to the farmhouse.

As soon they where seen all hell broke loose, children erupting from everywhere to greet Maria. Terry watched in amazement.

They stayed four days, horse riding and helping on the farm. The best of all was the evenings, cooking steaks on the open fire and being entertained by the children. Terry would always remember the walks they had alone, the lovemaking under the stars. The ship and the ocean seemed a million miles away.

Though Terry enjoyed his stay on the farm, he couldn't bring himself to like Herbert Weise. The man looked more like a typical German than an Austrian Jew. He didn't have a lot to say, and what he did say was distinctly anti-British. Terry wondered whether Herbert had in fact been using the children for cheap labour, not for the purpose of providing them with the loving home Maria believed in—but Terry said nothing.

It was good to return to Maria's flat. They spent the next three days sightseeing during the day and making love in the evenings.

Terry became very close to Maria and for the first time in his life began to consider someone else's feelings other than his own. He knew he had to explain to her why he was not returning.

The night before the ship sailed they dined in the square beneath Maria's flat. They finished off their meal with a brandy and coffee. Terry looked into Maria's eyes and a lump came to his throat. "Maria, this will be the last time I will see you for some time," he said sadly.

"Yes I know—three months." She gave a little smile.

"No," he said, feeling ashamed. "It may be a couple of years."

The shock on Maria's face upset Terry even more. When the shock turned to tears she stood up and ran towards her flat. Terry paid the bill and ran after her. Maria had locked the door from the inside. He could hear her crying and knocked on her door. "Maria, please let me in," he pleaded.

"Why should I? You're going away and not coming back!"

"I need to explain," he said, feeling guilty.

A few minutes later he heard the key turn in the lock. He tried the door handle and the door opened. He entered the room and closed the door behind him. She stood a few yards from the door, the streetlight from the window illuminating her and revealing the outline of her curves through the flared skirt. Her tears had caused her mascara to streak her cheeks, and her lower eyelids had become puffy. Her arms were folded across her red blouse covering her breast. In spite of her misery she looked sexy and vulnerable.

He walked towards her and put his arms around her. She tried to pull away but he held her tighter, leaned forward and kissed her. She wanted to scream and throw him out, but her love for him was too great. She responded to his kiss, her hands dropping between his legs and feeling the hard evidence of his desire for her. She dropped to her knees, unzipped his trousers and drew his urgent erection into the soft cocoon of her mouth. Terry was close to swooning, succumbing to the pleasure of her velvet lips and the electric cunning of her tongue as it insinuated its magic up and down his shaft.

He pulled away, picked her up and took her to the bed where he laid her down and undressed her slowly. He undressed himself and lay down beside her. His lips went directly to her breasts. His tongue played with her nipples, then gradually moved down her flat smooth stomach and further until it found the yielding damp between her legs.

The smooth inner flesh felt good on his tongue: he remained there until her body quivered with excitement. Her moans turned to a scream. He started to move up her body to enter her but she pushed him onto his back and opened his legs, her tongue searching out the sensitivity of his testicles. Then her mouth engulfed his penis once more. Terry lay there enjoying the exquisite sensation, her hand massaging his testicles, her mouth working up and down his shaft. All at once the sensation turned into unbearable pleasure as he felt his orgasm rising. He moaned, his whole body tensing and pulsing…

He thought, how could he ever leave this sexy lady? They made love once more that evening and again in the morning before he returned to the ship.

Once in his cabin he sat at his desk and wrote a letter to Maria. He knew she would be coming to watch the ship sail at 5 p.m. that day. During the afternoon in the first-class lounge while he was busy serving afternoon tea to the newly boarded passengers, Maria stood on the quay hoping to see him before the ship sailed. She had passed a message onto the ship and lucky for them both it had fallen into the right hands. A pageboy approached Terry and handed him a slip of paper. He opened it and read: "I AM WAITING ON THE DOCK—CAN I SEE YOU BEFORE YOU GO? LOVE, MARIA."

He made his way to the gangway. She was standing on the quay. He cleared it with the quartermaster and a few strides down the gangway he was on the quay. She looked beautiful in a white dress and a red neck scarf. He took her in his arms, then handed her the letter. "It will explain everything," he said. Her tears started to flow again. He took her in his arms once again and kissed her. A big cheer came from the upper decks and he looked up to see a crowd of about fifty grinning crewmembers, ready to cheer every embrace and kiss he made.

He left her standing on the quay sobbing her heart out. He knew he dared not look back as he made his way back up the gangway.

In years to come he would look back and wonder whether he did the right thing. He would never forget Maria.

CHAPTER 5

Maria 1958

Maria watched Terry walk up the gangway and out of her life. At four 4:45 the last of the visitors left the ship. At 4:50 the gangway was removed. At 5 p.m. the last of the mooring ropes had been released. The two tugs, one forward and one aft, took the strain. The twenty-thousand-ton liner was pulled away from the quay as the tugs manoeuvred her into midstream. There the towropes were released and the ship was under her own power heading for Montevideo and the open sea.

Maria made her way from the docks to catch the bus to La Boca. She reached the square just after six in the evening. She sat in her favourite restaurant just below her apartment, ordered a Cuba Libra and took out Terry's letter and started to read.

22nd Feb. 1958

My Dear Maria,

I am so sorry the way things have turned out. I never meant to hurt you. There will always be a part of me that will be thinking of you. Even now I do not know whether I am doing the right thing.

I am only twenty-one and I am not ready to settle down, there is so much I want to do and see. As long as I feel like this it will not be fair to you. The only thing I am ashamed of is I should have told you before you got too involved. I know I will never forget you. Perhaps I may regret my actions and return to Argentine sooner than later.

Maria, once again I am so sorry. Please forgive me. Have a good life.

Love

Terry

Maria sat in the bar all evening reading the letter repeatedly. The square had become busy with revellers enjoying the summer evening. All four restaurants had become busy. The smell of Argentine beefsteaks coming off the charcoal grills filled the air. She had not eaten but had overindulged on Rum and Coke. Two young street entertainers began to serenade her. Everything became too much for her and her eyes filled with tears. She ran from the square to the seclusion of her flat.

On the morning of 21st May, while she was being violently sick in the toilet, a knock at the door sent a chill down her back. The last person to knock in the same fashion had been Terry. She made sure she was presentable and rushed to the door, smiling and half-hoping to see Terry again. She unlocked the door and opened it wide, barely able to conceal the disappointment on her face when she saw the uniformed policeman standing in front of her.

"Senorita Menzis?" he asked.

"Yes?" she replied.

"You need to dress and come with me to the police station."

She looked at him in bewilderment, trying to think what she could have done wrong. "Why me—what have I done?"

"Please just dress and come with me." The young policeman's tone was apologetic.

"Wait there—I'll be fifteen minutes." She closed the door leaving him waiting outside. She knew better than to argue with the police.

Being the middle of May, the midwinter south Atlantic winds were blowing up the river Plate causing the temperature to drop well below average. She decided to wear a blue jumper over a white cotton shirt and a blue skirt. She finished applying her makeup, took her navy blue topcoat from the wardrobe and checked herself in the mirror. She looked good. Perhaps being three months pregnant had something to do with it—she just wished the morning sickness would stop.

She locked the flat and followed the policeman down the stairs to the car. He drove carefully to the main Buenos Aires police station where he conducted her into a small room. She sat and waited for a few minutes. The door opened to admit a man in his late thirties or early forties.

"Senorita Menzis," the man said with a kind but official voice. "My name is Inspector Rossi."

"What have I done wrong?" she asked anxiously.

"Could I see your I.D.?" He held out his hand. She extracted it from her purse and handed him her I.D. card. He checked the photograph, then handed it back to her. "I am afraid I have some bad news for you. Mr and Mrs Weise are your foster parents?" He stopped, waiting for a reply.

"Yes?"

"I am afraid they were killed last evening in a car accident." He waited for her reaction before he continued.

She sat there in disbelief. She had only seen them the previous Sunday. Rossi sat on the corner of the desk and gave her a handkerchief. She expected tears, but nothing came.

Inspector Rossi continued. "The reason we have brought you here is that you are their next of kin."

Maria blew her nose and looked at Rossi. "No, they only brought me up."

Rossi stood up and walked around the desk and sat down on the chair, leaned forward and read from a sheet of paper. "My colleague in Rosario has just returned from the farm. As far as they are concerned the paperwork left behind by Mr and Mrs Weise makes you the heir to the farm." He looked at Maria and liked the look of her. She was beautiful but had the innocence of a young girl. "You will have to go to Rosario to identify their bodies, I'm afraid." He wondered if she realised what it all meant. "I suggest, when you have done that, you go to the farm and organise the children and the day-to-day running—I reckon they're going to need all your help." He stood up, indicating that the meeting was over. He handed her a piece of paper.

"Those are instructions on how to get to Rosarios Mortuary and the address of your foster parents' solicitors. You will need to get in touch with them." He offered to shake her hand. She misunderstood and returned his handkerchief. He took it, replaced it in his pocket; and again held out his hand. "Well, Miss Menzes, I wish you well. I hope things are not going to be too distressing for you."

This time she took his hand and thanked him for all his help, then turned and left the building.

The cold winter wind hit her face as she went through the main doors onto the street. It felt refreshing. She sat on a nearby bench and suddenly her tears flowed. She sat there for what seemed an age but in fact was only twenty minutes. In that time she had planned the day ahead.

She returned to her flat, packed her old cardboard case, secured her flat and caught the train to Rosario. Within three hours she was entering the mortuary. Both bodies were easy to identify though her foster mother was badly disfigured, having gone through the windscreen. After signing that she was going to arrange the burials, she left and made her way to the farm.

As she approached the farmhouse the usual bedlam broke out, children rushing from everywhere—this time with tears and not the usual laughter. She went to the study and asked one of the girls to bring her coffee. She opened the desk and started going through paperwork.

There was a knock at the door. It surprised her since no one knocked in the house. "Yes?" she spoke gently. The door opened and two young boys stood before her. They were brothers, Lomas, the older by a year, and Pepe; both had been at the farm for ten years. Lomas was seventeen and his younger brother Pepe was sixteen years.

"Please Miss Maria, we would like a word," Lomas said nervously.

"Of course—what is the problem?" Maria said, feeling completely in charge of the situation.

Lomas continued: "Well, we are all very sad that Mum and Dad have died. We know you are in charge. Some say you are going to sell and leave us. What will happen to us?"

Maria, being the first orphan the Weises had taken in, realised what had happened. The children, on hearing the news, would have had a meeting, discussed the situation, voted on the subject, then picked a spokesman. That's how things were done at the farm—democratically.

"Well, for a start I will not be selling. All of us have got to rally around, to make a success of the farm, for all our sakes."

The smiles on the two lads' faces said it all. They didn't have to speak. They ran from the room and a moment later Maria heard a big cheer.

She arranged the funeral service to take place within the farm's grounds. There was nothing within the Weises' papers to show what religion they were. The local Priest performed the service. Only the children, Inspector Rossi and the Weises' solicitor attended the service. Both bodies where buried fifty yards from the farmhouse in a small woodland.

Under the watchful eye of inspector Rossi the solicitor read the will…The farm and its contents and a small amount of working capital had become Maria's as long as she carried on caring for the children.

Over the next few months she studied every book there was on horse farming. She wasn't happy with the return the farm was making. She realised there must be more to a stud farm than just supplying cattle farmers with the hardened Goutcho horses. She wanted go upmarket and specialise, but in what she didn't know.

One Sunday afternoon she sat on the veranda watching Lomas and Pepe playing their own version of polo. It was then the idea struck her—if she cross-bred her sturdy Goutcho horse with a thoroughbred racing horse, she could have the perfect sturdy polo horse.

On 18th October 1958 Maria gave birth to twin boys—Raul and Diago, both the spitting image of their English father.

The next twenty years Maria's idea proved a great success. Her polo horses became known worldwide and the rich came from all parts of the globe to buy her horses. She became well respected in high places. With her good looks and money, she was well sort after. She had become a high society lady. However, her only interests in life were her two sons first, then the working life of the farm that included the orphans. She helped many of the children to start a new life.

Maria had two regrets in life. The first was that Terry was not by her side. The second was that her two boys had no interest in the farm. Their fates lay elsewhere.

CHAPTER 6

Terry—March 1958

The MV. *Argentine* docked at London Royal Docks on the 18th March 1958. Terry signed off the ship and had fourteen days leave. As much as he missed Maria, he stuck to his plans and did not return to the M.V. *Argentine.*

He hoped that Maria would be able to move on from the job she was doing. The problem with countries like Argentina was that you were either rich or you were poor—there's no in between.

On Monday 4th April Terry reported to the Merchant Navy employment office in London's Royal Docks. An interview with the New Zealand and Pacific Line at their head office in Leadenall Street followed. His personality and immaculate record in his merchant navy discharge book impressed the shore side chief steward—so much so that he was offered employment right away. The shipping line's new liner was being fitted out in Newcastle and he accepted the vacant position of Second Steward without hesitation.

He spent the next two weeks serving food and drinks to the directors in the head office boardroom. He impressed the managing director so much that he was offered a contract with the company.

Two weeks later Terry took the overnight sleeper from King's Cross to Newcastle. He was on board the ship by 8 a.m. on the Monday.

The chief steward was a young man for the position he held. He was thirty years of age and had been with the company for fourteen years. Terry was impressed with the ship and the chief steward Mike Ryan.

The ship had just finished its sea trials. The Captain and the shipping line were impressed with the new style and line of the ship. On Friday the ship was to sail to the Royal Docks in London. The M.V. *Wellington* would then be loaded with cargo for New Zealand.

If the dockworkers kept to schedule the ship would then sail on the following Saturday for Auckland. Terry could not help feeling excited in anticipation of the journey that would take him westward to the Panama Canal, and then the Pacific Ocean followed by the long haul to New Zealand.

That evening the chief steward Mike showed him around a part of Newcastle. They ended up in a nightclub called the Jungle Bar where they sat at the bar. It wasn't long before Terry caught the eye of a young girl. Both smiled at each other: Terry winked and she moistened her lips with her tongue in a suggestive manner—and winked back. He told Mike he would be back in a minute. He walked over to the girl's table.

"My name's Terry. Can I buy you a drink?"

She looked up at him and smiled. "Yes please—a gin and orange." She spoke in a broad Geordie accent. He went back to the bar, ordered her drink, told Mike not to wait for him and rejoined the young girl.

She was slim with a long neck that seemed to go on forever before it came to a thin but singularly attractive face, the short haircut blending nicely with her high cheek bones. Terry had never seen anybody with such dark, magical eyes that seemed to emanate love and sex with every blink. She excused herself and made her way to the ladies' toilet. She was tall and thin, but her black mini skirt and black tights made her look incredibly sexy. The white shirt that hung loose outside her skirt did not conceal the fact that her breasts were small—indeed, it enhanced the impression of a flat chest. Terry smiled at the thought of what his father would say—"Tits like two fried eggs!" Terry wouldn't normally be attracted to anyone so thin, but her good looks and sexy eyes had captivated him.

Though Linda still lived with her parents, she was streetwise and sexually well educated. It did not come as a surprise to Terry when he invited her back to the ship and she accepted. What did surprise him was the excitement *she* showed. She was the one who became inpatient, who wanted to leave the nightclub and go aboard the ship straight away.

She even knew how to get into the docks without a pass. Taxis were plentiful outside the club. She gave instructions to the driver. She asked Terry for a ten shilling note which she passed to the driver who, in turn, handed it to the guard at the dock gate. The fitting out basin did not have the same security as the main docks.

Terry led her up the gangway and then to his cabin. He was pleased to see she had no inhibitions. Without saying a word she slipped out of her clothes and got into bed. It didn't take Terry long to find out she had a lot of experience when it came to lovemaking. In fact, as far as he was concerned, lovemaking didn't enter into their passion—it was just plain exciting sex.

The next morning she became a problem for he couldn't get rid of her, and she stayed until the ship sailed on the Friday. He had met his match when it came to sex and the hunger for it. He wondered what she told her parents.

CHAPTER 7

Linda—1958

Linda left the ship and decided to make her way home. Terry had given her a pound for a taxi. She walked a mile to the main bus route and waited for a bus for she hadn't had a pound in her pocket for some time. That pound could give her a couple of nights out! She'd enjoyed the last few days of luxury. She had really been happy—the happiest she'd been for some time. She'd spent the days in Terry's cabin that was spacious with an en-suite shower and toilet—luxury compared to her parents' house. Terry had brought her meals to the cabin three times a day, too. Nobody had spoilt her like that before, and in return she did his washing and ironing—something she would not do at home.

And the sex was great! In fact, he was the only man who had been truly able to satisfy her needs. She really could fall in love with this man. But she'd left it too late—the ship had sailed and she only knew him as Terry. She was not even sure of the ship's name.

Linda had turned twenty-one on her last birthday. She was unhappy at home, for her father didn't approve of her way of life. She was out to all hours and he never knew where she was. This caused many rows between them. The rows had become so bad she began to hate her father. The night she had met Terry she had had a screaming row with her father and had stormed out of their two-up two-down terraced house.

She hoped her father was worried sick! Perhaps he had been walking the streets looking for her. She hoped that was the case, but in her heart she knew he didn't care a damn. The bus stopped a hundred yards from the house.

She entered through the back door. It was just after midday. To her surprise her father was sitting at the kitchen table, a tin mug of tea in front of him and a cigarette hanging from his mouth. He looked at her with disgust.

"You little slut…!" he began with contempt in his voice. "You're no daughter of mine!" He took in her appearance and snarled: "Look at you—you look like a tart. I know where you've been and what you've been doing. The guard you gave the ten shillings to couldn't wait to tell me—he let you in the docks on Monday night." He took a gulp of tea. "Your bag is packed and in the hall. I don't want to see you in this house again. If you want to see your mother, you see her away from the house. Now get out of my sight!"

He picked up the *Daily Mirror* and turned to the back page, ignoring his daughter.

Linda looked at her father, stunned. She realised it would be a waste of time trying to reason with him. She walked through to the hall and found her small brown case next to the stairs.

"You needn't go upstairs—It's all there!" her father shouted from the kitchen. "Just leave!"

Linda couldn't hold back the tears any longer. She picked up the case and left the house. She only knew one person who had her own home. That was her good friend Amy. Although Amy was a prostitute, Linda liked her company and her stories about men and their inadequacies. She looked upon Amy with admiration: she liked her lifestyle, the nice well-kept flat, and the beautiful clothes she could afford. It was a short walk to Amy's flat. When she arrived her friend had only just got out of bed, having had a busy night.

Amy made tea and toast for them both and offered Linda the bed settee.

Linda never knew how it happened, but within a fortnight she was working alongside Amy. Being young and attractive, it wasn't long before she began to earn good money. Within a few weeks she was able to rent a flat of her own. Things were looking up.

In July she found she had a setback—Terry's lovemaking had left her three months pregnant. She refused to have a back-street abortion and made up her mind to work as hard as possible until she was too large to carry on. Even then, it was strange how some men get a kick out of having sex with a pregnant woman. She was still having clients four weeks before she gave birth. The money came in very handy. On 18th December 1958, with help from Amy, she gave birth to Kevin.

Two weeks later she carefully wrapped Kevin in a warm blanket, placed him in a cardboard box and left him in the telephone box outside the Newcastle Police station.

The next ten years were good to Linda. She had learned her trade well. She never walked the street and used the top hotels at top prices. Not only was she good at her profession—she enjoyed the power she had over men.

It was the spring of 1968 when she met Robert, a managing director of a shipping company. Within two months they were married. Linda moved from the North East to Robert's six-bedroom mansion house in Harrow. She never wanted for anything and gave birth to two children a year apart.

Every Tuesday and Thursday she would give the Swedish *au pair* instructions for the day, give her son and daughter a big hug, and then take the London underground to Piccadilly Circus.

Linda would walk into the Regency Palace Hotel, hand over ten pounds to the porter, sit in the lounge and wait. She limited herself to four clients a day. Her wages depended upon her clients' needs.

The worst day she only earned two hundred and fifty pounds, but on average she could earn five hundred pounds.

Robert never found out about her working trips to London. He assumed she spent her time shopping. He would have had a heart attack if he ever checked on her bank account! But Linda could never imagine herself not working. There was never an occasion when she felt guilty and she enjoyed her twice-weekly trips to London.

She thought of Terry and their lovemaking on many occasions, but never of their son, Kevin. When she did finely decide to search for her son, it would be too late.

CHAPTER 8

Terry 1958

On Friday 22nd April, at midday, The M.V. *Wellington* sailed from the fitting-out basin and headed for London and the Royal Docks. The ship arrived at the Thames estuary early the following evening. The ship anchored. The ship's berth would not be available until the early hours of Monday morning. The skeleton crew was disappointed. There was nothing worse then being at anchor and unable to get ashore, especially at weekends and in your homeport. Everybody felt cheated. As if that were not enough, the ship was dry, for the ship's bar had not yet been stocked.

At midnight on Sunday the anchor was raised and the ship made its way up the Thames. The loch master cleared the ship for entry through the lock gates that led to the Royal Docks. The ship berthed at shed 15 in the King George the Fifth dock.

Later that day the ship became a beehive for dockworkers. Pallet after pallet loads of Scotch whisky were hoisted aboard and stowed in the hatches. Then there were pallet loads of London Gin. When that was completed large wooden boxes with car spares were carefully loaded into three and four hatches. Finally, ten Landrover vehicles where placed on the open deck and secured.

At midnight on the 30th April the ship left her berth to catch the early morning tide. Earlier that day a fall complement of passengers embanked and were settled into their luxury cabins that consisted of seven double and two single berths.

Terry had the task of introducing the passengers to their cabins. Fifteen of the sixteen passengers were pensioners and Terry could not help thinking that one or two of them might not see the end of the voyage.

It became a pleasant surprise to see a smart and attractive woman walk up the gangway and introduce herself as Mrs Loveday. Terry checked the passenger manifest; her name was Irene Loveday, a forty-eight-year-old widow. He liked the look of her—well-dressed and sexy—and he wondered whether his sex appeal would work on a small ship like the *Wellington*. The only other single person travelling was a sixty-year old woman doctor. All passengers had a one-way ticket to Auckland.

The ship cleared the Thames estuary and headed for Dover; then by late afternoon passed the Scilly Isles and altered course for the Atlantic, the Dutch West Indies, and the Island of Curacao.

The catering crew consisted of the chief steward, a ship's cook and the second cook and baker in the galley, the four stewards—the captain's personal steward, the officer's steward, and two engineer stewards; and four catering boys who were there to assist and learn all aspects of the catering trade.

Terry struck up a friendship with the ship cook and the captain's steward; the three seemed to have more in common than the rest. In addition, their work brought them close together. Terry, being the working boss, had many varied duties to carry out. One of these was to open the passenger bar an hour before lunch and an hour before dinner.

From day one the first person at the bar and the last to leave was Mrs Loveday who impressed Terry—5ft 10 inches tall, blonde, with a figure any twenty-year-old would be proud of. If he had not seen her passport on her arrival he would never have believed her age. She looked at least ten years younger then her forty-eight years. Every day she impressed him. She always looked immaculate and her makeup was never overpowering, just enough to give her that little extra confidence. Her blonde shoulder-length hair had the ends flicked up to give a younger look. Her clothing came from all the top West End stores—nothing but the best for Mrs Loveday. But it was her come-to-bed grin followed by her cheeky wink that drove Terry wild.

Being a small ship, nothing went unnoticed. Terry decided to keep well away for he didn't want to risk his job. But his caution didn't prevent him from becoming jealous as he watched the officers making passes at her—which happened all night every night.

Three days into the voyage the ship ran into a force ten storm. For thirty-six hours the ship rode out the storm. The ship's cook had a bad time trying to keep things on the stove. The seaman spent their time in the hatches making sure the cargo was secure. The whole ship was like a corkscrew; if something wasn't battened down it ended up broken.

For the thirty-six hours the captain stayed on the bridge. At four in the morning the storm subsided and the captain left the bridge for a long-deserved rest. Though the storm had broken there was still a heavy swell.

At 6 a.m. Ron the captain's steward (nicknamed 'Dad' because of his age—at forty he was the oldest catering crew member on board) entered the bridge with the captain's breakfast. The chief officer politely informed Ron the captain had left the bridge and retired to his stateroom. Ron made his way to the stateroom, knocked on the door and walked in. There was nobody in the day room, so he walked through to the bedroom. The captain's bed had been used, but there where no signs of anybody. He put his head through the toilet door which was ajar—nobody. He knocked on the door to the office and walked in expecting to see the captain at his desk, but again—nobody.

Ron left the tray in the office and made his way back to the galley. Terry was helping the cook to prepare breakfast for the crew and passengers.

"What's up, Dad?" Terry asked, looking at Ron's worried face.

"I cannot find the old man," Ron replied with his Norfolk accent.

"What do you mean you can't find him?" Terry said with a smile. "The chief officer said he had retired to his cabin."

"I can't find him," Ron said, undoing his tunic.

"Don't take your coat off—come with me: let's see where he is." Terry removed his cook's apron and turned to the ships cook. "Get one of the boys to give you a hand, chef."

Terry followed Ron as they headed towards the captain's cabin. He performed a similar search—no sign of the captain anywhere. He reported to the chief officer on the bridge and the intern did a similar check. Still no sign of the captain. All heads of departments where informed and a search of the ship was put in action.

Terry had the task of disturbing the passengers and checking their cabins. He checked each cabin—Mrs Loveday's was last. It was ten passed seven when he knocked on the door.

Her distinctive voice of authority came from within: "Come in!"

Terry entered. She was sitting up in bed drinking tea.

"Sorry to disturb you Mrs Loveday, but we have mislaid the captain and I have orders to check all passenger cabins."

"Terry—what *are* you suggesting!" she said with a smile and a wink. She leant to one side to put her cup and saucer on the bedside table. As she straightened up the sheet covering it dropped away. Terry caught his breath as he stared at her magnificent breasts, full and firm—he had never seen such a beautiful pair. She looked at him, then at her breasts. "Oh? Do you like them?" She dropped her eyes as if she were shy. "Do you want to touch or…perhaps…suck them?"

Terry made a feeble excuse and left. He couldn't believe he had walked away from such beauty—and from such an opportunity.

All heads of departments met on the bridge at 7:30. Nobody had seen the captain since he left the bridge at 4 a.m. The chief officer had no choice but to turn the ship around and commence a search, as was required by maritime law. It took forty-five minutes to get the ship back onto the reverse course. Able seamen were placed at look-out points throughout the ship.

At 10:30, while Ron was cleaning the captain's cabin, he heard a noise from the bathroom. He put his head through the open door—nothing. Then there was a cough from behind the door where the bath stood. This time he checked behind the door. In the bath, fully clothed and covered with blankets, was the captain who was beginning to come out of a deep sleep. Ron stood there in a state of shock.

"Oh, it's you, Ron," said the captain, rubbing his eyes. "I'll have an egg and bacon toasted sandwich and a strong pot of coffee, if you please." He rubbed his unshaven chin.

The case of the missing captain followed Ron throughout his Merchant Navy career—he was never allowed to live it down.

It transpired that with the motion of the ship the captain had been unable to get to sleep in his bed. He had moved to the bathroom with a pillow and two blankets and placed them in the empty bath which acted like a cradle. Nobody had bothered to look behind the door. While everybody fretted the captain had six and half-hours of undisturbed sleep.

Ron was happy as a steward and never looked for promotion. He was six feet tall yet only weighed eleven stone. He was so thin everything he wore looked far too big for him. His face was thin and sallow, the eyes sunken back into his head, the dark skin around his eyes making him look unwell. The grey hair that parted in the middle made him look a lot older then his forty years. He made up for these handicaps with his zest for life and sense of humour. He had been in the navy since 1944, and lucky for him he had never come across real danger. The last year of the Second World War was exciting but uneventful. However, his stories and experiences kept people spellbound while relaxing in the crew bar over a pint.

One such evening he told Terry and Charlie, the ship's cook, about a little village just outside Willemsted, the capital of Curacao. It seems oil companies built the village for their workers' leisure time. The village, known as Happy Valley, was surrounded by a barbed wire fènce. The one and only entrance led to the main street, which consisted of bars, gambling houses and brothels. It was legal and well policed. All three decided a night out at Happy Valley was something not to be missed.

Ten days later in the early afternoon the ship docked at Curacao where it would refuel and unload a small amount of cargo—if you can call one and half tons of whisky and a fair amount of gin 'small.' The ship was scheduled to sail the next day at 4 p.m.

The captain decided to bring dinner forward to 6 p.m., which suited the catering department. This meant everybody should be finished for 8 p.m.

At 9 p.m. Terry and Charlie accompanied Ron in a large American motorcar they had hired. Dad told the taxi driver to take them to Happy Valley, and the driver laughed and nodded his head. The journey took thirty minutes, most of it though dense jungle. Suddenly the taxi arrived at a clearing where bright lights illuminated the tropical night sky. Terry looked in amazement—it was like a scene from a British war movie. It resembled a prisoner of war camp—barbed wire, lights and rows of huts. Entrance fee was two American dollars with a notice saying all girls were medically tested once a week. Terry found the notice hard to believe!

All three headed for the nearest bar. The whole place was buzzing! Terry felt alive with excitement and anticipation. The first bar they came to was a large wooden hut. Two steps led to an open-air dance floor where two couples were smooching to a Buddy Holly record. The dance floor covered about fifteen square feet. Further into the hut it was covered. There were ten tables, each occupied by men and their lady friends: if they were not drinking they were kissing. The main language seemed to be American. The atmosphere was electric.

At the far end of the hut stood the bar. The large mirror behind the counter made the place look bigger than it was.

The three men hurried towards the three vacant stools, passing the loud jukebox that stood against the left-hand wall. Dad ordered first: "Three rum and cokes!" he shouted, trying to compete with the singing of Buddy Holly.

Three long glasses full of ice were placed in front of them. The barman added lemon to each glass. The Negro barmen produced a free bottle of Barcadi and poured until the ice was covered, leaving very little room for the coke. The jukebox became silent. A few seconds passed. Eddy Cochren singing *Three Steps to Heaven* brought the place back to life. Terry liked it—it electrified the atmosphere. This was surely a night for drinking, not for chasing women. He turned to see a Negro woman making up to Dad. She was about 25 with a very large bust and an even larger backside—but with a very slender waist. The grin on Dad's face was a picture for anybody's album.

After two more drinks they moved on. Three hours later, after visiting the remaining bars, Dad guided them back to where they had started. By this time everybody had had a good drink, though all three were still in control of themselves.

Within minutes Dad's fancy girl reappeared and this time his grin expressed unadulterated lust. He turned to Terry and Charlie: "I'll be back in half an hour—don't go without me!" The girl took his hand and guided him out of the bar into the hut next door. The laughter from Terry and Charlie made Dad stop, turn and put two fingers up. He returned forty minutes later red faced, hair a mess but with a contented smile. By this time they had all had enough for the day.

They left the compound through the main exit and took a waiting taxi back to the Docks. They paid the taxi and went through the dock gates. Terry stopped and looked across at the ship.

"How far do you reckon it is to walk to the ship from here?" he said, looking at both Ron and Charlie.

"About two miles," Charlie replied.

Terry looked back at the ship and spoke with excitement. "We could swim to the ship from here. That would be less than a hundred yards."

"You can count me out!" Dad said in a tone that suggested Terry was mad.

"Right—you can carry our clothes," Terry replied, knowing he wouldn't change Dad's mind. "Come on Charlie!" The drink had gone to Terry's head.

"Hold on, who said *I* was going to swim!" Charlie looked at Terry with disbelief.

"Come on, it will be a giggle. I'll race you for ten shillings!"

Charlie thought for a minute. It was two miles to walk. "All right then."

They stripped off to their underpants, walked to the side of the quay and dived in with no hesitation. Dad gathered their possessions and, shaking his head and thinking to himself what drink could do to people, hoped both wouldn't come to harm. He started walking back to the ship. Lucky for him he got a lift from the ship's chandler, so he was waiting for them at the ship's ladder. Terry arrived ten yards in front of Charlie. Everybody thought it was a hoot.

The next morning, while preparing breakfast, the chief steward entered the galley. "Hi boys—I hear you had a bit of fun last night." He walked past both of them to a tray of meat that had been defrosting from the night before. He transferred the meat to another tray, the original tray being awash with about two and half pints of blood. The chief steward turned and looked at the two men. "Come with me!" He took them out of the galley to the open deck. The rich blue sea blended well with the clear blue sky. The chief steward emptied the tray of blood over the side of the ship into the water. Within minutes they counted five sharks, the smallest being about five feet in length.

Terry's legs turned to jelly. He would never forget how lucky he had been that night. He believed someone up there must have a soft spot for him.

The ship sailed on time and set course for the Panama Canal and the port of Cristobal. There the ship would pick up the pilot to take it through the lakes and canals to Panama City and the Pacific.

On the morning of the fifth day the ship anchored off the city of Cristobal. Within an hour the pilot was on board and the ship was underway.

The ship passed Colon through Limon Bay on the way to the Gatun Locks, where it was lifted 85ft to Gatun Lake. From there it travelled the excavated channel to the next set of locks, after which it was lowered 30ft to the Miraflores Lake. The other side of the lake another set of locks lowered the ship to the Pacific tidewater level. From there the canal ran past Balboa out into the Gulf of Panama, and Panama City. The journey took nine hours. The ship would dock at Panama City and stay overnight to top up with water and fuel before its long journey across the Pacific.

That evening at 7 p.m. Terry was on duty in the passenger bar. Again dinner had been served early, at 6 p.m. The older passengers had retired to the stateroom to play whist. The doctor was sitting in the corner of the bar reading a book. Mrs Loveday sat at the bar dressed in a tight fitting evening dress that made her figure even more desirable. She was holding a large bowl glass with both hands, twirling the Remy Martin and looking over the top of the glass at Terry.

"Terry," she smiled languidly, "I heard about your exploits in Curacao. I bet you really have a good time when you go ashore." She looked at him with blue eyes that would melt any man's heart.

"Well yes, but that night I had one too many drinks," he smiled while polishing a wine glass.

"I can't imagine you the worse for wear." It was meant as a compliment but Terry felt uncomfortable. "I suppose you'll be ashore tonight?" She flashed a wicked grin.

"I haven't made my mind up yet. I finish here at 8 p.m. I'll see how I feel."

She took a sip from her glass, never taking her eyes off Terry. "I haven't been off this ship since London. Will you take me with you?"

Terry couldn't believe his ears. "I don't think you'll like the places we tend to go to," he smiled.

"What type of places do you go to?" The excitement in her voice was plain to hear.

"Well, they're only bars, but it's the areas they're situated in that you may disapprove of." He chuckled. "It's the red light district."

She caught her breath. "*Please* take me—I'll pay for everything!" She put her glass down and gave Terry a pleading look.

He moved closer to her and lowered his voice. "There are a couple of problems. One, I'm not supposed to socialize with passengers; second, *no way* could you go dressed like that!"

"What do you suggest?" she said, her grin broadening.

"Well, I don't really know—perhaps trousers, some sort of top, definitely no jewellery." He felt guilty—was he doing the right thing?

She finished her drink and stood up. "Where will I meet you?"

Terry thought. "At 8.30 leave the gangway and walk towards the dock entrance. I'll be there waiting for you."

He closed the bar at eight sharp, had a quick shower and gave his apologies to Charlie and Dad. They in turn said they might bump into him and Mrs Loveday ashore.

He duly met Mrs Loveday at the dock entrance as planned. She was wearing white trousers and a pink blouse. The weather was hot and humid so she wouldn't need anything else. He was impressed with her youthful good looks and figure and proud to be in her company. Once they were through the docks taxi drivers surrounded them. Terry picked the one who spoke the best English after agreeing a price.

The taxi headed for the city centre. In the back Mrs. Loveday gave Terry a peck on the cheek and a twenty-dollar bill. "Let me know when that runs out—and please call me Irene."

The taxi driver stopped at the city centre. Following Dad's instructions, they made their way to the Calle Rafel, the street of bars. The first they came across was the American Bar. They sat and had a couple of drinks. Dean Martin's voice crooned from the jukebox. She took Terry's hands and guided him to the dance floor. Their bodies melted into one as they danced, her sinuous curves molding to his.

Within an hour Dad and Charlie entered the bar and joined them. The rest of the evening the four spent going from one bar to the next, drinking, dancing and generally enjoying themselves. Mrs. Loveday had been very generous to them all and when they tried to thank her she told them it was worth every penny—she had never had so much fun.

By 3 a.m. everybody had had enough and all four shared the Taxi back to the ship. Terry paid the taxi driver and as he turned to head towards the gangway Irene stood in his way. She put her arms around him and kissed him. "Come to my cabin," she said in a low voice. "I want to thank you properly." She didn't care that Charlie and Dad were listening—her desire for Terry was urgent.

He whispered into her ear: "Make your own way up the gangway. I'll see you in your cabin in thirty minutes."

The three men waited while she made her way up the gangway and out of sight. Then they followed. Terry made his way to his cabin first and showered, then wondered if it was wise to visit Irene's cabin. He looked at his watch—it was 3.30 a.m. He barely had three hours before going on duty. But the old saying crossed his mind—Never look a gift horse in the mouth! He dressed and locked his cabin behind him.

He reached Irene's cabin, knocked on the door and walked in. She was stretched out on the bed with nothing on, smiling provocatively. He undressed quickly and took his place beside her. She was a tall woman but her figure was in the right proportions. Her breasts where large and perfectly round, the nipples standing to attention, her waist tapered in at the right place. The thighs came out enough to match up with her breasts—she had a perfect hourglass figure for a woman her age. He could barely wait to explore her body with his hands.

But before he had a chance to do anything she was on top of him. Her whole body quivered with excitement. She had positioned herself so she could sit on his hard penis. The excitement was overwhelming—but then something happened which had never happen before: his erection went limp! Dismayed, he couldn't believe it! The more she tried to excite him, the softer it became. She gave up and lay on her back.

"Are you queer?" she asked.

Terry was so embarrassed he couldn't answer at first. "I…I don't go with men, if that's what you mean."

"What's wrong then?" she asked in a hurtful tone.

"I don't know…" He wished he were somewhere else.

He lay there thinking what could be wrong with him. Then it came to him—this woman was completely different from any woman he had been with. She was taller, had a fuller figure and an air of authority, plus she was twenty-seven years older than him. She was too intimidating! Other than his first encounter with Carol, he had always been in charge; but this lady had not only taken charge, she had dominated him. Clearly he couldn't handle this—and decided to take matters in his own hands.

He rose up, got on top of Irene, and wedged her legs apart, putting his head between them. His tongue found her vagina and took great pleasure in stimulating her. He worked his way to the clitoris. Her back arched and she began to moan—he could sense the pleasure he was giving her. This gave him the confidence he needed. He felt his erection return while his tongue flickered faster; while his tongue lashed her clitoris his fingers began to massage her vagina. Her moans turned to low whimpers that became louder until she finely let out a scream. He made his way up her body with an erection now firm and rampant—and was just about to enter her when a knock at the door stopped him. They both froze, their heavy breathing sounding like a whirlwind.

"Irene—are you all right?" It was Mrs Rice, the passenger from the next cabin—a retired doctor.

Irene caught her breath, then called out: "Yes, thank you, Elisabeth—just a bad dream!"

"Do you want anything?" the doctor's voice asked with concern.

"No thank you!" Irene was still trying to regulate her breathing.

"Good night, then."

Terry looked into Irene's blue eyes. "So I'm a bad dream?"

She giggled. "I couldn't say thank you Elizabeth I'm fine—I've just had the best orgasm ever!" She looked at him with a girlish grin. "It started in my toes, then ran up my legs, then shattered my body! Where did you learn to do that? If I were you I'd patent it—you could make a fortune."

He smiled, then wedged her legs apart with his knees and slipped his penis effortlessly into her, she was so damp and ready for him. She caught her breath and a few minutes later he collapsed on top of her, his heartbeat relaxing as his love juices jetted and flowed into her with an exquisite sense of relief.

In the next sixteen days it took to reach Auckland Terry performed his party trick several times on Irene. He loved performing the oral sex act on her for he knew how wild it drove her. Every time he finished she allowed him to do what he liked to her. It was an education for both of them; there were a few positions neither of them had encountered.

Irene left the ship in Auckland, leaving him a London telephone number with instructions to ring anytime after July. He never rang and never saw her again.

All passengers left the ship at Auckland and life became extremely dull. Terry couldn't get over the fact that the pubs closed at 6 p.m. The only way to drink was to buy a takeaway bottle, find a party or a dance hall and do a bit of sly drinking. There was nothing else to do other then a visit to the local cinema to watch an outdated film.

The ship remianed in Auckland for six days, then went on to New Plymouth. From that day life on the New Zealand coast became one big party. The ship docked at 7 a.m. on the 9th Friday, June 1958, breakfast finishing at 9 a.m. Terry had finished his own breakfast by 10 a.m. He went to his cabin and started making out the laundry list for the shore laundry when there was a knock at the door. "Come in," he said, expecting to see the ship's chandler and was surprised to see an able seaman.

"Terry, you're wanted on the ship-to-shore phone at the gangway," the seaman announced.

"Me? I don't know anybody in New Zealand."

The man shrugged. "Besides a couple of other people, they asked for you by name—you're the only Terry I know."

Terry thought it must be Irene and wondered what she wanted. He locked his cabin door and headed for the gangway where he picked up the receiver.

"Hello Terry."

He couldn't place the voice. "Yes?"

"Terry, you don't know me—my name is Betty. I work in the local telephone exchange. There's nine of us looking for a party tomorrow night. We were hoping you could fix up nine nice guys?"

Terry mulled this over. "Is this a wind up?"

Betty laughed. "Of course not! Can you organise nine blokes for a party?"

Terry's mind began to work overtime. The thought of women and a party sounded good. "I think I can manage that." He tried to think of nine crewmembers that would like a good time. It wasn't an impossible task.

"Right—we'll meet you all at the Globe pub tomorrow at 4 p.m."

Terry cut her short. "Where's the Globe?"

"You haven't been to New Plymouth before, have you!" she said in amazement.

"No," Terry said as if he were in the wrong.

"The Globe is the first pub you come to outside the dock gates. We'll meet you in the saloon bar at 4 p.m. tomorrow afternoon. When it closes at 6 pm we can all go back to my place."

In actual fact Terry found it hard to muster up nine crewmembers willing to take a chance on nine blind dates. Finally the chief steward, himself, Charlie the chef, two engineer stewards and four officer cadets decided to take a chance. Dad was top of the list—in fact he did most of the recruiting, like a child preparing for a birthday party.

On the Saturday the catering staff finished serving lunch at 2 p.m. The chief steward had worked a roster to allow the five to miss serving dinner that evening: they would work the following day and the ones working on the Saturday would be off on the Sunday evening.

Everybody made his own way to the Globe which was only fifteen minutes' walk from the ship. Terry, Charlie, and Dad arrived just after 3 p.m. The chief steward was already there with the four cadet officers. The saloon bar was small but empty. The noise coming from the public bar was tremendous—it sounded like a pigsty. The locals referred to the last two hours of the bar as 'open swilling-up time.'

At 3:30 p.m. four ladies entered. The first was about 5ft 8ins, very attractive but decidedly well built. Dad's eyes lit up.

"Hello—my name's Betty. Who's Terry?"

Terry came forward with his hand out, hoping she didn't fancy him—he didn't go for big girls sexually. She looked at his hand, laughed, pushed it away and gave him a big kiss. Dad walked forward, a big grin on his face—he was definitely impressed.

"Hi—my name's Ron. Everybody calls me Dad."

Betty was impressed. She took Dad's hand and led him to the bar. The door opened and five younger ladies walked in. Terry's attention was taken by a girl with long, bright ginger hair who was about 5ft 3ins, very pretty with the odd freckle. He couldn't take his eyes off her.

Within a very short time everybody was mixing as if they had known each other for years. It was like a working class cocktail party, except most of the women were drinking pints. Terry found out about the telephone call. It seems when a ship is in port and the girls fancied a party, Betty rings the ship and asks for the first name that comes to mind. Yesterday it was John. Nobody knew a steward named John, so she tried Tony, and once again there was no Tony. She was lucky in her third choice, Terry.

At closing time everybody was keen to start the party. A whipround brought enough drink to last the evening. Three taxis were ordered. Somehow eighteen people squeezed into the three taxis and made it to Betty's place. She shared a large bungalow with four work colleagues.

After about an hour everybody started pairing off. Terry made up his mind to try his luck with the attractive ginger-haired girl. He found out her name was Ruth. He approached her and asked her to dance and she accepted. They joined several other couples on the makeshift dance floor. Buddy Holly was singing *True Love Ways*. Terry cuddled her close and she responded.

"I'm glad you asked me to dance—my name's Ruth," she said, squeezing his ear with her right hand.

"I know," he replied, certain he was onto a good thing.

"How do you know?"

"I made it my business to find out. You're so attractive."

She giggled and he realised she was very young and very naïve—but he fancied her nevertheless, for her innocence was refreshing. He didn't want to hurt her, but then, again, what was she doing there—she must know the score. He would improvise.

The rest of the evening they never left each other's company. He found out she was eighteen and had worked in the telephone exchange since leaving school. She lived with her parents who had emigrated from Scotland in 1938. Their house was on the coast road about two miles away. That evening she had arranged to stay with Betty.

Ruth had only been out with one boy friend; she had given him the cold shoulder when she found out he was only after one thing—her virginity. By midnight she had had far too much to drink. She had become very amorous and was all over Terry. By this time the drink had taken Terry over and he only had one thing on his mind—Ruth's body and making love to it. All his earlier good intentions had vanished! They ended up in one of the bedrooms and made mad passionate love. Between her passion and tears he realised she had been a virgin. That had been a new experience for him and he lay there feeling guilty, ashamed and an out-and-out bastard. He left before she woke. The cold midwinter of New Zealand didn't help the bad feeling that accompanied him on the one-hour walk back to the ship. He still felt a bastard.

"Terry, you're wanted on the phone." It was midday. Terry was having a drink in the crew bar. He acknowledged the duty seaman and made his way to the phone at the gangway. It was Ruth. He had anticipated and dreaded this moment.

"Hello Terry—just thought I'd ring you and thank you for a lovely evening."

He hadn't known what to expect when a moment before he picked up the receiver. One thing he didn't expect was to have her thank him for taking her virginity!

"I was wondering—would you like to go to the cinema this evening?" Ruth asked with obvious delight in her voice.

Terry wanted to say no but couldn't help but say yes. She explained where to meet and hung up.

For the remainder of the ship's stay in New Plymouth they spent all their spare time together. Terry never did take advantage of Ruth. The ship sailed for Wellington on Saturday the 16 June.

The ship arrived at Wellington the following day at 10 a.m. To everybody's surprise most of the city had turned out to meet the ship. The two tugs with their fire hydrants spraying water hundreds of feet into the air was quite a sight. Sirens from other ships and the shore were sounding, while people on the quay were cheering. Terry hadn't witnessed anything like it. The chief steward explained to Terry that it was because the ship was on its maiden voyage and named after the city of Wellington. The people of Wellington were out to show their appreciation.

That evening Terry had another surprise. Ruth telephoned to say she would be arriving the next day. She was staying with an aunt for a week's holiday. Terry began to get worried—this girl was getting too involved. The ship was due to sail in six days' time for the South Island and the Town of Bluff. It would then take ten days to load the ship with chilled lamb for the U.K.

Terry had roughly two weeks to decide what he was going to do about Ruth. For the next few days he met her every evening. Each evening he wanted to tell her she was wasting her time and not to get involved, but he was too selfish, enjoying her company in spite of his conscience.

He didn't say a word. The ship sailed on the Friday and after saying their goodbyes on the quay she promised to telephone him every day while the ship was in Bluff. She kept her promise.

The day before the ship sailed from Bluff to the U.K. Terry wrote a letter to Ruth. He was too much of a coward to tell her on the telephone.

4th July 1958,

My dear Ruth,

I need to write this letter to thank you. You have made my first visit to New Zealand something I will never forget. I feel you want more out of our relationship than I do. I am sorry if I have misled you. You're a lovely girl and you deserve better than me. I am sure you will find someone who will love you as much as you will love him.

I do wish you all the happiness in the world.

Good Bye
Love

Terry

On the 5th July the M.V. *Wellington* sailed for London via the Panama Canal. It arrived at the Albert Dock, Z shed, on 8th August 1958.

CHAPTER 9

Ruth 1958

Ruth received the letter from Terry on Saturday the 7th July. All her plans shattered. In her mind she had hoped to marry Terry: he would come and live in New Zealand and they would buy a house, have two children and live happily ever after.

She left her house in tears and made her way to Betty's house where Ruth broke down completely. Her tears turned to uncontrollable cries for help.

Betty did everything she could to comfort Ruth. Nothing Betty could say would take away the hurt Ruth was feeling. Betty did what Betty did best—she organised a party for that evening. There was one problem—the port had been empty of ships for several days, so the only thing to do was to invite the local lads. The local lads weren't as much fun as the British seamen, but desperate measures were called for.

Betty made a special effort on Ruth that evening, applying extra makeup and putting up her hair with ringlets dropping down either side of her face. She wore a black low cut dress that was slightly above the knee in length. She looked stunning—a lot older than her eighteen years.

As soon as Ruth walked into the party Alex, a twenty six-year-old telephone engineer who worked in the same exchange as the girls, noticed her. He liked the new-look Ruth—it had sex appeal! Right from the start he kept Ruth to himself. At the same time he made sure her glass was never empty. He encouraged her—one rum and coke after another.

Alex was a small man, 5ft 2ins, very thin with receding hair. The weasel-like face, and the eyes bulging from the sockets, didn't help his looks. And he had a grudge against the world. He was bad tempered and a bully, though very good at hiding the fact, coming across as a little boy in need of mothering.

Betty encouraged the relationship, suggesting they should be alone. Ruth was feeling good: the drink had taken effect and she became infatuated with Alex. He was seven years her senior and she was flattered with the attention he was showing her. She didn't remember going to bed with him—only waking up next to him.

She never realised she was pregnant until September. The doctor said she had been carrying the baby for three mouths, so she knew the father was Terry. What could she do? She didn't have a clue how to get in touch with him.

She had been going out with Alex since the party—just over two months. After a few sleepless nights she come to the decision that would make the next twenty years the unhappiest of her life.

She informed Alex that she was pregnant and he was the father. To her surprise he never questioned the paternity of the unborn child—in fact, he was delighted. He asked Ruth's father for her hand in marriage and they where married on the 30th September 1958.

On the 5th March 1959 Ruth gave birth to David, an 8lb 8oz beautiful baby boy. For a whole week Alex celebrated being a father. His ego had grown so much he never thought for one moment David was not his.

CHAPTER 10

Terry 1972

The next two years were happy years for Terry. The ship had become a happy ship for the crew and passengers. The M.V. *Wellington* visited many countries and Islands in that period of time, giving Terry the travel experience he was looking for.

It was good news, but at the same time a feeling of emptiness when he was promoted to chief steward on board the M. V. *Auckland* (the newest addition to the company's fleet—in fact it was a sister ship to the *Wellington.*)

However, in 1966, his dream came true: he had made it to chief steward on board the company's flagship, the cruise liner M.V. *Pacific Sea*. Terry had been striving for this pinnacle for all his merchant navy life.

Six happy years on board the *Pacific Sea* suddenly came to an abrupt end when the ship was sold for scrap owing to the dwindling number of passengers and high running costs. Nearly all merchant navy liners where taking a hammering. It did not matter which shipping line it was—the passengers were just no longer there. The ships could not afford to sail.

'Cunard' sold both the Queen Mary and the Queen Elizabeth. 'Pacific Orient Line' were losing their emigrant ships, only keeping the *Canberra* and *Oriana* for cruising. 'Union Castle' was not replacing any of their liners. 'Royal Mail lines' had taken the three 'A' ships off the South American route. Their cruise liner *Andes* had seen better days—the repair bills were mounting and she was finally sold for scrap.

The merchant navy liner could not compete with air travel. The new Boeing 747 had made its first visit to Heathrow with over three hundred passengers on board with a flight time of eight hours to cross the Atlantic compared to the four days by sea.

Terry realised at thirty-five he needed to change with the times before it was too late. He applied for a position at British World Wide Airlines. After several interviews he was accepted.

In June 1972 he resigned from the company and the merchant navy, starting a new career with British World Wide Airlines.

It seemed that twenty years as a Chief steward in the merchant navy didn't carry much weight with the airline. He still had to start at the bottom of the ladder and he actually looked forward to testing his ability.

He found it strange starting a new life at thirty-five. He had only known the navy life, eating and sleeping at his place of work. To wake up in the morning, get in the car and travel to work on the M3 motorway with thousands of other vehicles was very strange.

The eight-week course was held at a converted hanger at the east side of Heathrow. Terry was the oldest person on the course of twelve women and eight men. There was an age gap of fourteen years to the next oldest, a twenty-one year old blonde who had just left the hairdressing trade.

The group nicknamed Terry 'Dad.' Terry's mind went back a few years—it didn't seem that long ago he nicknamed Ron Dad. He realised how life moves on, though he still felt young. The shock had come from the fact that the group of twenty and twenty-one year olds saw him as a father figure. But he enjoyed the group's company and not once did he feel fourteen years older then them. In fact, he enjoyed the challenge and he found the course easy.

He had spent a long time in a position of authority and it wasn't long before he took charge of the other students and before long they would come to him for advice and help. His experience made him a star pupil and he came away from the eight-week course with flying colours. He knew it wouldn't be long before he would be challenging others for promotion. The future looked good.

CHAPTER 11

Julie 1973

Julie sat in front of her dressing table mirror applying her makeup. Her short blonde wavy hair looked immaculate. Her 5ft 4ins figure was in perfect proportion to her height and she did everything to keep it that way. She ate the correct diet and exercised regularly.

Julie was excited because it was her birthday. She was twenty and her parents were treating her to an evening's entertainment. Her mother, Carol, had brought tickets for the Theatre Royal, Windsor. They would then dine at Julie's favourite Indian restaurant.

She knew how lucky she was to have parents who loved her and spoiled her.

They treated her like a goddess. She respected their love and never took advantage of the fact. She idealised her father who would do anything in his power to make her happy. However, it was her mother she felt closest to—she never knew why but accepted this as a natural relationship between mother and daughter.

She had left school at sixteen. Her one ambition was to become an airline stewardess with British World Wide Airlines—an ambition her parents had backed every step of the way.

When she left school she worked for her parents in their public house. This gave her the opportunity to learn the catering trade, while in her spare time she studied Spanish and German: all this would help her when applying to the airline.

She had applied to the airline two months before her twentieth birthday. Eighteen days had passed since she spent the day at their office in Knightsbridge. She felt the interview and medical went well, though up to now she had not heard the result.

She had spent the last two weeks waking up early and meeting the postman at the doorstep, hoping for the letter from the airline. Her mother was always there to comfort her. "No news is good news!" she would say, then go and make the tea. At least Julie cheered up the elderly postman—hers was the only address on his rounds where a beautiful young lady greeted him each morning.

For the last two days Julie had been frustrated, waiting in vain, for it was her mother Carol who received the confirmation phone call in the end. She received a telephone call from the airline and learnt that they had accepted Julie as a flight attendant—confirmation would be in the post! That morning it was Carol who was first out of bed and who intercepted the postman half way down the street. Julie was busy counting all her birthday cards when her mother climbed the stairs with the confirmation letter tucked safely under her dressing gown…

Julie finished applying her makeup, walked towards the full-length mirror and appraised herself. She adjusted her black cocktail dress and wondered if it was too long, though it only just covered her knees. At least it didn't hide her shapely legs. Her breasts were full and round and the dress revealed just the right amount of cleavage. She turned slightly to one side, looked over her shoulder so she could see her back; the dress was just tight enough to show the curves to the cheeks of her bottom and she smiled with satisfaction.

She made her way down to the saloon bar. Her parents stood in the bar and looked at her with admiration. Carol walked forward and put both arms around her. "I'm so proud of you," she said, holding back the tears of joy. Albert, her father, took both Julie's hands and looked her up and down. "If you don't succeed as a stewardess, you could always become a model." And he meant every word.

They arrived at the theatre with plenty of time to spare. The drama starred Michael Cane in a complicated 'whodunit' plot. Julie couldn't concentrate: she had other things on her mind—if only the airline would write! The waiting was driving her mad not knowing.

It was only a few minutes' walk from the theatre to the Indian restaurant. The table had been prepared for Julie. The owner of the restaurant, a smart but overweight Indian gentleman, greeted Julie with roses and Champagne.

When they had finished ordering Albert produced a small package. "That's from your mother and myself," he said with a lump in his throat and watery eyes that threatened to overflow at any moment. Julie had been expecting something like this to happen so it wasn't a big surprise.

The surprise came when she unwrapped the small parcel. Inside was a gold Rolex watch. She looked at her parents with embarrassment while tears welled up and spilled down her face. She loved them both so very much. "It must have cost you a *fortune*! It's lovely—how can I ever thank you!" She stood up and went first to her mother, then to her father, giving each in turn a big hug and kiss.

"Just be happy and successful—that will be thanks enough for both of us." Albert looked into Carol's eyes and, taking her hand in a gesture of togetherness, said: "Your mother has something else for you—something you've been waiting for." This time a tear did escape from his eye.

Carol opened her handbag and produced an envelope and handed it to Julie. "We both hope you will be very happy." Julie tore at the envelope in excitement. It was from the airline. She devoured every word over and over again. Uncontrollable tears began to flow. "It's the *best* birthday ever…" She smiled through her tears.

Julie began the airline-training course on Monday the 4th of November, 1973.

She had always thought of herself as a person who took orders, not a person to give orders. Her natural ability came to the surface more and more as the days passed by. It wasn't long before she rose to the challenging problems and took charge of the group. Her commonsense and intelligence put her head and shoulders ahead of everybody else.

She was so impressive throughout the course. Out of the twelve remaining students she stood out as the star pupil. She impressed the instructors so much that their reports recommended her for future promotion.

She would always be successful—until fate, or was it destiny?—took a hand.

CHAPTER 12

Raul and Diago 1977

Maria was putting the finishing touches to the salads and cold meats that were laid out on trestle tables beside the large swimming pool.

Lomas was lighting the large barbecue. Pepe had taken the Landover to Rosario station to pick up the two 'guests' of honour. Raul and Diago had spent the last two years away at the Military collage. This was their welcome home party.

It had been nineteen years since the twins were born in the back room of the farmhouse.

Maria's stud farm and her ideas had gone from strength to strength. Her polo horses were known worldwide and greatly sought after. She also provided racehorses that had raced and been successful in North America. Lord Downs had brought a colt from Maria that went on to win the English Derby.

Japanese and Australians had also been successful with her horses in Asia. Her biggest pride and joy was the horse she supplied to the British Government that went on to be the Queen of England's regular horse at the trooping of the colour. Besides the horse supplied to the English Queen, her horses had been sought after throughout the European countries. Many of her horses were bred to order.

Maria had the business brain, but she would never have been one of the top breeders in the western world if it had not been for Lomas and his younger brother Pepe; they had the Midas touch when it came to conception and delivery. The boys treated the horses as if they were family.

Both brothers were in their thirties, married with children. Maria had given them forty percent shares in the farm, twenty percent each. They lived in two separate farmhouses within the many acres of farmland they had acquired.

Though Maria loved the farm and the hard work it brought, her main inspiration in life were her twin boys. At first she was disappointed to see them seeking ambitions away from the farm. But she respected their independence and now she had become so proud of their achievements. They had passed out of the United States military academy with flying colours.

Raul had been accepted into the Argentine Air Force and was due to enlist as a cadet flying officer in two weeks' time.

Diago only had ten days before he enlisted as a cadet officer in the Argentine Navy.

By the time the two boys arrived home the party was in full swing. Maria had chosen the guests very carefully; beside the boy's old school friends and girl friends, the house was full of Buenos Aries society people (most of them hangers on). It always amazed Maria how these people emerged from the woodwork when there was a society party in progress.

Besides the 'hangers on' it was good to see the high-ranking officers from the government and the armed forces had accepted her invitation.

Maria did not like the Junta and his military government—it was corrupt and ran the country with terror. But, if it meant bowing to then to give her sons an easy ride through their training, so be it.

She insisted the boys wear their uniforms; beside the fact that they looked so handsome, she wanted to show them off to the military. She wasn't taking anything for granted—her boys were going to rise through the ranks even if it cost her money in bribes to do so.

The boys were identical in looks, but that was as far as it went. Raul loved attention—he stood out in a crowd and was always the centre attraction. Already he thought of himself as a young dashing flying officer. Diago did not like attention—he was a laid back young man, a scholar in every way so that everything had to be carefully thought out before he pursued anything. Unlike his brother he respected women and treated them accordingly.

The evening went well for Raul. He had met his future commanding officer and made a big impression on him. Maria once again didn't take any chances—she invited the commander for dinner the following week: she would dine him at no lesser venue than the Hilton. Her boy was going to be looked after—she would make sure of that.

Diago would be the problem; his commanding officer was five hundred miles away at the Naval military collage at the seaport of Puerto Belgrano. Not that this was a significant problem for she had already played up to the Admiral of the fleet who was joining her for Sunday lunch at the Hilton. She knew the Admiral had other things on his mind, but she knew all the tricks and would play him along.

She was pleased with the evening. Raul had made friends with his commanding officer—they had spent most of the evening drinking together. Diago mixed with the guests like a perfect host should and ended the evening in the company of an old girl friend.

In the end Maria had possibly wasted her time playing up to the high-ranking officers, for it became clear that her two sons had the ability and intelligence to make progress within the armed forces without her help.

CHAPTER 13

Kevin 1978

As a child Kevin assumed every child was treated the same whether they had parents, or like him, had been brought up in an orphanage. In the orphanage discipline seemed to be the main factor—discipline in the form of the twelve-inch slipper across the backside for being untidy or just having dirty shoes; or the cane on the backside for torn clothing or scuffed shoes; or, the worst punishment, reserved for answering back or insolence—the cane followed by several hours in the small dark cupboard under the stairs.

Kevin was glad he was not a bed wetter. The physical abuse and humiliation those poor boys went through must have been hell: not only had they suffered the cane, they had to sleep in their own urine until washday. If it persisted, they were given a plank of wood that covered the mattress and two plastic sheets.

Kevin remembered one boy who refused to sleep in case he wet the bed again. He would wait till the lights went out; then would get out of bed and walk up and down between the beds all night. Sometimes he would go days without sleep.

An incident happened when Kevin was twelve to change his future. Up until that day he had no ambitions and to him there was no future.

He had left school at 4 p.m. The June sun had made that Monday warm and pleasant. He was looking forward to the cricket practice arranged for the early evening. He walked through the village heading to the orphanage and stopped at the local television and radio shop. The television set in the shop window was tuned into the fourth day of the first test. England was trying to bowl out the West Indies for the second time. He watched as the English bowler John Snow delivered the first ball of a new over. Lance Gibbs was the batsman; the ball was a perfect line and length, just as he himself had been taught to do. The second ball pitched the same, and the third; the fourth ball was pitched up and landed an inch away from the batman's toe; the batman missed the ball and it hit middle stump. West Indies was all out. England needed ten runs to win the first test. Kevin grinned—he couldn't wait to try this tactic. He ran all the way back to the orphanage.

Forty minutes later Kevin and six other boys from the orphanage stood by the cricket nets waiting to bowl. Mr. Parsons, the 6ft 1in career officer, was in charge of cricket practice; in fact, that's all he did do—take charge; he never taught the boys anything. He used the hour and half to improve his own batting skills; he played for the village cricket team on a Sunday afternoon.

Mr. Parsons strapped on his two leg pads, selected his bat from the cricket bag and walked towards the stumps that had been placed inside the closed nets. The boys hated his swagger and cockiness. He reached the stumps, removed the bails, and placed two half crowns on each stump—the idea being if any boy knocked the coins off the stumps with the ball the money was theirs. As far back as Kevin could remember no one had ever knocked off a single half crown.

Mr. Parsons stood at the crease and took guard. Though he was tall he was very thin. His white shirt and grey flannel trousers looked far too big for him. He had a lizard-like face with ginger clumps of hair that unsuccessfully tried to hide his receding forehead. To Kevin he looked like a character out of a Walt Disney cartoon.

Kevin was the third boy to bowl. He ran up to the wicket at his usual speed and bowled. The ball was a perfect line and length. Mr. Parsons blocked the ball. The second and third balls were all just as good and each time Mr. Parsons played the ball with a straight bat. Kevin knew this was going to be his moment: his fourth ball was going to count! He took an extra couple of paces, ran to the wicket faster then he'd ever run before, and let go of the ball. It pitched one inch from Mr. Parsons' left toe; he was too slow with the bat and the ball squeezed through the gap between his left leg and bat, hitting middle and leg stump.

Four half crowns fell to the ground. Kevin's only thought was how he would spend the money—he had never had ten shillings in his life! The rest of the boys gathered around patting him on the back.

"Come to my room later," Mr. Parsons conceded. "I'll give you the money then."

Mr. Parsons was clearly upset with the whole incident. Each boy had a new lease of life. The next three balls clearly beat Mr. Parsons' bat though unfortunately none of them hit the wicket. Mr. Parsons lost his nerve, made an excuse and left the nets for the comfort of his room.

Kevin knocked on the door to Mr. Parsons' room.

"Come in!"—the voice was sharp and cold. Mr. Parsons didn't sound in a good mood. Kevin entered the room to find Mr. Parsons seated at his deck, a half bottle of Bell's whisky and an empty glass before him, and beside the glass the four half crowns. Mr. Parsons turned to face Kevin. "You got lucky tonight, boy," he said with a snarl. Kevin could smell the alcohol on the man's breath. "You don't think you're going to get ten shillings that easy, do yer?" Mr. Parsons stood up and walked towards the boy, stopping a few inches from him. He looked down at Kevin and unzipped his trousers, producing his erect penis. Kevin, frightened, backed away.

Mr. Parsons grabbed the boy by the arms. "You play with it and make me come—*then* the money's yours."

Kevin began to struggle. "No, leave me alone!"

But Mr. Parsons wasn't in the mood to give up. He dragged Kevin across the room and bent him over a chair. Then he pulled Kevin's trousers and pants down. The boy had no chance of escape, trapped by the man's strong grip and unable to break free. Mr. Parsons tried to push his penis up the back entrance into Kevin's body but the boy refused to keep still. Mr. Parsons' heavy breathing suddenly stopped, for the sound of the door opening froze him: he held his breath in fright.

In the doorway stood the chief care officer, a fifteen stone, retired sergeant from the Paratroops regiment. The man walked forward and smashed his right fist against the jaw of Mr. Parsons who stumbled backwards, hit the far wall and fell to the ground. Mr. Davies, the chief care officer, walked forward and swung his right leg so that his boot hit Mr. Parson between the legs. His erection had already shrivelled. "If I ever hear of you doing anything like this again I'll personally cut it off! Do you understand?"

Mr. Parsons' face was twisted in pain but he had the sense to nod his head.

"Kevin, wait outside," Mr. Davies said as if he were ashamed of Kevin.

It was several minutes before Mr. Davies joined Kevin in the corridor. "This incident is over, right? I don't want you to mention it to anybody—unless it happens again. Then you come straight to me, right?" Mr. Davies spoke with concern and Kevin nodded his head "I think it's about time we made a man of you. Tomorrow evening at six o'clock I want you dressed in your Sunday best and standing outside my room—is that clear?"

"Yes Sir," Kevin said, wondering what punishment he was going to have.

Kevin need not have worried. Mr. Davies took him to Newcastle and the Army Cadet center where he was enlisted as an army cadet. Over the next three years Kevin enjoyed life and the thought of his future and became proud of his cadet uniform that gave him the confidence he needed. When he left the orphanage at fifteen he joined the army as a boy soldier, thanks to all the help he had received from Mr. Davies.

At seventeen he enlisted in the regular army. Two mouths after his nineteenth birthday he applied to join the paratroops regiment.

He rose in the ranks to become a corporal in the Welsh Guards. The regiment had returned to their camp in Pirbright, Surrey, after a six-mouth tour of Ireland, when his platoon sergeant instructed him to report to the adjutant. The adjutant informed him he had been selected for a three-mouth selection course to become a member of the paratroops regiment. The course would commence at their Aldershot barracks in fifteen days' time. The adjutant granted Kevin two weeks' leave and wished him all the best.

The course was the hardest thing Kevin had ever come up against. There were thirty soldiers from all over the British army that started the course and only sixteen finished the twelve weeks of intense training. Kevin couldn't believe the thrill of jumping from an aircraft for the first time—the apprehension as he waited the few seconds before the canopy opened, the birdlike flight back to earth—there was nothing like it. He did seven more jumps including a night jump.

Then came the proudest moment in his life, receiving his wings on the parade ground at Aldershot. A lump came to his throat when he had time to look and recognised amongst the spectators the smiling face of Mr. Davies.

Kevin had been given a blue shoulder flash, which meant he would be detached to the Second Paratroops Battalion, better known as 2 Para.

Since the first night Mr. Davies had enlisted him in the Army cadets his dream had been to wear the Red beret of the parachute regiment.

There was only one unit better, the Special Air Service Regiment, which would be his next goal in life.

CHAPTER 14

David 1977

Ruth stood at the ironing board. Her youngest daughter's party dress was the last garment. The weekly chore was something she never looked forward to, but was her way of meditating. Indeed, many of her plans for the future originated from hours at the ironing board.

She looked a lot older then her thirty-seven years. The long ginger hair she had as a youngster was gone and now replaced by dull grey hair. She had neglected her hair and her clothes were drab—it had been years since she had brought a new dress. Eye makeup and lipstick were a luxury she could no longer afford.

After David was born her whole life changed for the worse. Her husband Alex had refused to let her go back to work; in fact, he wanted a large family. Ruth gave birth to four daughters within the next four and half years. It wouldn't have been so bad if she had support from Alex. Since their marriage, Alex had become a different man in Ruth's eyes. His drinking became a way of life. Every time she became pregnant he would have an affair—with any woman that would do.

She had never loved Alex, though she had worked hard at the marriage. It became an impossible task. Any respect she had for him was lost when he bragged about his conquest with other women. He was a chauvinist too—as far as he was concerned women were there to have children and to keep house. His heavy drinking caused tempers to flare. Recently the slaps he had been giving her over the years had turned to punches. She hated the man and couldn't bear him near her. She realised it was her own fault—that she should never have married him.

Ruth only had one aim in life—to bring up her son and daughters the best she could with the limited resources she had. Two days previously, while in the doctor's waiting room waiting for a check up, she read an article from an American magazine. It stated that New Zealand was one of the best places on earth to live. The climate was good, the scenery spectacular. The country had a small population where the standard of living was high.

The standard of living could be good, but to have that standard you have to have the money to go with it. Alex only gave her housekeeping money. Most weeks it was barely enough and anything she needed for herself came out of the housekeeping, and that made her feel she was stealing from the family.

The house was made of wood and needed a lot of repairs. Alex kept promising he would get the work done but nothing ever came of his promises. As long as he had his beer money—nothing else mattered.

Ruth had planned to leave Alex on several occasions. Each time she lost her nerve. She was frightened of what he would do to her and the children. She decided to wait until the children had had their education—then she would leave.

She thought of the person who wrote the article in the American magazine. He obviously hadn't done his homework. Her standard of living was well below the magazine estimates.

Her depression lifted on completing the ironing. She was pleased for David—it was his nineteenth birthday and he had the world at his feet. He had left school at sixteen and became an apprentice radio technician for the Radio and Wireless Company based in New Plymouth. She was so proud of him, though being an apprentice his wages were nothing to speak of—he could have earned more in the docks or on a building site. But he still made sure he gave his mother a third of his wages for his housekeeping: he knew she would struggle to manage without his contribution.

Six months before his birthday he informed his mother he had applied to Radio and Wireless to join one of their cable-laying ships as a junior radio officer. She didn't want to lose him, but at the same time she was proud that he wanted to make something of himself and not end up like Alex—a drunken bully who had never been further than the North Island.

The company accepted his application and was willing to sponsor his three-month introduction course as a junior radio officer in the United Kingdom. The course would start on the 1st June. He would have to make his way to Portishead Radio receiving station at Bristol, England. He would need two thousand pounds. This would be for his flight, course books and uniforms, and he would have to arrange his own accommodation. The only problem as far as Ruth was concerned was where the company ships were based and sailed from English ports.

When Alex found out what was going on he went into an uncontrollable rage. He grabbed David by the throat with his left hand and swung his right fist towards his jaw. David, who stood three inches taller then Alex, moved his head to one side and Alex's fist missed David's jaw by inches. Alex's drunken state caused him to fall to the floor. David knelt down beside Alex and looked into his eyes. He felt nothing but hatred for the man he thought of as his father. "If you touch me or any of the family again, I'll kill you!" he breathed through clenched teeth, not knowing where his strength and words came from.

David knew why his father was upset, of course—his wages would be missed and Alex would have to make up the shortfall.

It had been ten days since the incident. Both parties had avoided each other. Ruth and the girls never found out about the set to and

David was ashamed of the whole episode. Alex had been shocked by David's retaliation—his pride and ego had taken a beating.

Ruth's parents had arranged a dinner party at their house to celebrate David's birthday. Keith and Rita idolised David and were so pleased he was nothing like his father. They had disliked Alex right from the beginning, for they knew of his bulling and womanizing that had caused them to have nothing but contempt for the man. They would never be able to forgive him for the way he had ruined Ruth's young life and made her old before her time. Keith and Rita knew that without their financial help on occasions Ruth and the children would have gone without food. Brenda and Kate arrived home from school at 4 p.m. looking forward to the evening ahead.

Brenda was sixteen and Kate fifteen. They loved to get dressed in their best outfits. They would often borrow eye makeup and lipstick from their older sister, Diane. Tonight they knew the evening could be good fun provided their father wasn't there; their grandparents would certainly spoil them and let them drink wine.

Diane, the oldest girl at eighteen, arrived home from collage slightly late. She had stopped off at the chemist and bought some hair dye for her mother. That morning she had convinced Ruth into letting her 'dye' her hair and give her a complete makeover.

Tina, the youngest of the girls at thirteen, arrived home from her paper round just in time to answer the telephone. It was her father, Alex—he was unable to make the evening's dinner party due to work! Tina made her way to her mother's room, calling out to her as she went. "I'm in the bathroom!" Ruth replied. The door was open and Diane was standing over her mother massaging her scalp.

"Dad has just rang—he can't make this evening," Tina said with a smile. "He has to work!" She knew by the slurred voice of her father that he was drunk.

"Oh well, that will cheer your grandparents up," Ruth said wiping some dye from her forehead.

David arrived home at 5:30 pm. Ruth informed him that his father could not make the party. David never expected his father to be there so the news didn't come as a surprise. He knew he and everyone else would be able to relax and enjoy themselves all the better.

Ruth looked at David and suddenly realised what a grown up young man he was. Her heart ached painfully at the realisation that the dreaded day when he had to leave for England was fast approaching.

Diane finished Ruth's hair, then went to her own wardrobe and sorted out a dress for her mother. David and his sisters were the first to be ready and sat in the lounge waiting. They were overwhelmed when they saw the transformation in their mother! She entered the lounge with such grace with her hair pinned up and restored to its natural colour. Diane had applied the makeup so well—Ruth looked ten years younger and Diane's red dress fitted her like a glove! In spite of having had five children her figure had kept its shape. Ruth, for the first time in years, felt and looked good.

Keith and Rita were proud of their grandchildren and loved them as much as their daughter. They couldn't hide their dislike for Alex, but they never interfered with the marriage—apart from a few pounds here and there that helped Ruth to give the family some little luxuries.

Keith opened the door to the family and his heart jumped with joy to see his only daughter Ruth looking a wonderful picture. He knew without asking that Alex wouldn't be present and gave a sigh of relief—Alex would never allow Ruth out of the house dressed with this much class and glamour! Indeed, he would have regarded it as a threat to his marriage.

The meal was a great success—roast beef with all the trimmings. After coffee Keith produced a bottle of Tia Maria for the women. In addition he had a bottle of Bowmore Malt Whisky with its unique peaty flavour from the Western Isles—a special treat for David and himself.

For the first time since Ruth's marriage Keith stood up to make a speech. "First of all I would like to thank Diane for returning my daughter to me. It's been a long time to see her as she should look—young and pretty." He raised his glass and pointed it to Diane, then to Ruth. "Thank you both," he said, taking a sip from his whisky tumbler. "Now let's get down to the real business of the evening. I want to take this opportunity to thank David for being such a good son to his mother. I think you will all agree with me when I say we're going to miss him." He took his glass from the table and held it up to David. "I for one want to thank you for being there for your mother when she has needed you, son. We all know you want to pursue your own career." He looked at Ruth "I know your mother is pleased for you. However, none of us wants to see you go. I'm sure I'm speaking for all of us when I say thank you David and God go with you!" Keith raised his glass and this time pointed it at David—then swallowed the remaining malt in one go.

Everybody clapped. Keith looked at his wife. "You have something for David?"

Rita took an envelope from her bag. "We know you have been saving hard and we are very proud of the way you have gone about it. However, your granddad and me want to help you." She handed the envelope to David. "Happy birthday, David!"

David took the envelope and opened it. There was a cheque for two thousand pounds and an airline ticket to London Heathrow. David was speechless.

Ruth never forgave Alex for not being at Auckland airport to say goodbye to David. The rest of the family cried and hugged David right up to the last possible moment before he boarded the Qantas flight for England.

He arrived in England on the 14th May 1977.

CHAPTER 15

Diago 1980

Maria sat on the wooden bench facing the parade ground of the Argentine's Navel Academy at Puerto Belgrano. It was the passing out parade of her son Diago.

Twenty-two years had passed since Terry had left her on the quay in Buenos Aires. She had told both her sons that just after they were conceived their father had died in a sailing accident. Strangely neither of them talked about him nor asked questions. She had a large photograph of Terry and herself on the sideboard, taken on the farm when he visited. Everybody accepted that he was their father and the story that went with it. Lomas and Pepe never said anything to the contrary.

For the last three years Diago had been a cadet officer at the academy. Today he was passing out as a junior officer. After the parade Diago met his mother in the officer's mess. A buffet and drinks had been laid on for all guests. Maria explained she had arranged a car to take them to the airport. There they would fly to Buenos Aires. She had booked them both into the Hilton hotel for three nights. She wanted three days alone with her son. She wanted to take him shopping, then to the theatre—in fact thoroughly spoil him.

Diago had been back at the farm for five days. He was sitting alone beside the large family swimming pool making the most of his free time. It felt good lying in the sun on this lovely autumn morning. Salvia the housemaid approached him. "Senior Menzis, I have a telegram for you—I've also brought you iced coffee."

"Thank you Salvia," Diago replied as he reached for the telegram.

Salvia put the drink on the table next to him. "Would you like anything else, sir?" She looked down on his tanned body, thinking he was so much like his brother Raul and wondered whether he would be the same in bed as Raul.

"No thank you Salvia—the coffee will do nicely." He was more interested in the telegram and tore the envelope open and read:

TO: JUNIORY OFFICER DIAGO MENZES

REPORT TO THE NAVAL SHIP GENERAL BELGRANO NO LATER THAN NOON ON 28 MARCH 1980 AT PUERTO BELGRANO.

That evening he showed the telegram to his mother. She was immensely pleased with his appointment and immediately began organising a going away party. He had six days before his joining date. Within six mouths of being on board the Belgrano, Diago had earned his promotion to Lieutenant. The ship had spent most of its time in port. Every so often it put to sea and patrolled the Argentine coast between Mar del Plata and Punta Arenas. Two days before Christmas 1981 the ship docked at the military naval base at Buenos Aires. Most of the crewmembers, including Diago, were granted Christmas leave.

The Taxi pulled into the farm and Diago looked and admired what he saw. The farm had never looked better. The midsummer sunshine following an early morning rainfall had freshened the grass. The horses were taking advantage of the recent downpour and were grazing in the lush green fields while the surrounding trees gave the setting a 'postcard' look.

It came home to him what he was missing. The life in the navy was a great disappointment and was not what he expected. He started to wonder whether he should resign his commission and work the farm; for one thing, he knew his mother would be pleased.

To everybody's disappointment Raul was unable to join the family for his Christmas leave had been cancelled. For the first time in many years Diago spent a family Christmas and New Year at home. Maria had invited his school girlfriend Sonia. He and Sonia had kept in touch since military college. He had no idea Sonia was madly in love with him—as far as he was concerned they were just good pen friends and met whenever he was home on leave and had the occasional good night kiss.

Until now Diego's life revolved around the navy. This Christmas leave had opened his eyes and gave him more than a twinge of homesickness. It was the first time he didn't look forward to returning to his ship. He wanted more out of life—a family life, in fact.

The night before returning to the ship he took his mother and Sonia into the lounge and poured three large brandies. "I've asked you to join me for a nightcap because I've something to say to you both." He took a sip of brandy. "I have six months to go on my junior commission. I then have to decide whether to renew my commission." He paused, looking at them both, one at a time. "I've made up my mind to resign my commission. I want to return to the farm and work beside you—if you will have me?" He smiled at Sonia. "Sonia, my feelings have grown for you over the last few days. I want to ask your parents for us to start dating officially—that's if you want to?"

Sonia beamed. She had been waiting for years for this to happen. Her prayers at last had been answered.

Diago took the final sip from his glass, then looked at his mother. "Well mother, do you want me to come home and work the farm?"

Tears filled Maria's eyes. She stood up, then walked towards him and put her arms around him. "Thank you—thank you," she said between her sobs, basking in her knowledge that she had made the perfect gentleman out of Diago. Maria knew Raul would never approach the same situation in this manner. He would have been like a bull at a fence.

On the 30th January the *Admiral Belgrano* was ordered to sail from Buenos Aires to the Port of Comodoro Rivadavia. On the 5th February the ship had orders to put to sea and head for the Malvinas. After doing a wide berth of the Malvinas the ship was to make its way to the Argentine port of Ushuala, making notes of all ship movements in the vicinity.

The *Admiral Belgrano* docked at Ushuala on the 2nd March 1982. The next day Diago was surprised that extra ammunition was being loaded onto the ship. The following day a team of French workers came on board. He was soon to find out they were working on a new missile system. He had read about the system, which concerned the French Exocet missile. Within fourteen days the ship had been fitted with eight Exocet missile launchers. Diago wondered why there was so much secrecy. Perhaps it was because of the relationship between Chile and Argentine. The territorial dispute concerning the Beagle Channel had raised its ugly head again. Surely the Argentine Junta was not thinking of going to war with Chile?

By the end of March rumours were rife aboard the *Belgrano*. There was so much activity going on within the docks. Argentinean warships that had not left their moorings for years suddenly made steam and put to sea.

On the 2nd April 1982 it was official—the Argentine Forces had invaded the Malvinas Islands.

Diago had mixed feelings regarding the taking of the Malvinas. Like all Argentineans, they where taught to regard them as Argentine territory. Seeing the barren islands from a distance, he didn't think they were worth fighting over. Some said the Islands had oil that had never been drilled out. If that were true it could mean millions of American dollars to boost the much-needed economy for his beloved country. Yet he wondered if even this were a good enough reason to go to war.

In any case, it was argued, Britain would hardly send a fighting force half way round the world to protect a couple of small barren islands.

It was the 11th April before Diago and the ship's crew found out that the British had sent a task force to the South Atlantic. It was hard to believe that the Junta had risked losing popularity by putting the country on a war footing with Britain!

On the 26th April the *General Belgrano* and two destroyers, the *Hipolito Bouchard* and *Piedra Buena,* put to sea and headed for the Malvinas.

By the afternoon of Sunday 2nd May the ship was at action stations. At 1600 hours Diago had orders to check the emergency steering gear situated aft of the ship. He had just reached the aft poop deck when the first torpedo hit the ship forward. Three seconds later the second torpedo hit the ship astern. The blast sent Diago thirty feet in the air and his body became a pincushion for hot steel shrapnel from the ship's hull.

He landed unconscious in the ice-cold water forty feet from the ship's port side. Within seconds he regained consciousness. The first thought he had was his heavy winter topcoat was dragging him under the cold black sea. He thought about taking it off when he noticed the right sleeve had disappeared taking his arm with it. Three inches of bone and tendons were where his arm should have been. His immediate thoughts were to look around to see where his arm was. There was no sign and then suddenly the pain hit him. Pain like he'd never experienced before gripped his entire body. His mind flooded with thoughts, of Raul his twin brother, wondering what he was doing. Then his mind drifted to his father, the man he never knew. To his surprise he could see his mother a few feet away waving to him. He tried to swim towards her but she disappeared under the waves. He must save her! He reached out for her and the black sea engulfed him. His heavy waterlogged topcoat dragged him down to a watery grave.

CHAPTER 16

Raul 1980

Raul sat on the terrace overlooking the pool, enjoying his breakfast. He was in the middle of ten days leave before returning to the Rio Gallegos air base for his final year of training which would consist of six mouths at base, then six months combat training in Israel. He had just returned from Germany where he had been training on light aircraft with the German Air Force.

Ex-Luftwaffe pilot Adolf Galland had advised the Argentinean Air Force since 1947. Galland's influence on the Fuerza Aerea (Argentine Air Force) and the Argentine government was so entrenched that the Argentine government based their air force on the German Luftwaffe. When possible the Fuerza Aerea paid for their young pilots to have six months training in Germany.

In 1974 tension began to build between Chile and Argentine over the ownership of the Beagle Channel. The Argentine Government embarked on a re-equipment programme to bring their air force up to date. At this time they probably had the largest Air Force in South America—19,500 men and over 400 operational aircraft.

Raul had five days remaining before he was due to return to the air base. He would then start training on the Douglas A4P Skyhawk. The American aircraft had been built originally for the U.S. Navy.

Raul's thoughts were interrupted by Salvia. "Would you like more coffee, Senior Mendaz?"

"Yes please, Salvia." He watched as she picked up his dirty plate and returned to the kitchen. He was alone in the house with her. Pepe had taken his mother to the capital on business and Lomas was at the stud farm with the rest of the staff or orphans. Raul could never tell them apart.

He remembered the first day Salvia came to the farm. She was five years of age—which is what she had told everyone. Captain Rossi, an old police friend of his mother, had arrived at the farm holding the hand of Salvia. The police had found Salvia on the streets of Buenos Aires, begging. Raul couldn't believe how ugly the child was. That was fourteen years ago.

As she got older she seemed to take over the household chores automatically. At fifteen Maria offered her full-time employment as housekeeper with a wage and her own room. Salvia had proved what a good housekeeper she was ever since.

She returned from the kitchen with a jug of hot coffee. Raul watched as she came towards him. He couldn't help but admire her now mature body. She was approximately 5ft 5ins tall with a 34-inch bust that stood out like two lovely round oranges. Her waist was just 25 inches! Her long legs reached up to her round, tight 36-inch bottom that was shaped like a peach. Raul knew her body was beautiful. Nevertheless it didn't stop him thinking how ugly she was. Her nineteen-year-old face looked a lot older. Her colour and features were that of an Argentine native Indian. Her nose was flat against her face: the fact that her nostrils were very large and raised up did not make her the prettiest woman he'd seen. She wore her black and silky hair pulled backwards and tied into a bun.

In spite of her facial appearance Raul had become infatuated with the body of Salvia—so much so that he couldn't take his eyes off her dark slim figure. He knew if she'd been prettier she might have been a super model.

She reached over the table and poured a fresh cup of coffee. He could no longer restrain himself. He slipped his hand up her flowered flared skirt. To his surprise she wore no knickers and he found his hand come into contact with the thatch between her legs. She looked down at him, smiled and pulled away—and returned to the kitchen as if nothing had happened. Raul followed in a fever of excitement. When he reached the kitchen she was standing over the sink with her back to him. He went up behind her and started to kiss her neck. She turned and his mouth found her lips. She was unresisting and he lifted her, placed her on the workbench and she lay back. The height was just right for his erect penis to enter her, but she was too tight. He spat in the palm of his hand using the saliva to lubricate his penis and tried again. He thrust into her and she screamed in pain. Raul had never been with anybody so tight and the tight pressure forced the sperm out of him within seconds. He never thought for one minute that she had been a virgin.

For the remainder of his leave he would wait until his mother had gone to bed, then creep out of his room, make his way to Salvia's room and take his sexual pleasures. Salvia, being naïve, believed that one day Raul would marry her and she would become lady of the house. Lucky for Raul her body was not ready for pregnancy.

Raul received his pilot's wings in February 1981 and his mother attended the handing over ceremony. She had arranged to spend three days with him in Buenos Aires, as she said, to 'spoil him.' He loved his mother but he didn't want three days walking the streets of Buenos Aires shopping. His idea of celebrating his wings would be a few days holiday in Rio de Janeiro or Montevideo with nice young women—now *that* would be spoiling him! The problem was she always treated him the same as Diago: they may be twins and look the same, but Raul was much more adventurous than Diago.

After three days in Buenos Aires they returned to the farm. Raul felt uncomfortable when Salvia was around for she made it quite clear what she wanted—which was Raul. Having already got what he wanted from her he no longer wanted anything to do with her and life was becoming unbearable for him. Maria could sense something wrong though she had no idea what. It was no surprise when Raul told her he was going away to Montevideo for a week's holiday. Maria was disappointed when he didn't invite her.

Ten days later he returned to Rio Gallegos air base. He had been given an A 4 p Skyhawk that made him a part of the Fuerza Aerea defence system patrolling the Chile-Argentine border. Raul loved the thrill of flying and compared it with all-night sex with a good woman. He found it hard to separate the two.

He knew his mother was looking forward to Christmas. Diago had been granted leave and Maria wanted everybody together for the fist time in years. To please her he applied for leave. He had it granted, though, in truth, he wasn't looking forward to it.

Two days before he was due to leave for the farm his leave was cancelled and he was confined to base. No one could or would answer his question why. The next day at 10.00 hours Five French built Super Etendards flew into the base. He had proved to be the most promising pilot they had flying Skyhawks so he was selected to fly the new Etendard and to be trained on the new weapon system, the AM39 Exocet missile.

The training took place just off the Argentine coast. All through January and February the training went on. Raul enjoyed the low-level flying which was like riding a roller coaster, only a thousand times better.

At the beginning of March the training changed. The plane would leave the air base, climb to maximum altitude, fly four hundred miles out into the South Atlantic, then return. This went on day after day. The pilots didn't have a clue why. But it wasn't long before the whole country knew they where at war with Britain.

Raul had just returned from a morning recognizance flight over the Malvinas before having a late lunch, then retired for an afternoon siesta. He woke just after 4 p.m., his right arm stiff with pins and needles, his whole body soaking wet with sweat. He tried to move but the pain throughout his body was tremendous. He reached out to the bedside table for a glass of water, took a sip and choked. He felt as if he were drowning. He had never felt this frightened in all his life! He wondered what was happening to him, and then he passed out.

Lami, a friend and fellow pilot, woke Raul later that evening. He had news that the *General Belgrano* had been sunk that afternoon by a British submarine. Lami had no idea that Raul's twin brother had been serving on the ship. Raul's thoughts went back to the afternoon. Did he dream the event or was it real?

On Tuesday 4th May 1982 Raul and two colleagues took off from the Rio Gallegos air base and headed out into the South Atlantic. All three aircraft had a long-range fuel tank under the port wing, and the AM39 Exocet anti-ship missile under the starboard wing. Fifty minutes later all three approached the Malvinas from the west. Raul, the lead pilot, made his way to the north of the islands, banked to the right and at the same time pushed the controls forward so the aircraft lost height.

As the plane dropped he could make out Pebble Island to his right, then Ajax Bay to his left. He flew between the north and south island at ground level. At the end of the channel he switched his ship detector radar on. Two blips showed and Raul fired his missile at the first blip, banked to the right and pulled back on the stick. He turned to see his missile hit a war ship. The last he could see before turning towards home was black smoke billowing from amidships. His missile had hit a British Destroyer.

Raul flew many more missions over the Malvinas with many more probable hits, but his first hit was the only one confirmed. Each mission became harder. The problem was the distance and the weather. The eight hundred-mile round trips only allowed the aircraft fifteen to twenty minutes to carry out their missions. This meant they could not afford to get involved in dogfights with British pilots. The weather played a big part as well: it would be perfect on the main land, yet thick fog over the Malvinas.

Each day the Argentine aircraft became fewer and fewer. Most of the aircraft had been shot down either by enemy aircraft or by superior land-to-air missiles. The remaining aircraft were unable to take off owing to the lack of spare parts. The British had successfully put up a blockade. Everything that had been imported was hard to come by, even for the Military.

By the time the land war had finished on the 15th June the Argentine Air Force was completely demoralised. Raul, who was still after revenge, tried time and again to penetrate the British defences, only to be turned back by RAF Phantoms now based at Port Stanley.

In December 1984 Raul's time in the Argentine Air Force ended. He returned to his mother's farm, still eager to avenge his brother's death.

CHAPTER 17

Kevin 1982

Four mouths before Kevin's 23rd birthday his dream came true. He becomes a member of the elite Special Air Services. It was the 2nd May and Britain had been at war with Argentine for 31 days. Since becoming a member of the SAS, Kevin had spent the last eight mouths in the classroom at Stirling Line Barracks and had been studying many different functions. Today he felt extremely proud of himself—he had just passed his Spanish language exam. Before leaving the classroom he had been given a message to report to the Warfare Office and Captain Brown the next day at 800 hours.

Kevin was a part of the Boat Troop D Squadron 22 SAS. He arrived at the office on the following day to find seven other members of D Squadron, Including a Captain Knight. The office had been set out with eight chairs in a half-moon shape facing Captain Brown's desk. Everybody was standing in one corner helping themselves to coffee from a percolator.

Captain Brown stood up from behind his desk. "Right gentleman, we seem to be all here. As soon as you've had your coffee please take a seat and we will start." He sat back down and waited for them all to be seated. A few seconds later the buzz of conversion stopped and everybody was seated, waiting in anticipation.

"Thank you gentleman. I have some good news for you all. You're off to war and the South Atlantic." Everybody in the room had been waiting for this moment since the 2nd April. The Captain continued: "We have a main raiding force on board H.M.S. *Hermes*. The forty-five men from D Squadron are preparing to land on Pebble Island to destroy the radar station, fuel dump and airstrip. By doing this it will minimise the main task force casualty list on D day." Captain Brown took a sip of coffee and continued. "Now your job is to go in a couple of days before our main unit, do a complete reconnoitre, pinpoint the objectives, then advise on the best time to attack—to maximise the impact of the raid. Once you've marked out the landing zone and the main force have landed, you get the hell out of there—your job will have been done." Captain Brown looked at the men in front of him. Everyone had a smile on his face. They were like a class of schoolboys that had been informed they were playing football for the school team. "Captain Knight will be in charge of the group. He will now give you a rundown on the next few days." Captain Brown sat down to the right of his deck and beckoned Captain Knight to take over.

Kevin couldn't believe his luck when war broke out and Second Para were deployed to the Falklands. He couldn't help being envious—he wanted to be with them. But now seven colleagues and he himself were going to be in the thick of it.

Later that night the SAS unit with full equipment flew from Brize Norton on board an R.A.F. D.C.10. The men and their equipment filled the large aircraft.

Kevin had time to think about his first operation. The unit was to fly to Ascension Island; once there they were to familiarise themselves with the new equipment supplied by the American forces. A Hercules aircraft would then take them to the South Atlantic. The C130 Hercules would be making essential equipment drops to the Task Force Fleet. At the same time the SAS unit would parachute and rendezvous with H.M.S. *Glamorgan*. Once on board they would have their final briefing.

At Ascension Island they familiarised themselves with the Stinger, an American shoulder-launch missile (recommended to the SAS for its lightness and size); and also an attachment to the High Frequency radio sets that looked more like a small computer terminal—invaluable for its use to encode and digitise messages: when used the message would be just a short burst of speech or Morse. At Brigade H.Q the message would then be unscrambled.

The flight down to the South Atlantic was uneventful other then the refueling done by a Victor K2 Tanker while in flight. The Hercules flew over the Task Force and dropped its load. The SAS unit was put on standby, the aircraft banked full to the right and straightened. The green light came on and all eight men jumped from the rear of the aircraft at 1500 feet and opened their canopies. It was easy from there to guide their kite-like canopies towards the orange flares that were burning brightly in the cold South Atlantic water.

A launch from H.M.S. *Glamorgan* picked them up and within fifteen minutes of leaving the aircraft they were on board the Destroyer. That evening they sat and watched a movie with the rest of the crew. Kevin could not digest the movie: his mind could only think of the task ahead.

The next morning, 11th May, Kevin and the rest of the SAS unit were shown to the officers' wardroom where they were briefed on the coming events.

At 20.00 that evening the eight men in four canoes left the H.M.S. *Glamorgan's* side and headed for Keppel Island. Twenty minutes later the guns of the *Glamorgan* began shelling Pebble Island, the idea being to keep the Island's radar operators sufficiently preoccupied. The group landed on Keppel Island at 21.35, unopposed—the Island looked, and was, unoccupied. They hid their canoes and took up a position so they were able to observe Pebble Island's airstrip. All the next day they observed and made notes. At sunset they sent back all the information to H.M.S. *Hermes*. They then informed H.M.S. *Glamorgan* the group was to continue across the Keppel Sound to Pebble Island. Again, the *Glamorgan's* guns bombarded the Island. They reached the Island, again unopposed. They hid their canoes and made tracks to a hill they had observed earlier that day. The hill was about a thousand feet above sea level and north-west of their objective. When dawn came they were able to survey the whole area. The airstrip lay nine hundred feet below them; to the right was the radar station; at the other end was the fuel and ammunition dump. During the day supply aircraft brought in more fuel and ammunition and flew off again. The airstrip itself only had two spotter aircraft, nothing like they had expected. Captain Knight decided to wait another day.

On the 14th May the airstrip suddenly became the busiest place on the island when Twelve Pucara aircraft landed and took up station. Pucara aircraft where designed and built at the Argentine Military Aircraft Factory. Designed for ground attack, the aircraft had a considerable punch, armed with two cannons, four machine guns and up to 3300 lbs of bombs and rockets.

It would be quite something to have these aircraft destroyed before lay could take off and cause carnage among the British forces. A workforce began to refuel and arm the ugly but dangerous aircraft.

Captain Knight prayed they would not take off until the next day—and his prayers were answered. The aircraft, though armed and refueled, just sat on the tarmac.

That afternoon the group radioed H.M.S. *Hermes* and recommended the raiding party commence that evening. Captain Hamilton, the raiding party's Commanding Officer, agreed. Kevin and his group made their way to the rendezvous area and marked out a landing zone for the incoming helicopters. Once the Sea King helicopters landed, Kevin and his group made their way back to their canoes and headed out to sea and the *Glamorgan*.

Meanwhile the assault group split into two. The first party was to destroy the main targets—all aircraft on the ground, the radar station, then the fuel and ammunition dump. The second party's orders were to keep the Argentine garrison of army and navy personnel occupied. H.M.S. *Glamorgan* now had targets to aim for and kept up a barrage of 4.5in shells at one a minute.

At 0745, SAS Squadron started their withdrawal, the operation a complete success. Only two miner injuries where sustained by the SAS, caused by shrapnel from a remote-controlled mine which, however, detonated too late to have much effect.

Kevin's exploits in the Falklands war were at an end. He was transported back to Hereford and the classroom. He had four weeks to learn to speak with an Irish accent.

In June he made his way to Dublin on a fake Irish passport. He spent the next six mouths trying to infiltrate the IRA and gathered vital information. However, the IRA never took him into the fold.

Being fluent in Spanish took him to Columbia in January of the following year. There he spent nineteen months playing havoc with the Colombian drug cartel. He and two colleagues destroyed millions of pounds worth of cocaine. They were brought home because the cartel had put a million dollars on each one of their heads.

Kevin decided he needed a holiday.

CHAPTER 18

David 1985

David climbed the stairs to the officer's promenade deck. He laid his towel on the first deck chair he came to. He had two hours before he had to take the ship's weather report to the London Meteorological office in Bracknell. He lay down on the deck chair and enjoyed the relaxing warmth of the sun.

The ship, a cable layer for Radio & Wireless Company, had sailed the previous day from Cape Town after five mouths in the South Atlantic. M.V. *Essex* was making its way to its homeport of Southampton where it would be laid up for six weeks for a major refit.

David was looking foreword to returning to Southampton and his home. He had applied for six weeks' leave and to his surprise it had been granted. He lay in the sun daydreaming about the last few years—years that had been good to him and his family.

Tina his youngest sister, to everybody's surprise, had a natural ability to learn languages: at the present she was fluent in Japanese, French and Italian and working for Auckland International Airport as an interpreter.

Brenda had married a sheep farmer from the South Island. She was very happy and had a son of eighteen months and was six months pregnant with her second child.

Kate had become a police constable with the Auckland's Metropolitan Police Department, at present sitting for her sergeant's exams.

Diane went to University and got a Degree in business studies and was now working as a consultant to the New Zealand tourist board—which meant travelling around the world.

His mother Ruth had divorced Alex and set up home in Auckland. Since Diane gave her the makeover for David's Birthday party she had grown in confidence: by the time Tina had left school in 1980 Ruth had her final divorce papers. She was now a supervisor at the Auckland Telephone exchange. The equipment may have changed but the job reminded her of her teenage years.

David joined his first ship with Radio & Wireless five months after arriving in England. Since then he had worked hard and studied even harder. Two years before, after sitting his final exams, he had become chief wireless operator on board the M.V *Essex*. To celebrate this he bought a two-bedroomed bungalow in Chandlers Ford, a town just outside of Southampton. The odd thing was he picked the bungalow because of its garden. At the time he didn't have a clue about gardening. He became friendly with his neighbour Harold, a retired train driver, who had the problem of being henpecked. His wife Doris had had their garden completely paved. Harold only had his allotment to look after. Therefore, when David asked him to tend the garden while he was away he was delighted. He also supplied a few gardening books for David to read while he was away at sea.

David was looking forward to getting home. This would be the first time since arriving in England that there would be someone to come home to. He had met Barbara while he was on leave from the previous voyage. They had met by chance in the local hairdressers.

He had entered the shop on the off chance, wanting a haircut without an appointment. As he approached the girl sitting behind the reception desk, an attractive blonde lady left the lady she was blow-drying and came towards him.

"Good morning—would you like a haircut?"

"Yes please," David said, feeling his face reddening.

"If you'd like to sit down I'll be with you in ten minutes."

The young girl behind the reception desk couldn't believe what she'd just seen: the owner had never acted like that before and she wondered why.

David sat in a waiting chair with his back to the window, picked up a magazine and began to flick through the pages. His eyes and mind were not on the magazine but concentrating on the blonde lady that had greeted him. Her beauty and elegance were captivating. Her hair was short and straight, just covering her ears, the front sides curled slightly up to cover her high cheekbones. Her green eyes sparkled and her warm smile never left her face. She wore a blue nylon overall that could not hide her lovely peach like bottom. Below this magnificent round bottom were the perfect long and shapely legs.

Barbara finished the lady's hair with a spray of lacquer. She turned and smiled at David and indicated for him to sit in the vacant chair. She followed the lady with the new hairdo to the reception desk. After the usual pleasantries she returned, tied a sheet around David's neck and looked at him via the mirror.

"Right, what would you like?" She flashed a smile that left him speechless.

"Er…oh…an all-over trim please."

She started to comb his hair. "Did you go anywhere nice this time?"

Once again he was speechless. She smiled again. "It's all right—I live in the bungalow facing you. Harold told me all about you—you're in the navy."

"Well, the Merchant Navy," he replied, feeling more at ease.

"It's still the Navy. When are you going back?"

"I have another ten days leave—then the ship is off to the South Atlantic."

All through the conversation their eyes never drifted from each other. David realized she hadn't even started on his hair. He also noticed she wasn't wearing a wedding ring.

"Do you live with your husband?" he probed.

She shook her head. "I'm not married. I live with my mother."

David was usually shy with women but this woman put him completely at ease.

"I don't suppose you'd come out to dinner with me one evening?" he said with a sudden surge of bravado.

"That will be lovely—how about this evening?" she said, finally starting to cut his hair.

"Great! I'll come across for you about 8 o' clock." David smiled and she nodded, carrying on cutting. It was not until he left the salon that he realised he had failed to ask her name. He would ask Harold, he thought.

That Monday evening in November they took a Taxi to Southampton and decided to have an Indian meal. By the end of the evening they both felt they had known each other for years. For the rest of the week they spent every evening together—the theatre, the cinema or just going for a walk to the local public house. On Sunday Barbara invited him for lunch with her mother. Her mother took an instant liking to David.

After lunch he invited Barbara to view his garden. The garden looked a picture in the cold sunny afternoon. They entered the large warm greenhouse and he picked a few tomatoes, then turned and handed them to Barbara. She accepted them, put them on the nearby bench and placed her hands around his neck and kissed him. Both their lips gelled together in what felt like a moment of eternity. Then she broke from the kiss and looked into his eyes. "David," she said huskily, "make love to me—here, and now?"

They lay on the greenhouse wooden floor. His hands lifted her dress and removed her knickers. He placed his right hand between her legs, feeling how wet she was. She sighed: "David…I'm so ready for you." He removed his trousers and underpants and slipped into her, smoothly and effortlessly. Their love for each other was so great and urgent they climaxed within seconds of each other.

The memory of that afternoon and the letters he received from Barbara gave him a new lease of life. If the weather kept fair the ship would dock in Southampton on the 15th April. The next fourteen days before then would seem like a lifetime to David. On the 9th April the ship had a brief stop at Las Palmas to refuel. Beside the usual letter from Barbara he received a letter from his sister Diane. She was coming to England in April on business—could she stay with him?

CHAPTER 19

Raul 1985

Maria had become concerned for Raul. All he seemed to do was sit around the pool and drink. She understood what he was going through because she was going through the same pain, for the loss of Diago had caused her so much heartache. The farm would have suffered if it had not been for Lomaz and Pepe, and without the friendship of Captain Rossi she was convinced she would have lost everything.

Everything came to a head when she caught Raul coming from the room of Salvia in the early hours. She decided she had to be cruel to be kind. She told Raul he was to work the farm or find a job—otherwise he would have to leave the farm. At first his reaction was to leave the farm: he reacted like a spoilt brat. But that night he didn't sleep a wink and he tossed and turned. By the time the sun came up he realised what a fool he had been. The one thing in life he needed to do was fly again.

Within minutes of the sun breaking through he was up. He started the coffee percolator, went to the lounge and sat at the desk, selected writing paper and wrote a letter to the Argentine National Airline. His excitement at the thought of flying again compared to re-living the whole of his sex life over again. For the first time since leaving the Air Force, his future looked promising.

He was on his tenth lap of the pool when Salvia appeared on the terrace. She stood there with the sun to her back and Raul stopped at the edge of the pool looking up at her. With the sun to her back he could see through her dress. She still was not wearing any panties or bra. He climbed the ladder, walked towards his sunbed, took a towel and sat down. Salvia came towards him and handed him a letter. "Senor Menzes—for you!" she said in a churlish tone. Since Maria had caught Raul leaving her room Salvia had been threatened to find other employment if she ever had sexual contact with Raul again. She stood in front of him waiting for some sort of reaction when suddenly a gust of wind lifted her dress. The thick thatch of black pubic hair was just a few inches from Raul's face. She thrust her pelvis foreword and before long Raul had buried his face into the bush of pubic hairs, overcome by the tantalising smell of womanhood, his tongue finding the damp slit.

"Salvia—go to your room!" It was his mother's voice. "I'll speak to you in a moment." Her fury broke loose on her son: "Raul! How could you! It looks like I came along in time!"

"Sorry, mother," he said meekly, embarrassed and full of shame. "It will not happen again."

Maria sat in the chair and faced him. "Don't you realise what she's up to? She wants you—so she can become lady of the house. I won't have it! You could have anybody!"

Raul let her carry on without answering her. He opened his letter and the shock on his face stopped Maria in her tracks.

"What is the matter?" she asked with genuine concern in her voice.

"The airline has rejected me—they will not give a reason."

The next morning Pepe drove Raul to Rosario's main train station. There he took the train to Buenos Aires. At 11:30 a.m. he hailed a taxi. He told the taxi driver to take him to the offices of Argentine Airolinas, the national airline. Their offices were about fifty yards from the Hilton Hotel. He made his way to the personnel office on the second floor. In the small outer office a lady in her mid-forties sat at a large desk busy typing on an electric typewriter.

"Yes, can I help you?" she asked, looking up.

"Yes—I want to see someone regarding my application." He pulled out the letter he had received the previous day and handed it to her. She opened it and read it.

"You have been rejected," she said, handing him back the letter.

"I *know* that!" he replied in a loud voice. "I want to know *why*." The tone of his voice alarmed her.

"We do not give out reasons," she said, going back to her typewriter.

Raul was becoming angry at her tone of voice. "Now look *here*—I'm a qualified *pilot*. I fought for this country to regain the Malvinas Islands! Now I want to speak to someone who dealt with my application! They must have made a mistake."

She looked at him. The hurt and strain in the man's handsome face touched her sympathies. "Take a seat—I will see what I can do." She pointed to two chairs next to the door and he sat in the chair nearest to the door.

After three internal telephone calls she informed him that someone would see him at 2 p.m. if he wanted to return at that time.

He returned an hour and ten minutes later, fifteen minutes to two. At twenty past two the lady at the typewriter showed him into a side room. Two gentlemen sat at the one and only desk: both men were in their forties. The man to the left of Raul wore a dark grey suit, the other white overalls with black trousers and a white shirt. A red tie badly knotted was partly hidden under his white overall.

They both and shook hands with Raul. "My name is Captain Bonneti and this is Doctor San Josa. Please be seated, Mr Menzis." The man in the dark grey suit pointed to a chair situated in front of the desk. "We have taken these unusual steps to see you, in respect of your war record." He looked at the papers in front of him. "Are you sure you want to hear why you have been rejected?"

"Of course—that's why I'm here!"

The man in the white coat cleared his throat. "Raul—may I call you Raul?" Raul nodded. "Raul, it's your discharge report from the Air Force that concerns us; it's not good."

Raul looked surprised. "I resigned my commission, I was not discharged."

The doctor continued: "Yes, we know that—we have your discharge record here. It was completed by your commanding officer after you left the Air Force." The doctor looked back at the papers in front of him. "It states here you were grounded seven mouth before you resigned." He looked back at Raul and waited for a reply.

"That's correct—the reason being the Air force were unable to get spare parts for aircraft. So they were unable to take off—hence I was grounded." Raul honestly believed this statement told to him by his commanding officer. He continued: "All I lived for was flying—so when they grounded me I resigned, hoping they would see sense and make me operational again; but they just let me go."

The doctor looked at Captain Bonnetti, then back at Raul. "Your discharge report gives a completely different version. It says you became obsessed on revenge for the death of your brother." The doctor once again referred to the document in front of him. "It says you constantly put yourself and your aircraft in danger, flying into the no exclusion zone set up by the British after the war. On the last occasion you convinced a colleague to escort you. His plane was attacked by British Phantoms and shot down—because of this action your friend died. This was the last straw—you were finally grounded."

Raul sat there in disbelief. He had had no idea they blamed him for Lami's death. It did explain a lot that went on in the last few months at the air base. Colleagues deserted him. There were closed doors to anybody in authority. He wondered why it had never become known until now.

Captain Bonnetti interrupted his train of thought. "I spoke to your Commanding officer this lunch time. It seems you put the country at risk with your exploits; you could so easily have brought further conflict with the British. Our Air Force was concerned that the British could have retaliated with a bombardment on our mainland bases. That in turn gives us no defence against anybody. This would give Chile the opportunity to take advantage of our situation. So you see—you had become an embarrassment to the Air Force." Captain Bonnetti leaned back in his chair and contemplated the ceiling. After a few seconds he leaned forward and scribbled on a piece of paper that he passed to the doctor. The doctor studied the note. "Raul—would you mind waiting outside for a few minutes?"

Five minutes passed before the doctor opened the door and invited Raul to return. Raul sat in the same seat and Captain Bonnetti looked at him. "You understand, under the circumstances, we cannot employ you as a pilot with our airline; what we can offer you, however, is to train you to become a member of our cabin staff."

Raul looked at them with disbelief. He loved flying as a pilot, not as a waiter! He left the building after telling them both what he thought of them and their airline.

He walked for what seemed an age but in fact was only twenty-five minutes before he found himself in the red light district. The first bar he came to had a sign in lights over the main door: *Trebol.* He pushed the door open and walked in. It was dark to his eyes after the bright autumn sun. The only person in the small bar was a woman behind the bar—about 5ft 4ins and very slim. The light from behind the bar showed she had dark red hair that covered her shoulders and wore blue denim jeans. Her white nylon shirt matched the blue denim waistcoat. She was very attractive—her head should be on the body of Salvia, Raul thought.

"A bourbon and coke," he said, taking a seat on one of the stools at the bar. A wall jukebox at the end of the bar kicked in and Johnny Cash's voice filled the small room with the song *A Thing Called Love.* The barmaid placed the glass of bourbon and a bottle of coke in front of him, turned and placed an ice bucket in front of him. "It would be nice to get a please and thank you," she grumbled as she walked towards the jukebox.

"You're English?" he said, disgust in his voice.

She turned and walked back and stood in front of him. "How dare you insult me—I'm Irish," she said with contempt.

"You're still British! Why don't you go home—don't you think you've killed enough Argentineans?" He drank his bourbon down in one gulp without adding any coke, then stood up to leave.

She raised the bar flap and placed herself between Raul and the door. "Now you listen to me! I'm Irish and a member of the Irish Republican Army. We've been fighting the British for two hundred fucking years—to unite Ireland. You've fought the British for ten weeks and given up!"

Raul couldn't believe the sprite in this petite lady. "Argentine may have given up! *I* will never stop fighting the British!" He realised he had an ally and continued: "So you're a terrorist?"

She was furious. "I'm a *soldier*! The British may call me a terrorist, but I'm fighting for my country's independence. That makes me a *soldier*, okay?" She gave a half smile. "Look, since we have a lot in common I suggest we sit down and have a drink. My name's Mary—Mary O' Donald."

She held out her right hand. Raul took it with both his hands, kissed the back and then shook it. "My name's Lieutenant Raul Menzis. I was a pilot in the Argentine Air Force during the war. I had a confirmed kill—a Destroyer. I hope that makes me a hero in your eyes?"

Mary was impressed. They spent the rest of the evening in each other's company, exchanging exploits against the British. The last thing Raul could remember was the bar being very busy and dancing to Irish music.

He woke trying to remember the evening before. Where was he? He lay in the bed trying to focus on things around him. The window had shutters admitted just a sliver of light. The room was small with just a double wardrobe and a double bed. Mary lay next to him, her long dark red hair covering her face. He wondered whether anything had happened. The bourbon had not only given him a sore head, his mouth tasted as if he had eaten a plateful of bad cabbage. And he needed to go to the toilet. The door was next to the wardrobe. He made his way to the door and opened it to find a small corridor with three more doors. The first door had a light coming from underneath. He opened the door to find a toilet and bathroom. The light came from the skylight. He looked at his watch—7:55 a.m. After relieving himself he washed his mouth and drank straight from the tap. The water tasted good! Then he realised he had no clothes on. He made his way back to the bedroom and climbed into bed. Mary was awake.

"Are you all right?" she asked with genuine concern.

"A bit of a sore head," he said, looking at her thin body. She lay on her back, her hair covering the whole of the pillow. Her thin trim body fascinated him. Her breasts resembled two fried eggs with currents poking out of the yoke.

Mary misread the look on his face. "It's all right—you don't have to worry, nothing happened last night."

Raul felt embarrassed. "I'm glad—I like to remember when I make love." He felt his penis begin to swell and she looked down at him.

"Mm…that looks nice." She placed one hand on his testicles and the other on his shaft. She manoeuvred her body so she was kneeling next to him. She bent down and ran her tongue up and down his shaft before her mouth engulfed the head. After only a few seconds she stopped and lay back on the bed. "I want that in me—please." She smiled.

Raul got on top of her, levered her legs open and entered her. Automatically her legs rose up and wrapped themselves around his waist in a viselike grip. It was a strange feeling: with her thin wiry legs and her thin petite body, it felt as if his penis were supporting her whole body. At the same time she was saying in a loud voice: "Faster, faster!" She finely arched her back and gave a scream of relief. Raul still had not come. He turned her over, placed her into a kneeling position with her head on the pillow, face down, and entered her vagina from the rear. He reached a climax with her head turned to one side and looking up at him, grinning with satisfaction. She released Raul's penis and he fell to the bed exhausted. Within minutes he was asleep.

Mary bathed and dressed, putting on maroon corduroy trousers and a cream shirt covered by a maroon cardigan. The autumn mornings in Buenos Aires could be chilly.

She made her way down to the bar. She was glad she had paid the evening bar staff to clean before going home. She went behind the bar and picked up the telephone, checked the dial tone and dialed twelve digits. The connection took two minutes before the phone rang. It was answered after the fourth ring.

"Hello—is that you Sean?"

"Yes," came the response.

Mary spent ten minutes on the telephone speaking to her brother Sean who lived in a town called Ballygowen, twenty miles south of Belfast. Her brother looked at his watch—12:25 p.m.—and sat in the lounge armchair digesting Mary's conversation. At 1:40 p.m. he made a telephone call and was connected within seconds. "It's me—Sean. I need to speak to you—it's urgent." The voice on the other end of the line replied: "Meet me at the Harp and Angel at seven this evening"—and hung up. Sean was pleased. It gave him more time to work on his plan.

* * *

Sean locked the door to his terraced cottage and walked the half-mile to the Harp and Angel. He walked into the one-bar public house, greeted the landlord and walked directly to the door marked 'toilets.' Through the door was a corridor with three more doors—one marked 'gents,' the second marked 'ladies,' and the third 'private.' Sean knocked on the door marked 'private.'

"Who is it?" the soft voice of a man came from behind the door.

"Its me—Sean." There was the sound of a key turning in the lock and the door opened.

Peter Driscol, the Commander of the South Belfast branch of the Irish Republican Army, beckoned Sean in, closed the door and locked it. The wood-panelled room measured fifteen feet by fifteen feet. At the far end was an open fire with burning logs. In the middle of the room was a wooden table with four wooden chairs; a green checked tablecloth covering the table. An old briefcase, an office lamp and a pint class half filled with Guinness were on the table. An old floral two-seater sofa was against the near wall.

Peter was thirty-six years of age, 5ft 8in tall, and his twelve stone made him a stocky man. His black hair and ruddy face gave him a healthy look. Sean, in contrast, was six feet, thin and wiry with ginger hair. They had been friends since nursery school.

Both men made their way to the table and sat down. Sean was second in command to this unit and the main planner. Any plans put forward had to be cleared and sanctioned by both Peter and Sean.

"What's so important that can't wait for our weekly meeting?" Peter asked.

Sean took out a packet of Chesterfields and offered the pack to Peter who took a cigarette, stood up and went to the fireplace where he picked up an ashtray that he placed on the table before sitting down. Sean lit his cigarette, then leaned over and lit Peter's. He looked at Peter. "I had a phone call from Mary this mourning."

"Oh? How is she?" Peter blew a smoke ring in the air.

"She's fine, but can't wait for the day she can come home. I told her it's too dangerous now—the British are still looking for her. She told me about someone who could help our cause." Sean took a drag from his Chesterfield. "At first I couldn't think how he could help, but I've come up with a simple plan. The idea is to get maximum world-wide publicity at minimum cost, right?"

"Go on." Peter leaned forward, flicking his ash into the ashtray. Sean started to explain his plan.

"Well, to start with, Patrick O' Hare and his son are waiting to be sentenced by us for robbing a bank in the name of the IRA, then pocketing the money for themselves. They know they're under a sentence of possible death. As a reprieve, we offer them both a mission. Knowing them both as we do, they'll accept. Their only other option is to go to the U.D.I and grass us all up." Sean looked at Peter who was leaning back in his chair, studying the ceiling. Sean continued: "Patrick and his son join up with our man from Argentine. They then drive from Dublin through England to Spain. Before they leave, we let it slip to the SAS or the Special Branch that an IRA cell is active and on the move. This should keep two or three of their top men occupied for a couple of weeks. That will do for starters. The mission itself will be to make their way to Gibraltar. They arrive there as tourists and wait for the official visit of the H.M.S. *Invincible.* Prince Andrew is making an inspection visit to the Rock. They then attempt to assassinate the Prince or cause as much havoc on the Rock as possible."

Peter looked at Sean and interrupted him. "Other than getting rid of Patrick and his son on a suicidal mission, I can't see the point."

It irritated Sean that he had to explain. "The thing is, an Argentine terrorist joins the IRA on a combined mission, right? They combined to fight the British Forces because of their occupation of their respective Islands, thousands of miles apart. The British will worry that the IRA is moving abroad in their fight. Above all, they will be concerned that Argentine has started a terrorist movement. This should tie up more of their undercover agents. The rest of the world will condemn Britain on their Colonial bulyling of two miner nations. The IRA can only get good publicity out of anything that happens. It doesn't matter what the outcome, the IRA can't lose—right?"

❦ ❦ ❦

The next morning Mary made her way back to the bedroom. She had just finished speaking to Sean on the telephone. She stopped at the kitchen. The coffee had percolated. She had started it before telephoning Sean. She fixed up a tray with two cups, sugar, milk and the coffeepot and pushed the door to the bedroom open. Raul was sitting up in bed smoking.

"I've brought you coffee." She put the tray on the bed and sat beside it, poured two cups and handed one to Raul. "I've just been speaking to my brother. Do you still want revenge on the British government? There's an IRA cell being put together for an important assignment. My brother is willing to train you and guide you. If he's satisfied with the outcome you'll be able to join the cell." She added sugar to her coffee and took a sip.

Raul put his coffee down and looked at Mary. "What's the assignment?"

She shook her head. "Because of security I don't know. They won't tell you until the last possible moment. I can say this, though—they told me it will give you and your cause plenty of publicity."

Raul crushed his cigarette in the ashtray next to the bed. "If I say yes, then what?"

She took the coffeepot and topped up both cups. "We'll fly you to Dublin via New York. There you'll be trained in our methods before starting the mission."

Raul got out of bed and made his way to the bathroom. He showered and returned to the bedroom, drying himself. He stood in front of Mary, the towel around his neck. "Right—when do I start?"

❖ ❖ ❖

Raul had been away from the farm for six days. Maria had asked her friend Captain Rossi to try and find him but he had no success. When Raul walked into the lounge of the farm Maria was on the telephone, speaking to Captain Rossi. "Thank you, Antonio, he has just walked in!…Yes, I will…thank you. Good bye." She replaced the receiver. "That was Captain Rossi—the police have been looking everywhere for you! Where have you been? I have been worried!" She walked forward and kissed him on both cheeks.

"Mother, I'm a grown man! I don't need you to keep checking on me. I've come home to pack a suitcase. I'm off to Europe. I have a job with a Spanish airline and I'm flying from Buenos Aires this evening."

Maria was shocked but not surprised. She prayed for him to settle at the farm, but the war had changed him: he had become distant and was no longer the son she knew and loved. She often thought it would have been kinder to everybody if Diago had survived and Raul had died.

She drove Raul to Rosarrio station. He didn't want her to come to the airport, for Mary would be there with his tickets and a forged Irish passport. Maria wished him good luck, said her goodbyes and drove back to the farm where she gave way to tears. Why did she have the terrible feeling she would never see him again?

CHAPTER 20

Julie 1985

Julie sat in the front row of the Brookwood Crematorium holding her mother's hand, watching Albert's coffin being lowered to the underground furnace. The chapel was full of friends and customers from the Jolly Farmer public house.

Ten days earlier when Julie was preparing for her next flight to Australia via Singapore, her mother had telephoned her in a blind panic. Albert had had a fatal heart attack while cleaning the cellar.

British World Wide Airlines were very understanding and gave her four weeks compassionate leave.

Her mother had been in a state of shock since Albert's death. Julie took responsibility. The funeral arrangements were easier to arrange than she had expected. The funeral director organized every detail and all Julie had to do was invite the mourners and arrange the wake. Albert had always stated that on the day of his funeral the Jolly Farmer would be an open house to all his regulars. It didn't take a lot of work on Julie's part to organize open house for the day.

Carol had insisted she didn't want anything to do with the public house ever again and instructed Julie to arrange for its sale. Julie had been in touch with the Licence Vintners Association and the pub was placed on the market. A relief manager and his wife had started work at the pub two days earlier. Carol had moved back to her cottage a hundred yards from the pub.

Julie had become concerned about her mother's health. She had never seen her in such a state. It was understandable, of course, for Albert was not only her husband but also her soul mate. They had spent the last twenty-seven years doing everything together.

Julie spent the next two weeks caring for her mother. She felt it strange that her feelings were not the same as her mother's; of course, she loved her father and it had come as a shock, but she had been able to accept his death. Perhaps it was because she worried more about her mother that her thoughts for her father were relegated to the back of her mind.

She had four days left before she had to report to the airline. Val, who was the family friend and neighbour, had said she would check on Carol every day. Julie knew her mother would be in safe hands.

Julie was glad to be back in her own house. The last three and a half weeks had taken their toll and she was tired. The three-bedroomed terraced house situated in Ruislip was cold to walk into and Julie turned the thermostat up to seventy degrees.

She had bought the house eighteen months earlier. The company had just promoted her to Purser and the house was her way of celebrating.

The next morning she drove her Ford Escort GTi. to Heathrow. She parked the car in the World Wide British Airways cabin crew car park and reported to the dispatch office. She knew she would have to have the usual medical before they would allow her back to work. She had been off work for more than fourteen days. The medical officer was satisfied with her condition and that her father's death would not affect her ability.

Her next flight would be a Boeing 747 to the West Indian Island of Antique, leaving Heathrow at 9 a.m. the next day.

CHAPTER 21

Terry 1985

Terry left his Camberley Luxury flat at 6 a.m. and drove to Heathrow. This was only his second flight as Cabin Service Officer. He parked in the staff car park and took the airline bus to the reporting office. The cabin director gave him his brief and wished him a trouble-free flight.

He made his way to the restroom, poured himself a cup of black coffee from the ongoing coffee percolator, sat in the nearest armchair and studied his brief. He had the usual complement of crew, twenty-one cabin staff and two pursers. There was a footnote regarding one of the pursers—Julie Lyons had just returned from four weeks compassionate sick leave owing to the death of her father. Terry had never flown with or met Julie before, which is not surprising since there were over eight thousand-cabin staff that worked for the airline.

He hoped she was over her grieving. He did not cherish the prospect of her bursting into tears every two minutes. Other then Julie, the briefing was straightforward. The passenger list indicated a variety of needs—the usual vegetarians, a couple of bad legs, one neck in a brace and three children in carrycots. The one good thing about this particular flight was that most of the passengers were holidaymakers—they'd be out for a good time.

At 7:30 a.m. the crew for flight BWW 416 to Antigua were called to the security point. Terry checked them off one by one. He couldn't help noticing the beauty and self-confidence that emanated from Julie. He was automatically impressed and knew she wouldn't be a problem.

The flight to Antigua was uneventful. Terry had become increasingly impressed with his purser Julie. Passengers and crew alike took to this confident lady which all helped to make a pleasant and enjoyable flight for everybody.

The crew were booked into the Hilton and would be there for two nights before flying back to Heathrow. Terry shared a room with the other male purser, Steve Stuart. He unpacked, put on his swimming trunks, grabbed a towel and made his way to the pool.

After five laps he climbed out of the pool and sat on a sun bed and ordered a Planters Punch from a passing waiter. He noticed Julie walking towards the pool, impressed by the movement of her body: she walked with the grace of a tiger stalking its prey. Her figure fitted her yellow bikini like a glove. Her blonde hair, tied into a ponytail, went well with her bronzed skin.

Terry couldn't take his eyes off her good looks and shapely legs. He stood up and waved at her and she smiled back in recognition. He beaconed for her to join him. She came over and put her bag and towel on the sun bed he had placed next to his.

"Can I get you a drink?" he said as the waiter returned with his drink.

"What's that you're drinking?" she asked, pointing to his drink on the waiter's tray.

"Planters Punch—would you like to try one?"

"Why not?" She took her sunglasses from her bag and adjusted them to fit.

Terry handed her his drink and addressed the waiter: "Sorry to be a nuisance, Adam—could you do me another?"

Terry sat back on the sun bed and looked at Julie. She was so lovely it made him feel twenty years younger just being by her side! After an afternoon of non-stop conversation and two more drinks they both decided to sleep before dinner. He invited her for dinner that evening and to his surprise she accepted.

He arrived in the foyer at two minutes to eight, feeling and looking good for his forty-eight years. Just after 8 p.m. he watched Julie's elegant movement on the stairs. She was wearing a primrose dress that was not tight fitting, yet which outlined her flowing sinuous figure. She wore white shoes that matched the white handbag she was carrying. There was something about the primrose chiffon necktie around her neck—it had a knot like a noose and reminded him of someone, he couldn't think who. One thing he did know, the glamour and style of this young lady stirred up feelings that no person had ever done before—feelings he couldn't explain, not the feelings of lust but of genuine affection or love. He knew deep inside they would never make love—why, he couldn't say.

It took ten minutes in a taxi to get to the Lobster Smack, a restaurant overlooking the beach. The table Terry had booked was the nearest to the beach. They sat facing each other, the Caribbean Sea stretched out beside them. The moon reflected off the sea made the scene a romantic paradise.

Their friendship may have only begun that day, but the conversation was that of two people who had known each other for years.

On the way back to the Hotel they arranged a full day's hire with the taxi driver for the following day—for a tour of the Island.

They arranged to meet the next morning after breakfast, again in the foyer. This time Julie was waiting for him. He stepped out of the lift and she was the first person he saw. It took his breath away, again, seeing how lovely she was.

Again her blonde hair had been tied back into a ponytail. He felt slightly embarrassed, for the ponytail made her look even younger then she was. His eyes moved from her face to her body, admiration replacing embarrassment as his eyes took in the round breasts semi-hidden by a turquoise blouse tied in a knot under her bust. Her white shorts fitted her pert bottom like a second skin.

Again, she reminded Terry of *someone*—but who?

The taxi driver took them to all the usual tourist places, then into the hills for lunch. Twenty minutes later they passed through a ranch-like gate, the narrow dirt road leading to a large house on the side of a hill. The driver explained the house, now a hotel and restaurant, used to belong to the sugar plantation which the government now owned. The restaurant overlooked a swimming pool; beyond the pool was a backdrop of green sugar cane dropping away to the blue sea of the Caribbean.

After lunch they sat drinking coffee and a local liqueur. "Julie, there's something I want to ask you." Terry took a sip of cane liqueur that tasted like syrup until it reached his chest when the burning sensation brought a glow to his face. He continued: "You've had a rough time other this last month. I was wondering whether you'd like to come on holiday with me? When we return to Heathrow I have a couple of days before flying to Gibraltar. A friend of mine has a two-bedroomed flat he's letting me have for ten days. You're welcome to join me." He smiled. "You'll have your own room. Don't worry, there'll be no hanky-panky—just friends!"

Julie looked at him and smiled.

"That sounds terrific, Terry. Let me think about it, will you? I'll let you know before we arrive home."

For the rest of that day and the flight back to Heathrow his mind never went further than Julie and the prospect of spending ten days with her. He still couldn't fathom why his feelings were not sexual.

Two hours before the aircraft touched down at Heathrow Airport Julie had accepted his invitation.

But they were destined never to find out just how close the bond between them was.

CHAPTER 22

Kevin 1985

Kevin took eighteen days leave and made his way to Heathrow. The first available flight was a Pan Am flight to San Francisco. He had hoped for a flight to the Caribbean and the sun. As this wasn't possible, the United States West Coast sounded the best option. He had never been to San Francisco, so why not?

The flight landed at 2 p.m. local time. He took a taxi from the airport to the Holiday Inn, about a mile from Fisherman's Wharf. He spent the next four days seeing the usual tourist sites. Two places really impressed him—the Golden Gate Bridge and Alcatras.

On the fifth morning he hired a rental car and drove to Las Vegas. Three days later and two hundred dollars out of pocket thanks to the Blackjack table, he decided to drive to Los Angeles.

He spent a day at Universal Studios and the next day on board the Queen Mary. He decided you needed two people to enjoy Disneyland and America. He had become bored and wanted to return home and a bit of action.

He drove to Los Angeles airport. The first available flight was first class on the Air New Zealand Airline to Gatwick. He returned the car to the hire office at the airport. It was midday and the flight would not be boarding until 3 p.m. with a scheduled take-off time of 4 p.m.

He made his way to terminal three where he booked himself into the first-class restaurant and took two hours over lunch.

Just after three the speaker system called for all passengers on the Air New Zealand flight to board. As he was a first-class passenger there was no queuing. He went through security to the main boarding entrance and entered the aircraft. The first-class cabin was to the left and forward in the nose of the Boeing 747. He made a mental note: twelve-luxury seats one side and the same the other, with six in the centre in three rows. The steward showed him to his seat in the centre aisle at the front of the cabin, port side.

He sat down and made himself comfortable. His eyes wandered to the port side front two seats. A pair of shapely legs in pattern black high heel shoes and black stockings or tights made him sit up and take notice. The airline seat obscured the rest of the lady's body, except the long brown hair that cascaded over the top of the seat. He wondered what she looked like; perhaps she was a film star. From were he was sitting she could easily pass as Jackie Collins. He sat there wishing she would turn around to satisfy his curiosity. It was thirty-five minutes later while the plane was climbing to thirty thousand feet, after the seat belt and no smoking signs had been turned off, before he was able to satisfy his curiosity. The lady stood up, straightened her black skirt and matching jacket, and turned round. She looked very smart and businesslike, the tanned skin and brown hair going well with the bright yellow blouse. Kevin was very impressed: she looked and presented herself as if she were a model.

She opened the forward locker and took out a green Jaguar sports bag and walked towards Kevin. As she walked by him a surprised expression flashed across her face and for a moment Kevin thought she was going to speak. He watched as she walked past him and into the first vacant toilet. Five minutes later she returned. She had changed from her black business suit and was now wearing pink slacks and a matching top. She returned to her seat but just before sitting down she glanced at Kevin and smiled. A short time later a woman that had been sitting next to the lady in black stood and looked at Kevin, her mouth dropping with surprise. She made her way to the toilet and a few moments later returned to her seat.

Kevin made up his mind before the plane landed at Gatwick that he would get to know the lady who was now in pink.

CHAPTER 23

Ruth 1985

Ruth sat in front of the mirror putting the finishing touches to her makeup. She was looking forward to the evening. Diane, her eldest daughter, was taking her out to celebrate her forty-fifth birthday. Since her divorce she had become a different woman—she looked ten years younger, the makeup and red hair dye contributing a great deal to the transformation. She was enjoying life to the full, making up for all the drab years she had spent with Alex her ex husband.

She and Diane and tried to meet up at least once a week. This was not always possible owing to Diane's work, travelling a great deal with the New Zealand tourist board. Diane had done more then most to open New Zealand to the travelling public.

The doorbell rang. Ruth pressed the button on the intercom, spoke into the machine and waited for a reply.

"Mum, it's me—Diane; are you ready?"

"Yes, do you want to come up?"

Ruth checked her makeup in the mirror next to the intercom. "No, I have a taxi waiting."

Ruth selected a warm coat for the autumn nights had started to get cold. She checked the windows and secured the door to her two-bedroomed luxury apartment. She was proud of her new home. Two minutes later she joined Diane in the taxi, kissing her on the cheek. "So where are you taking me?"

Diane looked at her mother's broad smile and felt very humble in the presence of a woman who had dragged herself from dismay to an attractive middle-aged woman with everything to live for. Diane enjoyed spoiling her mother—something her father had never done.

Ruth asked again: "Well, are you going to tell me or not?"

"You're like a little child! Well, I thought we could go for a drink first, then see a show." Diane took her mother's hand and squeezed it.

The taxi stopped outside the Imperial Hotel. The five miles' journey from Mount Eden to Symondes Street took ten minutes. Diane paid the taxi, took her mother's arm and they entered the foyer. Ruth became even more excited for the musical *Evita* had been performing at the Majestic Theatre, situated next to the hotel, for eight weeks. Ruth had been planning to see the show for weeks.

Diane guided her mother through the foyer past the Rangitoto Cocktail bar and down a flight of stairs.

"Where are we going?" Ruth said with concern.

"To the downstairs bar—it's quieter."

At the bottom of the stairs was a sign, 'Banqueting Suite.' Below the sign were double doors. Diane pushed open one door and held it for her mother. Ruth entered and the place was in darkness. Ruth protested just as the beam of a spotlight blinded her and a big cheer of. "Happy Birthday!" echoed around the Hall. The chandelier lights went on, revealing eighty guests with smiling faces.

Ruth's mother and father came towards her. Behind her parents were her three other daughters and her grandchild.

She was speechless. In her whole life nothing like this had ever happen to her. She didn't know how she would be able to thank everybody. She prayed David would appear from a dark corner.

Ruth met many old friends that had travelled from all over New Zealand just to be at the party. Everybody seemed to be there except David.

An hour later Keith, her father, appeared on the small stage at the far end of the hall. "Could I have your attention please?" He paused and waited a few seconds. The hall became quiet and he continued. "Before the Disco starts I would just like to ask you all to raise your glasses and wish Ruth a happy birthday."

Three big cheers and a salute from the party revellers brought Diane to the stage. Keith spoke into the microphone again. "Please could I have your attention once more! Diane would like to say a few words." Keith held the microphone in front of Diane.

Diane leaned forward and spoke into the microphone "Mum, as you can see, friends and family have come from miles to help you celebrate this evening. They have come because they love and admirer you. I know the one person you would have loved to have been here would be David, but as you know his ship is not scheduled to arrive in Southampton for another twelve days." Diane gave a mysterious smile. "So as he can't come to you, the family's sending you to see him. We've brought you a first-class return ticket to London Gatwick, leaving in two weeks' time. There's one problem, though—the family don't trust you by yourself, so they're sending me with you."

Diane watched her mother sit down. Ruth could not control her emotions and sat there and cried. It seemed an age before she could control her tears. When the tears stopped flowing she knew this was the best present she could ever have wished for.

After the party Diane explained to her mother she was going to London on business, so she was using the business trip to be her companion. Ruth was delighted.

❧ ❧ ❧

Ruth's excitement boarding the Boeing 747 was something she had never experienced. A handsome but effeminate steward welcomed her on board the large aircraft, introducing himself as Ashley and pointing to the nametag pin on his clean white shirt. He was so professional at his job he made Ruth feel like royalty. Ashley showed both women to the first-class cabin, then to their luxury airline seats. It was something Ruth always dreamed of but never thought would happen. She felt nervous but happy.

The twelve-hour flight to Los Angeles passed quickly for Ruth—the in-flight movies, the first class food and champagne—she never wanted it to end.

On arrival at Los Angeles passengers were informed they would disembark during the four-hour stopover period. They would be spending that time in the transit lounge. Diane had already informed Ruth she had a business lunch with American Pacific Airlines to discuss a possible package holiday to New Zealand. They both made their way to the first-class restroom in terminal three. Ruth washed and applied fresh makeup, then waited for Diane at the entrance. Diane emerged from the restroom a different lady to the one that went in. The white slacks and tight fitting tee-shirt had gone. The black suit with black stockings and black shoes went well with the yellow blouse. Ruth looked at her and realised just how beautiful and business minded she was. "I can see why you're so successful at your job. I'm so proud of you!" She moved forward and gave her daughter a big hug and kiss, careful not to damage the little makeup that Diane was wearing.

They both met up again two hours later in the first-class bar. Diane was very pleased with her meeting. Ruth had been duty-free shopping, mostly window-shopping. At 3 p.m. they made their way back to the aircraft just in time to hear the announcement to board.

The aircraft took off on schedule. Diane waited for the seatbelt and no smoking sign to go off. She stood up, took a bag from the forward locker and turned to glance back up the cabin. She couldn't believe it! David was seated in the first row of the middle aisle. She moved towards him and was just about to speak when she realised it wasn't him. Five minutes later she returned to her seat. Before she sat down she glanced back at the man who smiled. She felt embarrassed but smiled back at him. She sat down and looked at her mother. "I've just had a shock! There's a gent sitting in the middle aisle who's the spitting image of David! At first I thought it was him."

Ruth could see her daughter wasn't her usual composed self. "Let me take a look." She stood up and made her way towards the toilet. She looked at the man and her heart missed a beat. David did not come to mind but Terry, David's father, did—as he was twenty-six years ago. She entered the toilet and tried to compose herself, then returned to her seat. Diane realised it had genuinely upset her mother. She was flushed and shaking. "Mother—are you all right?"

"Yes—I'm fine; it was just a bit of a shock."

"Well I did tell you he looked like David," Diane said with a smile.

Ruth was tuning her headset to the comedy channel, hoping to clear her mind of Terry and the past.

Diane was reading the proposals made by the American Pacific Airline. She suddenly felt the presence of somebody standing over her and looked up.

"Hello, my name is Kevin. May I get you a drink?"

She recognized the gent from the middle aisle. She liked the good-looking face and the body that had obviously been looked after. She was pleased he had made an effort to introduce himself. She couldn't believe her choice of words, spoken in a very businesslike manner and without smiling: "This is first class—you'll find all the drinks are free and usually served by the steward or stewardess."

"Take no notice of her—she's wrapped up in business," Ruth said standing and holding out her hand. "My name is Ruth and this is my daughter Diane. We'd love two Champaign cocktails before dinner."

Kevin smiled, disappeared and returned two minutes later to find Ruth and Diane standing at the front of the aircraft stretching their legs. "The drinks are on their way," he said with a smile. Diane apologised for being rude just as the steward approached with three Champagne cocktails.

They spent the rest of the journey in each other's company. Ruth wanted to know everything about him and his past. Some of her questions were so in-depth Diane became embarrassed—she could only assume her mother was trying to pair them off.

Her speculations could not have been further from the truth. Ruth was only interested in why this young man was so much like her first and only love…Terry, the English steward from twenty-six years earlier.

CHAPTER 24

David 1985

The M.V. *Essex* docked at Southampton new docks at 6 a.m. on the 15th April. David hoped to be off the ship and start his leave by 9:30 a.m. Just after 9 a.m., while packing his case, he was interrupted by a knock on his cabin door. It was the Radio and Wireless shore side engineers. They needed access to the radio room. A part of the ship's refit included a new radio satellite system. David spent the next two hours being updated on the new equipment to be installed over the next six weeks.

He made the gangway just minutes before it was taken away; the ship was being moved to dry dock.

He walked through the customs shed and the green channel. Unchallenged, he made his way towards the door with the sign WAY OUT. The door led to the car park. He was walking towards the taxi rank when someone called his name.

"David!"

The voice came from his left. He turned to see Barbara, wearing a cream trouser suit, standing beside her car. The smile on her face made her high cheekbones even more prominent. With her blonde hair cut short she looked fresh and lovely with the spring sun shining on her. He stopped in his tracks, spellbound. For five months he had been waiting for this moment! Now it had come he wasn't sure what he should do. But he didn't have to do anything—she ran the twenty feet to him, flung her arms around him and both their lips joined in passion. She pulled back and looked into his eyes. "Oh David, I've missed you!"

"Not as much as I've missed you! There hasn't been a day I haven't thought of you."

She realized he still had his suitcase in one hand and a travel bag in the other. "Come on—let's go home and make love!" She turned and headed back towards her Ford Sierra.

"What about your mother…?" he began, putting his case in the boot.

"You want to make love to my mother as well?" she asked with a shocked expression.

He looked at her in surprise and she laughed. "Don't look at me like that! Only joking! Mother's gone out for the day with her social club."

She drove back to David's bungalow. She'd kept house for him while he was away. The double gate to the small drive was open and she parked the car in the drive, walked to the side door and unlocked it, holding it open while David took his case and bag from the car and entered the door to the kitchen. He deposited his luggage in the hall and turned towards Barbara. She was still in the kitchen standing by the sink, filling the kettle. He walked towards her, put his arms around her and started to kiss her neck. The smell of her perfume was pervasive as his lips explored the velvet skin of her neck. The excitement electrified him and he became aware of his erection against her. She put the kettle down and turned to face him. "I think the tea can wait, don't you?" She smiled, took his hand and led him through the kitchen to the hall, then to the bedroom. Within minutes they were undressed and in bed.

Their love for each other was so overwhelming that nothing seemed sordid. Barbara wasn't a virgin when she met David, but she'd never have dreamed of giving way to the wanton behavior with anyone else which she did with him that morning. David in return found it quite natural to kiss and lick the juices from between her legs. It was the first time he'd experienced a climax three times on the same erection and in such a short time. She enjoyed his lips and tongue between her legs, and it was a pleasant surprise to find out she enjoyed doing the same to him. To her delight the time in bed became one big orgasm.

David sat on the settee wrapped in a towel, both having just finished showering together. He was going through mail that had accumulated over the last five months. Besides the junk mail most of the letters were bills. There was one from New Zealand in Diane's handwriting. He read it twice just to digest the contents.

Barbara had been making tea and sandwiches and entered the lounge with a tray that she placed in front of David. "Are you all right?" she asked with concern.

"Yes—it's a letter from my sister. She's arriving on the nineteenth, and she wants me to meet her." David was worried that it might upset Barbara and any plans she may have made. But she returned a reassuring smile, genuinely excited at the prospect of meeting his sister.

"That's great! I'll get to meet one of your family. Is she staying with you?" She sat down next to him and put her arm a round him.

"She wants to, but doesn't say for how long."

Barbara took her arm from him, leaned forward and started to pour the tea. "The nineteenth—that's this Saturday. Perhaps I can come with you?" She handed him a cup of tea.

David held out his hand and took the cup. "What about your business?"

"I've left Helen in charge and told the staff I'm taking two weeks' holiday." Her eyes twinkled. "If a certain man is nice to me, I may even take longer."

The next three days were like a honeymoon for the two of them. The lovemaking was so intense that nothing else mattered. Barbara's mother was pleased for her daughter. She had never approved of any of the other so-called boyfriends, but David was different. She could see the love he had for Barbara and knew they where meant for each other.

Friday evening David had booked a table at the Bar Gate restaurant in Southampton. After the meal they drank Irish coffee. He leaned forward and took her hands in his. "Barbara," he said, a little nervously, "I know we haven't known each other long, but will you marry me?"

She smiled while her eyes filled with tears. "I can't think of anything I'd like better, David. Of course I will."

The next morning David checked with Gatwick Airport. The Air New Zealand flight was on time and should land at 11 a.m.

The ninety-mile drive took Barbara ninety-five minutes. They arrived at Gatwick at 10:35 a.m., parked in the short-stay car park and went for coffee. At 11:25 a.m. the television monitor indicated the baggage was in the hall. They made their way to the reception area and waited.

Both stood at the arrival barrier. Barbara couldn't believe her eyes—if David had not been actually standing next to her she would have mistaken the gentleman who was pushing a trolley laden with suitcases for him. Two ladies accompanied the man.

The younger of the two ladies suddenly waved, called David's name and ran towards him. David couldn't believe that the skinny seventeen-year-old student he had left at Auckland airport had become this desirable auburn-hair beauty! Their embraces turned to tears of joy. Meanwhile the elder of the two women came up behind David, covering his eyes with her hands. "Guess who?"

He turned; without saying a word he took his mother into his arms and cried.

Barbara, feeling out of things, turned to the gentleman who was standing bemused by all that was going on. "Hi! My name's Barbara,

David's fiancée." She held out her hand, aware of the likeness between him and David and assuming they were related.

"My name's Kevin. I've just been helping these ladies with their luggage."

Diane, overhearing, interrupted: "David wrote and told us all about you. He didn't say you where engaged!"

Barbara blushed. "It only happened last night. Perhaps I shouldn't have said anything." They looked at each other and knew they would be great friends.

It took an age for everyone to calm down. Diane introduced Kevin to everybody and explained he was a civil servant. He arranged to telephone Diane the next day.

Ruth took an instant liking to Barbara and couldn't wait for the wedding day.

David, still in a state of shock, was pleased to see his mother looking so young and attractive; and even more pleasing was that Diane and his mother had taken to Barbara.

Diane was pleased that David had found such a lovely lady, and to see the happiness on his face as he walked the length of the terminal exit, Barbara on one arm looking likes a typical happy bride, his mother on the other with so much pride on her face. It was as if David had just been to the palace and been knighted. Diane kept in step with Kevin and every so often glanced at him. Since he introduced himself twelve hours earlier, her admiration for him had grown every minute. She stopped walking and held him back, though the moving walkway continued to carry them forword. "Are you serious—will you telephone me tomorrow?"

He looked into her eyes. "I've not got to go back to work for another eight days, so I'm going to hire a car and drive to Southampton and book into an hotel for a week. How does that grab you?"

Diane leaned forward and kissed him. "I'd like that."

It was two days before David and Barbara had a chance to be alone. Kevin, who was staying at the Southampton Hilton, had taken the ladies, including Christine, Barbara's mother, for a drive in the New Forest. The plan was to have lunch and return in the early evening.

David and Barbara watched the hired Nissan Bluebird pull away from David's bungalow. Then, rushing to the bedroom, undressing and getting into bed at 10:30 in the morning, to make love, made them both feel like guilty teenagers. They spent the next couple of hours exploring each other's bodies and making mad passionate love. Both of them had never been so happy.

They lay there both on there sides gazing into each other's eyes. David pushed himself up. "Have you thought about getting married? We haven't discussed a date, and whether you want a big white wedding or a small but fashionable wedding." He smiled down at her, thinking she was the most beautiful person he had ever met. She raised herself and pushed him so he ended up on his back. She sat astride his stomach and put her hands on his shoulders. "David, I love you and all I want is to marry you. So name the time and the place and I'll be there." She bent forward and kissed him, then sat up quickly as a thought struck her. She smiled. "David! Why don't we get married while your mother and sister are here in England?"

That evening, while everyone was having dinner, David spoke of their plans. As long as there were no gremlins in the works, they hoped to arrange the marriage for the 10th May, two weeks from the coming Saturday. Ruth and Diane were asked to be Maids of Honour while Kevin was overwhelmed, being asked by David to be his best man.

The next ten days were hectic for all the family, but with hard work and determination everything fell into place.

Barbara and David were able to book Southampton registry office for eleven o'clock on Saturday 10th May.

The wedding lunch was to follow at the Bar Gate Restaurant. Barbara was willing to wait for a honeymoon until David returned from his next trip. But David had other ideas: after a short telephone call to the shipping company, he spent twenty minutes at Barbara's hair salon talking to Helen.

He spoke to the rest of the family in New Zealand and explained the situation. Nobody could accept the invitation at such short notice, but wished him well.

The registry office grounds looked magnificent on the beautiful spring sunny day. Everybody started to arrive at 10:30 a.m.

David and Kevin looking very smart in their matching grey suits. They could have passed as identical twins. However, Kevin's physique made him look taller than David.

David's next-door neighbours, Harold and Doris, were handing out carnations. The staff from the hairdressing salon and there companions were gathered in a group, taking photographs.

The first wedding car arrived. Ruth emerged wearing a lilac suit and a large brimmed hat, mauve so that it matched the mauve blouse. Diane followed wearing an identical suit with an unusual colour. Both of them looked stunning.

Two minutes later the second car arrived. Christine waited for the driver to open the door, then stepped out. The mauve suit with lilac hat and blouse was a masterstroke by Barbara. The colour combination of the three ladies made a brilliant impact. The three stood back as the driver held Barbara's hand as she also emerged from the car. She was wearing a white trouser suit, the trousers slightly flared, which were designed to go with the slightly flared jacket. Her lilac blouse was partly hidden by a white waistcoat, and her large white hat and white high heel shoes finished off the well thought out effect.

David stood there with pride and admiration. He couldn't believe this beautiful woman had consented to be his wife. She looked as if she had just walked off the front page of Vogue.

The wedding went without a hitch, the sixteen-strong wedding party making their way to the Bar Gate restaurant. The champagne was at the right temperature. The Fillet of beef Wellington, the Chef's speciality, was cooked to perfection. The fresh strawberries from Spain were ripe and juicy. The best Cognac from France finished off the excellent meal.

Kevin made the usual best man's speech. David followed with the groom's speech. The wedding gift he had for Barbara surprised everybody except her mother and Helen her manager.

Helen had agreed to manage the salon. David had arranged for Barbara to accompany him on the next five-month voyage.

But sometimes fate takes over and alters the best-laid plans.

CHAPTER 25

Raul 1985

Raul paid the taxi and made his way to the Bar Peron in the main airport lounge. Mary was sitting at a table reading the English printed-paper, the *B.A. Herald.* Raul put his case next to the spare seat facing her.

"Would you like a drink?" he asked as she looked up to greet him.

"Yes please, Canadian Club ice and a slice of orange."

She folded the newspaper and placed it in her carrier bag. She waited for Raul to return from the bar. He had ordered the same as her but topped his up with soda, placed the drinks on the table and sat on the spare seat facing her. She took out an envelope from the carrier bag and placed it on the table in front of Raul.

"That's your airline ticket to New York. You'll be travelling with Pan Am via Rio de Janeiro and Miami. As soon as you get to New York, go to the Aer Lingus ticket desk for departures and show your Passport. They will have a first-class ticket for you to Dublin. My brother Sean will meet you at Dublin."

She looked at Raul with envy, for he was going to the country she loved. How many more months or years did she have to stay in exile? Life just wasn't fair, she thought, taking a sip from her glass.

Raul leaned forward and spoke in a whisper. "What about the forged passport you talked about?"

"That will be ready for you in Dublin. You won't need one till then." She finished her drink, stood up and stepped towards him. "I've got to get back to the bar. Your flight departs in two hours. So, I'll say good-bye—and good luck! The last few days have been fun. I hope you find what you're looking for." She kissed him on both cheeks and walked towards the exit.

Thirty-six hours later he was met at Dublin airport by Sean, then taken to a cottage in Bray, fifteen miles south of Dublin. Peter and Sean didn't want to take the risk of exposing Raul to British intelligence at that early stage.

Sean was impressed with the young man's perfect English and commented on it. Raul explained, his mother had insisted English should be the family's second language. Their school was chosen because 75% of lessons where taught in English. The military college he attended was based on the American style where, again, English was the dominant language.

It was midday on Friday the 9th of May when Raul went to bed in the back room of the small cottage. The flights had taken their toll and jetlag had taken over his body.

After what felt like a couple of hours of restless sleep, he struggled out of bed, washed, dressed, and made his way downstairs. The hall led to a small kitchen. A lady in her fifties was standing beside the cooker. She looked up at Raul. "Hi, you must be Philip, Sean's house guest? I'm Nell the housekeeper. He's just gone to the corner shop for the papers. Sit down at the table. Breakfast will be ready in a jiffy!" She turned back towards the cooker. Her Irish accent was so strong it took Raul several minutes to digest what she was saying.

"What time is it?" he asked, completely confused as to what was going on around him.

"Ten past eight, my love."

He was even more confused. Why did she call him love and what day was it? He hoped she wasn't making a pass at him.

"What day is it?" he asked her as she placed a large plate in front of him. He looked in amazement at the plate that was full with two eggs, bacon, two sausages, mushrooms, tomatoes and baked beans. He had heard of it but never experienced the full British Breakfast.

"It's Saturday of course," she said, returning with toast and a pot of tea. "You get stuck into that lot while I go and make your bed."

He looked at the feast in front of him and thought there was no way he could eat that amount for breakfast, but decided to have a couple of mouthfuls. He was on his second sausage before he realised how tasty the food was and how hungry he was.

Sean arrived with the papers just as Raul was mopping up his plate with the last piece of toast.

"I was hoping I'd be back before you got up," he said, placing his hand on the teapot to check the heat. "Good—still warm." He poured himself a mug of tea. "Have you said anything to Nell?" Sean held the mug in both hands and took a sip that sounded like water going down a drain.

"Other than passing the time of day, no. However, I gather my new name is Philip?" Raul wiped his mouth with a piece of kitchen roll that served as a table napkin.

"Yes—sorry about that. I meant to get to you first, before she had time to quiz you. As far as she's concerned, you're an Englishman with roots in Ireland that's here to check your family tree—okay?" Sean collected the dirty plates and stacked them in the sink.

"Why all the secrecy?" Raul asked.

Sean looked at Raul and for the first time realized he didn't have a clue about the IRA movement and their enemy, the British.

"The Irish Republican Army is at war with the British—though the British and a small minority of Irish people will not accept we're a fighting army. They brand us as terrorists; this originates from the colonial British government at Westminster. Your country has suffered the same fate. They have taken the Falklands, or should I say the Malvinas Islands from your inheritance and placed British subjects there—just as they have separated our Island and put the Westminster Government in charge of the north of our Island. Like you, we should be united."

Raul was impressed with the dedication in Sean's voice and determination on his face.

"Have you had a enough to eat?" Sean said, pouring himself another cup of tea. Raul nodded. "If you pack your things together, we can move. We're being picked up by a driver and taken to a new address until the mission begins."

At ten that morning the driver collected them. Two hours after setting off the Volkswagen camper pulled off the back road that led to Ballyfoyle. At the end of the dirt track stood a fifty-foot high rocky hill. At the base was a small farmhouse and barn. The camper parked next to a metallic green Range Rover. Sean indicated to Raul that they were at their destination and informed the campervan driver he needn't stay—they were finished with him. They made their way to the open door. Peter Driscol, a commander in the IRA, sat at a wooden table smoking a cigarette. Sean introduced Raul and after the usual formalities the three sat at the table. Peter, without asking, poured out three large measures of Jameson's Irish Whiskey. He looked at Raul and was surprised how young he was for an ex-Argentine fighter pilot. "We're just waiting for your two companions who will be with you on this mission." They didn't have to wait long. The throbbing beat of a diesel engine came from the dirt road that approached the farmhouse. The engine stopped followed by the sound of two doors slamming. The front door opened. A large balding man in his fifties entered followed by a small and younger man in his twenties. Raul wasn't impressed with Patrick O'Hare or his son Steve.

Peter began to explain the plan. The three were to take the Range Rover and make their way to Gibraltar. They must arrive before midday on June 9. At 11 a.m. that morning Prince Andrew would be inspecting the Rock's garrison. At midday, the Prince was scheduled for a public walkabout in the square and Main Street. The mission was to assassinate the prince; and if this proved impossible, to cause as much havoc as possible to disrupt the visit. They were then to make their way to a small inlet south of the Rock where they would rendezvous with the *Mediterranean Queen*, an ex British Royal Navy patrol launch registered in Morocco and owned by an Irishman. The launch would then speed them to Morocco. From there they would fly by private jet to Libya. Colonel Cadaffe had promised twenty thousand pounds per man if the mission proved successful.

Raul was impressed by the simplicity of it all. The air force had taught him the simpler the plan the better. For the first time he felt at ease and eager to get started.

Peter finished giving his lecture and asked Patrick and his son to show Raul the armory, after which the three left the farmhouse and made their way to the barn.

Sean took the whiskey bottle and poured himself and Peter two large measures, then leaned back in his chair. "Right," he said, "now tell me what's *really* going to happen?"

"It's exactly as I have said, except there's no launch, no Morocco and no Cadaffe. The mission will only be a success if the three men are captured and taken prisoner or, better still, killed. That is the only way we'll get the maximum publicity." Peter swallowed his whiskey in one gulp. "As long as Special Branch is informed, everything will fall into place."

Patrick opened the barn door and walked towards the far end of the building. Both he and his son moved four bails of hay. This exposed a hidden door. Patrick unlocked it and stood back. He then indicated to his son and Raul to go through the hidden doorway. Steve went forward and switched on the lights that illuminated a stairway.

Raul followed. Patrick shut the door and brought up the rear. The twenty-five steps led down to a natural cave. Raul looked in amazement at the amount of arms and ammunition that had been stored in the cave. Not even the armory at his old air base had this amount of arms.

But he was concerned about Patrick and his son. They were not genuine fighting soldiers—to him they where just petty criminals. He watched as Steve handled a 9mm sub-machine gun. The grin on Steve's face gave Raul a chill. As far as he knew he had never met a psychopath—until now; and to him this young man gave a good impression of one. It wasn't hard for him to realise Patrick was ignorant and uneducated. The one thing that did surprise him was the fear they showed when in the company of Sean and Peter. He wondered what hold they had on the father and son.

Further into the cave was a firing range. Raul tried several guns before he selected a German machine pistol. He was impressed with the thousand rounds a minute the gun fired.

For the next twenty-three days Raul shared the small farmhouse with Patrick and his son Steve. Each day he spent in their company got worse. The belching and the breaking of wind disgusted him. The stench of body odour made him feel sick. He had never come across such people. Argentine had poverty and slums, but Raul was convinced the unfortunate people who lived in those places would not act or perform like these two undesirables.

They were supposed to be members of the Irish Republican Army, but Raul thought they were more like a bad version of Butch Cassidy and The Sundance Kid. He prayed that one day they would take a bath.

As the days passed the routine became the same. The early morning light was a new experience for Raul. In Buenos Aires the dawn never broke until after six in the morning. It seemed strange to have the light and dawn chorus start at four thirty in the morning. Once he was awake, he was up and out by 5 a.m. He would be running the local hills, returning around 7 o'clock. The scenery that surrounded the farm was breathtaking. He never realised there were so many different shades of green. It was hard for him to realise that this beautiful country could produce so much violence. The British had a lot to answer for.

Every morning at 10 a.m. the campervan arrived with the daily papers, fresh milk, bread and anything they may have asked for the previous day. It was always the same driver; Raul got to know him as Murphy, a man in his late twenties with a broad Irish accent.

Thursdays Sean would arrive and go over the plans repeatedly until everybody was bored stiff.

As the days passed Raul started to make plans. It was his gun—his bullets—that were going to kill the English Prince: the revenge for his brother's death would be sweet. The money he would receive from Caddaffe would help buy a small aircraft—the land his mother owned was ideal for a small landing strip. The business opportunities for a pilot and aircraft could be tremendous. For the first time in his life he felt excited at the thought of going home to the farm and his mother. He knew she would give anything for him to move back into the farm: she wanted nothing else. The only thing now was to get the mission out of the way. Suddenly life and the future looked good.

On Wednesday the 4th June, Sean and Peter arrived at the farm just after 9 a.m. followed shortly after by Murphy and the campervan, earlier then usual.

Again, Sean went through the plans. The only thing different this time was that Murphy and Peter were there. Sean finished by telling them they were booked on the evening ferry from Dublin to Holyhead the following evening. Peter opened a bottle of Jamison's Irish Whiskey and poured everybody a drink. Murphy stood and explained he needed to bring in the shopping from the campervan. As he left the room Peter stood up. He went to the window and watched, doing it in such a way that nobody realised what he was doing. Murphy collected two carrier bags from the campervan and on his way back stopped behind the Range Rover. He took something from his pocket and placed it behind the rear bumper. Peter smiled to himself, realising the first part of the plan was working.

Sean gave them a telephone number to ring in case of an emergency. He would be manning the telephone until the mission was over. Sean and Peter wished everybody good luck and drove off in Patrick's old Landrover.

Murphy drank his whiskey, then poured himself another. He sat at the table discussing their mission. He explained how he would have loved to have gone with them. He finally stood up and wished them well—and left. Within minutes Steve said he was going into the local Village to do a bit of shopping. Sean had insisted that nobody was to leave the farm until it was time to depart for the ferry.

Raul couldn't be bothered with confrontation so said nothing. Patrick just grunted and carried on drinking.

Steve drove the Range Rover through the narrow lane that led to Ballyfoyale. After a few minutes he saw the campervan fifty yards ahead parked beside the road. Murphy was inside a telephone box with his back to Steve. Steve stopped the Range Rover and walked the remaining distance. He opened the door to the telephone box just in time to hear Murphy telling someone that the Range Rover would arrive at Holyhead on the Friday morning. The accent was that of a well-educated Englishman. Murphy turned to see Steve at the door holding a Magnum pistol. Murphy replaced the receiver. "What's happened to your Irish accent?" Steve asked, pulling the trigger four times. All four bullets entered Murphy's stomach and within minutes he was unconscious. He died two hours later propped up in the telephone box. Nobody found him until the following day.

Sean and Peter didn't find out about the murder for three days. They guessed what had happened. They had known from day one that Murphy was really an SAS infiltrator. They had fed him just the right information. The chance of this ever happening again was most unlikely. Sean and Peter knew that if Patrick and his son came back from this mission there wouldn't be a trial—the execution of both of them would take place immediately.

The Range Rover left the farmhouse on Thursday 5th June. They made the ferry with plenty of time to spare. The overnight crossing was uneventful and docked on time at Holyhead. Just after 8 a.m. Patrick manoeuvred the four-wheel drive down the ramp and through the docks. Patrick had his eyes on the road and Steve was reading the sport pages of the *Sun* newspaper. Raul was pleased with the opportunity to see a part of England. He tried to take in as much as possible. That's when he noticed the large black car parked at the side of the road. At first glance, the car didn't look any different to any other car, until his eyes focused on the person sitting in the rear. His heart began to race and it took several minutes for him to regain his composure. The likeness between the man in the rear of the car and Diago made Raul feel uncomfortable.

Patrick stopped the car in a layby just outside Shrewsbury. Raul watched as Patrick started inspecting the outside of the car; within seconds he was back in the car holding up a small metal disc. "It looks as if you were right, my boy; our friend Murphy has planted a bug. I'll call Sean and see what he has to say." He made his way from the Range Rover to the telephone box situated in the layby. After a short conversation he made his way to the rear of the car, then to the driver's side. He opened the door, climbed in and took hold of the steering wheel. "Sean says to leave the bug in place and to carry on as normal. He thinks we could use whoever is following us to our advantage later on in our mission." He started the car and checked his watch. They had been in the layby for six minutes. He put the car in gear and pulled back onto the A5 heading for Wellington.

They were on the M5 when Raul noticed the large black car pass them. Once again his heart missed a beat when he saw the man in the rear seat. Now he knew it was true that everybody had a double. He had seen Diago's double for the second time in one day.

Fifteen minutes later Patrick drove off the motorway onto the forecourt of a service station and stopped beside the petrol pumps. It wasn't until Raul made his way to the toilets that he noticed the large black car. A closer look showed him it was a Mercedes and he wondered why it was a left-hand drive. He couldn't bring himself to look in the rear of the car. He followed Steve to the toilets. The Black Mercedes was no longer at the pumps when he retuned to the Range Rover. The driver had moved it to the car park situated in front of the cafeteria. The three men who occupied the car were just sitting there waiting. Raul finally decided to inform Patrick. Before starting, Patrick studied the Mercedes. "Yes, that's our boys—we know who we're dealing with now. Strange—they're driving on German number plates. I've never come across that before." He put the Range Rover into gear and drove back onto the M5.

They came across the Mercedes again at the Portsmouth ferry terminal. When the ferry arrived in Spain the Range Rover and its passengers were clear of Bilbao before the Mercedes had found its way out of the dock area.

Patrick didn't see the Mercedes again until the next morning. He noticed it in his rear view mirror five miles from La Linea, the Spanish town that connected Gibraltar to the Spanish mainland.

While waiting in the queue Patrick telephoned Sean from a local call box. Steve edged the Range Rover forward when necessary.

Patrick returned ten minutes later, indicating for Steve to move over to the passenger seat. Again he climbed in behind the steering wheel. He turned to face Raul. "The plans have changed. It seems the *Invincible* and the Prince are held up in the Spanish port of Vigo. The ship called at Vigo on a courtesy visit and while it was docking a gust of wind took the bow into the quay and damaged the hull. They have no idea when the ship will be ready to sail again." Patrick noticed the disappointment on both faces. "Never mind—Sean has come up with another idea. We trap the Mercedes, assassinate the SAS men, set fire to the Mercedes as a diversion, then make our escape as planned."

Raul had been working himself up to assassinate the Prince for the last four weeks and had thought of nothing else. It was the only thing that had kept him going. It wasn't the IRA and certainly not Patrick or Steve. It was personal revenge—and now the possibility had gone he felt relieved. He was not even sure he wanted to go through with the killing of British soldiers. But he thought of his twin brother and knew he *had* to have revenge. He looked at Steve, then at Patrick. "Right—let's go for it."

CHAPTER 26

Kevin 1985

Since Kevin arrived back from his holiday in America his whole outlook on life had changed. When he joined the Army from the orphanage the army had become his home and his family. He had no idea what family life was.

He had spent eight days staying at the Southampton Hilton Hotel. It was a wonderful feeling to be included in all the plans that were being made by Diane's family. When David asked him to be best man at his wedding the feeling of being a part of a family was a new and wonderful experience for him. In such a short time he had fallen in love with a beautiful lady, been accepted into her family and became a good friend with David who was like the brother he never had. For the first time in his life he cared for someone more than he cared for the army. He wondered whether he should plan to leave the army and move to New Zealand. Perhaps Diane would marry him and they could settle down and have children.

He returned to Hereford and back to duty. The love he had for Diane was so great he had trouble concentrating. He needed to concentrate—he was back in the classroom learning Arabic.

He had been granted ten days' leave from the 9th May so he could attend David's wedding. He telephoned Diane every day of the ten days that remained before the wedding.

The wedding was small but very enjoyable; in fact, Kevin was envious—he wished it were himself who was getting married—to Diane.

After the wedding lunch Kevin told everyone he was going back to the hotel to change clothes. He would meet as planned at David's house for drinks and the knees-up later that evening. Diane kept him company.

He opened the door and invited her in. The room was on the fourth floor. As she walked into the room the view from the large window in front of her took her breath away. The panoramic vista of Southampton docks and beyond surprised her. She stood there for several minutes taking it all in. With all the drink she had had at the wedding lunch, she felt a bit tipsy. She made her way to the double bed, arranged the pillows and made herself comfortable. Kevin sorted out a change of clothing, placed them on the nearby armchair and entered the shower room. After several minutes he re-appeared wrapped in a large bath towel. It took Diane's breath away—she liked the look of his body; though she felt frightened and nervous, she was excited deep inside.

He lay next to her and started to undo her mauve blouse. She drew away, stood up and undressed, then lay back down beside him. After a passionate kiss and his fondling of her breasts it was second nature for him to want to kiss her breasts. After several enjoyable minutes he climbed on top of her and felt her go tense. His penis had never felt so large and urgent as he placed it between her legs and tried to enter her. Her vagina seemed to contract. It didn't matter how much he tried—he just couldn't penetrate her. His bone-hard penis grew floppy and he pulled away and lay on his back, staring at the ceiling. He wondered what he had none wrong. She put her head on his chest and sobbed. "I'm so…so sorry," she said between her sobs. "I just felt so scared…please don't ask me why…" How could she tell him the truth?

It was in1980, when her mother and father were going through with their divorce. Her father had moved out and was living in lodgings. The house was up for sale but still occupied by Ruth and the four girls. Diane was away at Auckland University most of the time, studying for a degree in business studies. This particular day she was home on summer vacation. It was late afternoon and she was in the house alone. She had just taken a bath. She wrapped the large bath towel around herself, just under the armpits, making sure none of her private parts where showing. She sat at the dresser blow-drying her hair when suddenly she had the uncomfortable feeling someone was watching her. She stood to go to the wardrobe. The smell of alcohol reached her nostrils. She sensed someone at the bedroom door.

She turned quickly and her towel fell to the floor. "You f—whore, you're just like your mother!"

It was Alex, her father. He was in his usual state of drunkenness. "Look at you! Standing there with nothing on—you're a f—prick teaser!"

Red faced, she bent down to pick up the towel. He stepped forward and put his foot on the towel.

"Dad, let me cover myself!"

"Oh, *Dad*, you say? You're no child of mine! You're just a slut like your mother!" He grabbed her left arm with his right hand and twisted it up her back. He then unbuckled his belt and dropped his trousers with his left hand. He tried to enter her while they were both standing; after several minutes he realised without her help this would be impossible. He wedged her arm further up her back and grabbed her hair with his left hand, pushing her to the ground. She was too frightened to scream—she couldn't believe this was happening to her. He was her *father*—how could he *do* this! By this time she was on her knees he had to let go of her arm in order to use both his hands to hold her head and hair. She thought he was going to pull all her hair out, it was so painful. "Open your mouth, you bitch!" She shook her head. He pulled more hair and she screamed again. "I said, *open* your *mouth*, if you want any hair left!" She did what he said and he pushed his penis into her mouth. The smell of stale urine and bad cheese made her wretch. Hate and disgust overwhelmed her and she knew exactly what she was doing when she bit down hard. He screamed like a wounded pig and pulled back—but she wouldn't let go. He punched her on the side of the face. The force jerked her mouth open and he ran from the house, calling her all the names he could think of.

The family never saw him again. All legal matters regarding the house went through the solicitors.

Diane never told anybody of the incident—she was too ashamed. When her mother asked about the bruise on her face she told her she had slipped in the bath. Diane was convinced that if her mother ever found out the truth Alex's life would be in danger—and she loved her mother too much to implicate her in an action that would ruin her life.

Kevin cuddled her and kissed her and didn't ask any questions. He'd take things easy and help her the best he could.

After the wedding party they returned to the hotel. It seemed natural for the two of them to go to bed together. He massaged her back and felt her begin to relax. He turned her over and massaged the front shoulders. His hands went to her breasts and massaged them gently. After a short while he stopped and lay down next to her, both their arms around each other and drifted off to sleep.

For the next three nights it was the same; when he had finished massaging, they would go to sleep in each other's arms. On the fourth night he let his hand wander down between her legs and very gently he ran his finger along her vagina. Again, they fell asleep holding each other. The next evening he went though the same procedure. As his hand went between her legs her sex juices began to flow and her pubic hairs became moist. This pleased Kevin—he knew he was winning. The trouble was how long could he control himself? He was very careful not to rush things. Slowly he slipped a finger into her, massaging gently. After what seemed an age they fell asleep.

The next evening they met Ruth and Christine in Southampton's town centre and ate at the local Indian Restaurant. The two bottles of wine followed by liqueur coffees gave everybody a mellow feeling.

By the time Diane and Kevin had got into bed the drink had suffused and relaxed their bodies. He still had the sense to take things easy. First, he massaged her back, gradually turning her over. He put his hands on her shoulders and began to massage, then worked his way down to her breast. His hands left her breasts and slowly stroked her stomach; from there it was natural to end up between her legs. The whole of her crotch was awash with juices. He entered her with two fingers and slowly began to caress. She sighed.

"Kevin, I want you—please. I don't want to wait any longer." Her voice sounded so sexy to his ears. He climbed on top of her and her legs automatically parted. He entered her gradually, making sure it was only a little at a time. He never took his eyes from her face. Her eyes were tightly closed, her lips pushed together as if she were in pain. He stopped. "Are you all right, Diane?" he whispered with concern. She pulled him closer and her love juices made it easy for the whole of him to enter her. She relaxed, her eyes opened and she gave a tight smile. "Oh Kevin, that feels so good…thank you so much." When here smile relaxed he knew all her inhibition had gone.

The next few days were like a wonderful dream for them both. The lovemaking had rounded off a perfect friendship. The problem was Diane's return to New Zealand was in a few days. Both refused to think about it until the final day, when panic set in for both of them.

The morning of her return they woke early. After an hour of blissful, tender lovemaking, he told her how he wanted to spend the rest of his life with her. If she agreed, he would arrange to move to New Zealand.

She couldn't believe her ears! She'd hoped and prayed that things wouldn't end in a hotel room in Southampton. Kevin had become everything to her. The love she had for him she found very hard to take in and digest. Since their first meeting he had taken over her mind. At first it had became any excuse to be with him. Then she found she was thinking of him every minute of the day—so much so that she couldn't think straight: she would walk into a room and have to think why she was there. She had become concerned when he wasn't there—for there was something about his job that frightened her. He would disappear for a few days, then return as if nothing had happened. He had told her he was a civil servant and she left it at that. On the last occasion he had been away for five days; when she questioned him he became defensive and changed the subject. She hoped whatever he was doing was within the law.

She lay in his arms and looked into his eyes and knew he had meant everything he had said. Oh, how she wished he could return with her! But she was a realist and knew this couldn't be so. They made love again and when they had finished they lay in each other's arms, looking into each other's eyes, the admiration and love they had for each other overwhelming. A tear of happiness filled both Diane's eyes: the future looked good for both of them. Of course, neither of them realised, Diane had become pregnant that morning.

Since the age of fifteen the army had become Kevin's love and life. The regiment had become his wife and it dawned on him now that now was the time for a divorce. Diane was his new love and life—nothing else mattered. On his return to Hereford he would start to put the wheels in motion and make an appointment with the regiment's adjutant. Diane had become his life and future and his only thoughts were to be with her. He drove off the M23 and onto the slip road that led to the South Terminal.

He checked in his rearview mirror for Barbara's Ford Escort, confirming that she was following. He could see David with his head turned, busy talking to his mother who was sitting in the back of the car. Kevin prayed that one day he would be a part of this family.

He indicated and then drove into the airport's short-stay car park. Barbara followed. They had just over three hours before the Air New Zealand flight was due to leave. Being a Saturday morning, both cars had made good time.

Ruth and Diane checked in their luggage and were informed the flight was on time and would be taking off at 1a.m. The tears and kisses became natural to them all. Kevin had never experienced a farewell like this before. The love he had for Diane had come to the surface and he couldn't control his emotions. Memories of the orphanage flooded back—how he would lie in bed at night and pray that one day he would have a family and a feeling of being wanted. Slowly his prayers were being answered—it was a good feeling, though sad that it could be months before he saw Diane again.

Kevin took Diane's hand and led her to an isolated corner. "Diane, I'm not going to stay any longer. I find it too much to take. I'm going to say goodbye now. I promise to write every day." She put her arms around his neck and kissed him passionately. He responded in the same passionate way. After several minutes she pulled away and looked into his eyes.

"Telephone me on Tuesday. By that time I'll have recovered from the flight."

Kevin took her by the hand and led her back to the group. He said his goodbyes to everybody and made his way back to the car park.

He drove back to Hereford in a daze. His mind was on one thing only—Diane and the thought of spending the rest of his life with her.

On Monday morning he was back in the classroom. Again Arabic was on the agenda. The sergeant of the guard had informed him the adjutant was on leave, so his planned interview had to wait. This made him feel guilty and unhappy. He had hoped to telephone Diane with news that would bring them together. Instead, they talked for twenty-five minutes, like teenagers, both excited about the love they had for each other.

On the morning of Thursday 5th June Kevin entered the classroom and was surprised to be informed the lessons had been cancelled and he was to report to Captain Brown' s office as soon as possible.

The last three days in the classroom had been hell for Kevin. He had always been a good student, but since his return from leave and his new-found love, Diane, he could not concentrate; the last three days had been a waste of time for he had learned nothing. He was convinced the order to report to Captain Brown was a reprimand for slacking in the classroom.

He wondered how he was going to explain his lack of concentration. He knocked on the office door. The cool self-controlled voice of Captain Brown responded to his knock with a polite "Come in." Kevin was surprised on entering to find Sergeant Ian Marshal sitting facing Captain Brown. He had never been assigned to work with Ian before; he wondered whether the nickname 'Pickle Ian Marshal' and the regiment's story behind it had any truth—he certainly had never seen the pickle jar with the so-called testicles! He looked at Ian closely: his long brown hair matched his nanny-goat beard; his thin face with a large thin nose and green eyes made him look like Kevin's idea of Jesus Christ. He was wearing a white grandfather shirt outside his fawn trousers, white socks and brown sandals. When Kevin looked into the man's sad eyes he knew the stories were true and wondered how *he* would have dealt with the situation Ian had found himself in.

"Oh Kevin, come in—be seated," Captain Brown said, pointing to the vacant chair next to Pickle. Pickle looked up and nodded to Kevin. Kevin sat and smiled to himself. He couldn't help stealing another look at Ian and thinking he looked like a dropout—instead of being here he should be on a street corner selling the Big Issue.

Unknown to Kevin, five days earlier Ian Marshal had been doing exactly that. For sixteen weeks he had lived in lodgings in the Kilburn area of London. His task was to live and mix with the Irish community, gathering as much information as possible. He had lived as an Irish dropout by day, standing on street corners selling the Big Issue. The evenings he spent making friends in as many Irish public houses and clubs as possible, making it known he was an IRA sympathiser. Ian was finally enlisted as a fund-raiser for the IRA. Ian knew this was just a test for beginners, but it was a step in the right direction. The job consisted of visiting clubs and public houses and blatantly collecting money, just like a charity collection.

Ian had worked hard at his new role. His Irish accent was that of Belfast—he had perfected the accent over the years. His new-found friends where from Cork and very clever at fund raising.

They would not use force or intimidation, unless a gun wedged in the trouser belt where everybody could see it could be called intimidation. Ian was amazed at the amount of money he and his new-found friends had collected. Friday's collection always trebled, when the Irish labourers, straight from the building sites, became very generous with their wage packets after two hours of drinking Guinness and Irish Whiskey.

Things were going well for Ian until the last Sunday. He and his new Irish friends had just finished collecting at the King's Arms in Kentish Town. The three of them made their way to the Wheelwright Arms in Kilburn. The public house was large with a lunchtime disco with topless dances, and as many as eight hundred customers had been known to attend. It was a good picking ground for collecting. Before they had time to collect any money, however, a smartly dressed Irishman approached them and warned them off, saying that special branch had several men under cover at the disco.

Ian's heart began to race. The smart Irishman with dark greasy hair was Martin Driscal, a known active member of the North Belfast IRA. Three years previously, while serving as a sergeant in the Third paratroops regiment stationed in Northern Ireland, he had arrested Driscal on a firearms charge; though the man he had arrested had ginger curly hair, there was no mistaking the blue piecing eyes. After an hour in Ian's custody special branch had taken over. The last Ian had heard of him was that he had escaped to Southern Ireland. Lucky for Ian he didn't seem to recognise him. That evening Ian contacted Captain Brown who in turn gave Ian orders to vacate his room and return to Hereford for debriefing. Captain Brown didn't want to jeopardise any Special Branch undercover work.

For the last four days Ian's debriefing consisted of a full report, detailed descriptions of suspected IRA members, followed by a few hours spent looking at the mugshot file putting names and places to faces. It was good to finish the debriefing. It was one part of the job he really detested.

Kevin looked back at Captain Brown and waited for him to continue. Captain Brown leaned back in his chair and began to speak. "Two hours ago I had a part-message from one of our men in the field. I'm afraid he was cut off before he could finish." Captain Brown leaned forward and put his elbows on his desk, then continued: "The part-message we have indicates the IRA have a cell on the move and they're heading for the mainland. It seems they're booked on this evening's Dublin ferry, arriving at Holyhead tomorrow morning." He leaned back, rotating on the swivel chair and looking out of the window. He spoke with concern in his voice. "I'm afraid our man was cut off before he could give us any more information." He just sat there looking out of the window. Both Kevin and Ian wondered who it was that had passed on the information; it didn't look good for their unknown colleague. They knew not to ask questions, however. In time the regiment would be given information of any deaths that may have occurred in the field.

Captain Brown turned away from the window and faced Kevin and Ian. "Right, let's get down to business. You're both assigned to meet the Ferry, locate the cell and follow them. I want to know what they're up to." He opened a green file that was on his desk. "We have one problem—the only surveillance car I have for you is one I commandeered from Special branch. It was being returned to Berlin for work in the Eastern sector and comes with a driver." He studied papers from the file. "His name is Corporal Paul Quinley, a driver with the RCT stationed in Berlin, well respected by MI5 and MI6. We have him as long as the assignment lasts." Captain Brown closed the file and looked directly at Kevin. "Kevin, Quinley should arrive this afternoon. I want you to take him under your wing and look after him. Tell him what you think he should know. Try not to let anything happen to him." Captain Brown stood up, indicating the meeting was over. "I have a bad feeling regarding this IRA cell. Let's stop whatever they are up to, right?" He walked towards the door. "I'll call you both for a full brief as soon as corporal Quinley arrives." He opened the door and Kevin and Ian where dismissed.

Kevin returned to his billet and felt a lot easier. The assignment was just a straightforward surveillance job—no big deal. He sat and wrote two letters—one to the adjutant expressing his wish to resign from the regiment, the other to Diane telling her he had no idea when he would be able to write again.

He took an instant liking to Paul Quinley. Paul was overweight but reliable, a soldier from the old school. Over the next few days Kevin relied more and more on Paul. His mind was on other matters: Diane was never out of his thoughts.

The next few days were like a dream to Kevin. There was the meeting of the ferry from Dublin, the tracking device that allowed them to follow the IRA's Range Rover through southern England to Portsmouth Harbour, the sea crossing to Bilbao and then the long journey through Spain. Their final destination would be the Rock of Gibraltar. And all the time his mind was elsewhere—in the hotel bedroom in Southampton with Diane.

When the Mercedes pulled into the main square on Gibraltar it was greeted with machine-gun fire. Kevin wasn't the well-trained SAS man that fought in the Falklands, the undercover man in Columbia. He was a lovesick young man who only wanted to be with his new love. Everything was like a slow motion film. He stepped out of the Mercedes holding the Browning pistol in both hands; he fired one shot that hit the young terrorist between the eyes. The older terrorist appeared from behind the Range Rover and Kevin took aim and pulled the trigger twice. He knew before the second bullet left the gun that the terrorist was dead.

From then on everything happened in spilt seconds. Twenty yards away Kevin noticed David, Diane's brother. He froze, wondering what on earth *he* was doing there! Then he realised there was yet another terrorist to deal with. That was when he felt the unbearable pain in his back—and he died with the image of Diane in her black business suit. Her hands had reached out for him, drawing him into her arms.

He had loved her so much.

CHAPTER 27

David

David put his one arm around Barbara's waist and waved farewell with the other arm as he watched his mother and sister walk through passport control into the duty-free area at Gatwick. The tears had dried up. He suddenly felt guilty, looking forward to being alone with his new bride. It was the first time since the wedding day that he had been alone with Barbara. He looked at her beautiful face, put both of his hands on either side of her high cheekbones and pulled her towards him. He kissed her and the excitement grew within him. He looked forward to getting home. He looked back at the duty-free area, just in time to see the last wave of farewell from his mother and sister.

A strange empty feeling passed through him. It was as if he would never see them again.

His mind scanned the last five weeks—the happiest of his life. It was the surprise of his life, seeing his mother again and out of the blue like that. Then there was the meeting with Diane's boyfriend Kevin and the instant friendship that bonded them together. He felt it strange how similar they were, not only in looks but in mannerisms. Both could have passed as brothers, though Kevin was broader in build and had the weather-beaten face that made him look five years older than David.

Their thick brown hair, the brown eyes that seemed to smile, the slightly wide mouth, the top lip slightly thin compared to the bottom lip which was full—the resemblance was uncanny. There was the nose, too, not too big, not too small—anybody would be proud of it. These features made both of them equally attractive to the opposite sex.

The drive home to Southampton was uneventful. Barbara, realising David must be feeling low, left all conversation to him. It was not until she drove the car into the driveway of their bungalow and turned the ignition off that David turned and looked directly at her. "I love you so very much," he said, leaning across and kissing her.

That evening David showed the passion and love that he had to offer. Since their wedding day Barbara had found her lovemaking with David a new experience; nothing was sordid and she liked to do things to him she had never dreamt of with anybody else. She was becoming addicted to his lovemaking.

On Monday the 26th May they received a letter from the Radio and Wireless Company. He was to report to the ship no later than the following Monday when it was scheduled to sail—on Tuesday the 3rd. The ship's first port of call would be Las Palmas.

David made a point of returning to the ship several times that week to familiarise himself with the new satellite radio system.

The ship's refit had made life a lot easier for David. The cabin he had used on the previous voyage had become a control room for the new system. His new cabin was now next to the radio room that used to be the officers' bar! The new officers' bar was located next to the dining room.

The Ship's radio room was located one deck below the Ship's Bridge. He was now able to leave the radio room on the port side. Two strides took him to his cabin on the starboard side. The cabin now in effect had two rooms, which included a day room measuring fifteen feet square that was furnished with a three-seater settee and a matching armchair. Both settee and armchair were placed in a position to overlook a small fourteen-inch television set and video recorder. Both items stood on a pine cabinet. A matching pine coffee table separated the armchair and settee. Behind the main entrance door was a small alleyway that led to a toilet and shower; beyond that was the bedroom that contained a built-in double pine wardrobe. On the opposite side to the wardrobe was a single but large bunk bed. On inspection David found the two handles he thought belonged to a draw were in fact a bunk bed extension. As you pulled the handles to the drawer a mattress came into view; four spring legs raised the drawer to make the bunk bed into a large double bed. He looked forward to Monday and the coming five months.

On Monday 2nd June Barbara made her final check of the hairdressing salon and said her goodbyes before joining David and her mother for a light lunch. At 3 a.m. the Taxi arrived to take them to the docks. She had spent the previous day on the ship unpacking and trying to make the cabin as homely as possible. Their only obligation now was to report on board and wait for the ship to sail.

At 6 a.m. Tuesday morning the ship left Southampton Dock and made its way down Southampton Water. It took ninety minutes for the ten thousand-ton vessel to reach the Isle of Wight's Needles. The morning sunshine on the water made the calm sea look like a mirror. The ship entered the English Channel at six that evening before passing Ouessant Island and sailing into the Bay of Biscay.

Barbara had spent most of the day on the open deck just forward of their cabin. The whole experience was like a fairy tail. It was something you always dream of as a child. She wondered what she had done to deserve all this happiness. She realised David had brought this happiness into her life—and how she loved him! He was only yards away in his radio room working, but she wanted him next to her—she wanted them to be as one. She could not imagine her life without him. The future was theirs and it looked good. Of course she did not know she was three days pregnant.

Strange how fate can change the best laid plans.

The Bay of Biscay did not live up to its stormy reputation and the eighteen-hour crossing was like crossing a pond. The ship passed Finisterre at twelve minutes past noon on the 5th June, then set course and headed southwest to the Canary Islands.

That afternoon David was in the radio room receiving a shortened version of the world news put out by Reuters. In the past he would have to type it out. Now, with the new satellite system, the newssheet was printed automatically.

He didn't hear the knock on his door. It opened, the sunlight flooding in. The Captain stood in the framework of the door. That morning the word had come from the bridge—the rig of the day was white—and the Captain looked immaculate in his white starched shirt with matching shorts, the sun reflecting off his highly polished white leather shoes. The white long socks were pulled up to just below his knees. The two black epaulettes, each one with four gold bars, made his shoulders look much larger than they were. The black and gold amongst all that white made David's uniform look shabby. The Captain had removed his peaked cap on entering the room and had it tucked under his right arm. His fair hair and fair complexion made him look a lot younger then his forty-two years.

He closed the door behind him. His voice sounded even younger. "Afternoon, David—how is your new satellite system?" Before David had time to answer the Captain continued: "The new navigation system has packed up, so we're back to the old compass. What I need you to do is to send this message to head office as soon as possible." He held out a piece of paper for David. "I need an answer as soon as possible. I'll be on the bridge for the rest of the afternoon, so let me know as soon as you have a reply. Sorry I don't have time to talk. Perhaps you and your lovely wife will join be for dinner this evening?" He turned, opened the radio room door and left.

David had sailed with Captain Roberts on several occasions since becoming a radio officer. At first he thought the man very rude, but he quickly realised he was just shy and lacked conversation. But what he lacked in personality he made up as a Captain. The shipping company regarded him so highly that ten months earlier they had made him Commodore of the fleet. David looked at the message.

TO HEAD OFFICE:

NEW NAVAGATION SYSTEM HAS BROKEN DOWN. NO PROBLEMS USING COMPASS. PLEASE ADVISE AS SOON AS POSSIBLE.

CAPTAIN ROBERTS

Thirty-five minutes later a reply came through:

TO M.V. ESSEX

ALTER COURSE FOR GIBRALTAR. MUST KNOW YOUR E.T.A. AS SOON AS POSSIBLE. SENDING A COMPONANT MANAGER AND ENGINEER TO DO WORK ON YOUR ARRIVAL.

IAN BRADY M.D.

David climbed the outside companionway to the bridge; the captain sat in his chair looking at the ship's progress against the slight swell of the Atlantic. He took the message David gave him. After reading it twice he stood up and walked towards the chart room situated at the rear of the bridge. Without turning to face David he said, "David, wait here. I'll work out an E.T.A. and you can get it off straight away." David loved being on the bridge; the view of the bow rising and falling to the motion of the sea gave him goose pimples! He became impatient—he wanted to let Barbara know the ship was on its way to Gibraltar.

Five minutes passed before Captain Roberts returned and handed David the new message for head office:

TO HEAD OFFICE:

E.T.A. FOR GIBRALTAR. 4 P.M. FRIDAY 6th JUNE.

CAPTAIN ROBERTS

David sent the message, then went to find Barbara who was sunbathing on the deck just aft of the funnel. Both were excited at the thought of visiting the Rock of Gibraltar and eating with the Captain that evening. Barbara felt honoured for she knew from David that the Captain liked to keep to himself.

David returned to the radio room just in time to receive another message from head office:

M.V. ESSEX:

BERTH NOT READY FOR YOU UNTIL 6A.M. SATURDAY 7 JUNE. ENGINEERS WITH YOU A.M. SAME DATE. MUST VACATE BERTH BY MONDAY 9 JUNE OWING TO ROYAL VISIT OF H.M.S. INVISABLE.

IAN BRADY M.D.

David returned to the bridge and passed the message to the Captain who ordered adjustments to the ship's speed to bring it into anchorage in Gibraltar at 4 a.m on Saturday.

The seas were light to moderate over the next 36 hours, allowing the ship to arrive at the anchorage on time. The pilot and the tug had the ship docked at its berth at 6.05 Saturday morning.

Two pieces of news that morning sealed David's fate.

The first piece of news came from the components manager and his engineer. They had spent two hours locating the problem. They informed the Captain they needed spare parts. These had to be flown out from England and would not arrive until Monday morning.

The second piece of news came from the company's representative in Gibraltar. The H.M.S. *Invincible* had hit the quay while visiting the Spanish port of Virgo. The ship was slightly damaged and the aircraft carrier was unable to make its scheduled call at Gibraltar. The *Essex* could remain at its berth until her repairs where completed.

Barbara and David took full advantage of the ship's stay in Gibraltar. By day they were sightseeing while they spent the evenings eating in a little back street restaurant.

At 8 a.m. Monday morning the Captain informed the crew all shore leave ended at 11 a.m. The systems engineer had informed him that if the spare parts arrived on the first flight, the repairs should be completed by midday. This being the case, the Captain wanted to sail as soon as possible afterwards.

Barbara suggested to David they go ashore for a last minute bit of shopping. They left the ship just after 9 a.m. and strolled through the docks towards the main street.

The first shop they came to was a chemist. Barbara stopped, contemplatively, and looked at David. "I think I should visit the chemist and top up on a few toiletry items I need," she said, straightening his white collier. "You stay here—I won't be long." She walked to the shop, opened the door and disappeared inside while David waited outside. His loving thoughts of Barbara were interrupted with the sound of screeching brakes, followed a couple of seconds later by the sound of gunshots. David walked the 25 yards that led to the main square out of curiosity. His first sight on entering the square, to his amazement, was his new-found friend Kevin.

Kevin was standing next to a large black car, his arm stretched out in front of him and holding a gun. David watched as Kevin pulled the trigger once and a young man in his twenties fell to the ground. He noticed movement behind a parked Range Rover fifteen yards away and saw a balding man in his fifties. At that point Kevin pulled the trigger of his gun twice. The balding head of the man exploded. Stunned, David looked back at Kevin. Their eyes met, the surprise on Kevin's face a mixture of pain and bewilderment.

David couldn't take it in before it was too late: a man appeared behind Kevin firing a machine pistol. Bullets from the gun entered Kevin's back, killing him instantly. The man who fired the machine pistol walked forward. David couldn't believe his eyes—the man was the spitting image of Kevin! Someone else appeared from behind the black car and pulled the trigger of his gun repeatedly. The last thing David saw and heard was the man with the machine pistol falling to the ground, firing his gun indiscriminately around the square. Two bullets had entered David's heart and ten minutes later he died.

Barbara left the chemist shop to the noise of a car backfiring, as she thought. David wasn't in sight and she followed the noise. As she entered the square the noise stopped. The carnage around her took her breath away. Then she saw David, his white shirt awash with blood, his throat rasping as he fought for breath. She sat down beside him and cradled his head. She screamed, and then screamed again—and again. The screams turned to anguished cries for help.

CHAPTER 28

Julie 1985

Julie drove off the M25, joined the A3 and headed towards Bagshot and her mother's house.

The flight back from Antique was pleasant, thanks to the understanding and friendship from her new friend, Terry the Cabin Service Officer.

The Boeing 747 landed at Heathrow on time at 9:30 a.m. on 4th of June. Julie had telephoned her mother from the BWW debriefing room. She had arranged to travel to Bagshot late evening for dinner and stay the night. It had been ten days since her father's funeral and she wondered how her mother was coping. She sounded fine on the four occasions she had spoken to her on the telephone.

Julie drove her Escort Gti through Lightwater, thinking of Terry and their forth-coming holiday to Gibraltar. She hoped she was doing the right thing. She knew he had feelings for her—she could tell by the way he looked at her with his strong brown eyes. She had never met anybody before who could talk with their eyes like Terry; those eyes, she felt, had invited her to bed on a couple of occasions over the last few days. He was such a lovely man but not really her type. She liked the tall dark gypsy type with curly black hair and a day's stubble, whereas Terry was clean-shaven with brown wavy hair that was always well groomed and skin like a baby's bottom. He looked a lot younger than his forty-eight years. She had told him they could be friends but nothing else and he was willing to except the friendship. She knew he was only accepting the situation, hoping that one day she might change her mind.

They were both booked on the 8:30 Sunday morning flight to Gibraltar and she was looking forward to her holiday.

The Escort stopped outside the little cottage. She took her overnight bag from the boot and locked the car as she turned. Her mother was standing in the doorway, her dyed blonde hair looking fresh and shiny. She had obviously been to the hairdressers that day. She wore a black dress, the hemline just reaching her knees. Carol still wore plenty of makeup. This pleased Julie for she had been frightened that her mother would go into a shell and let herself go.

They held each other tight, kissed, then cried. The emotions from both ladies were to console each other. After what seemed an age they entered the house. Julie went straight to her room and unpacked her bag, then freshened her makeup and returned to the living room. Carol poured out two gin and tonics and placed both glasses on coasters to protect the expensive glass coffee table. She sat with her legs crossed on a brown leather chair. Julie sat opposite on the matching sofa and looked at her mother. "Well mother, how have you coped since the funeral?"

Carol picked up her glass and took a sip. "The day after you left I felt really sorry for myself—in actual fact I felt suicidal. I fell asleep in this chair that afternoon." Her eyes became moist. "Then something really strange happened to me." She took another sip from the glass. "Albert came to me—he came to say his final farewells." She looked at Julie, knowing she would never understand the experience she went through that afternoon. Though she was asleep she knew Albert had come to her to say his farewells. She continued: "He told me I was still young, to stop moping after him and find a new life for myself."

Julie put her glass down, stood up and walked towards her mother. She put her arms around her. "Mother," she said softly, "it was only a dream."

Carol took Julie's hand, held it tightly, and turned to look into her eyes. "You don't understand—he was *here*. Perhaps I was sleeping, but he was here. He told me he was breaking away from me and I needed to start afresh. As he left I awoke. I felt shocked and upset that he had left me completely alone." The tears ran down her face.

Julie held her tighter. "Mum, it was only a dream."

Carol dried her eyes and drew away from Julie, then looked into her eyes. "You still don't understand, do you? Whether it was a dream or not, he came to release me. He has given me peace of mind and released me from the terrible feeling of guilt."

Once again they put their arms around each other. "Mother," Julie said, "you have nothing to be guilty about." She took hold of her mother's shoulders and looked into her eyes.

Carol shook her head. "I'm still here—he's not. That's my guilt—but he's released me from it."

Mother and Daughter finished their drinks, then walked the five hundred yards to the only Chinese restaurant in Bagshot for dinner.

They spent the evening laughing and joking. The happy memories of their family life gave pleasure and contentment to them both.

Carol could never bring herself to tell Julie that Albert was not her real father.

They were having coffee and brandy when Carol asked Julie about her new-found boyfriend. "So are you going to tell me about him or you going to keep him a secret?" Carol smiled as she twirled the brandy glass in both hands and looked into Julie's eyes.

Julie returned her smile. "Mother, I know that look—you're trying to marry me off. I'm not ready to make you a grandmother."

Carol blushed. "You're going on holiday with him. I thought there must be more to it than just friends."

"Mother, he's a work colleague and a very nice man, but not my type. For a start he's nearly seventeen years older then me."

Carol butted in. "Your father was older than me."

Julie refrained from saying what she felt. If he had been the same age as her he would more than likely be here now. "Mother, when I get married, I'm going to marry someone younger. There's no guarantee, but the odds are that I will die before him. Therefore, I won't be left alone."

Once a gain Carol butted in. "But if you have children you won't be alone."

Julie responded with some impatience: "Mother, can we drop the subject? When we come back from Gibraltar and assuming we are still friends I'll bring him to meet you. You never know—you may fancy him yourself." They both laughed.

Just after 6 a.m. Sunday morning Terry rang the bell to Julie's Ruislip house. She was pleased to see how smart he looked in his light blue shirt and dark blue trousers and highly polished black shoes. She knew that, in spite of his age, if she allowed herself, she could so easily end up in bed with him. She wondered whether she could grow to love him, for she liked his charm and company. She felt safe and secure with him. Yet she knew, for now anyway, she just didn't fancy him sexually. Nevertheless she had to admit to herself she was looking forward to the next ten days.

Terry drove his car to the BWW staff car park at Heathrow. There they took the staff bus to Terminal 1 and checked in their baggage. The check-in staff informed both of them the flight would be leaving on time. After a visit to the duty-free and coffee shop, they made their way to the boarding gate. Julie always enjoyed boarding the plane as a passenger—it was always nice to be looked after by your colleagues. The custom amongst the company crew was gold treatment for their colleagues.

It was five minutes after the Boeing 737 had taken off that Julie realised the gossip that must be taking place in the crew's pantry.

Travelling as a companion with Terry on the same flight to Gibraltar will put the cat amongst the pigeons, she thought! She wondered how long it would take before the cabin crew had them married off. She looked at Terry in the next seat; he turned and looked at her and knew what was going through her mind. "Sorry if you're embarrassed," he said with a sheepish smile.

She took his hand. "Terry, there's quite a few ladies in the company who would love to be in my shoes—so let's have a good time and sod them all!"

The Taxi pulled into Main Street and stopped outside the chemist. The driver turned and spoke to them both "I-A. is the flat above the chemist shop—the entrance is in the main square. I need to drive you around the one-way system or you can get out here and walk the few yards in to the square."

Terry made the decision: "We'll walk from here." He paid the taxi, took both suitcases and walked the short distance past the shop into the square. At the rear of the shop an oak door with brass symbols stating 1-A was prominent. He placed the cases to one side, took out a set of keys from his trousers' pocket and opened the door. The stairs were situated to the right of the door—five steps, then a right angle, then fifteen steps led to the front door of the flat. The bright hundred-watt bulb made the wooded stairway seem dreary and old fashioned. At the top of the stairs was a small alleyway, then the main door: the same key that let him into the building opened the door to the flat. The light from inside transformed the dreary staircase, revealing the interior of a luxury apartment. The well-equipped flat consisted of two bedrooms, one at the front and one at the back. The back bedroom faced the main square. The front bedroom overlooked Main Street.

The twenty-five foot lounge had a three-piece suite nearest the door. Further into the room stood a modern dining room table and four chairs. Up against the left wall was a large wall unit, a record player and television placed on the centre shelf. At the far end of the room were patio doors that led to a sun terrace overlooking the main street. The table and chairs on the terrace made it an ideal suntrap and a perfect setting for breakfast.

That evening they ate in a small Spanish restaurant just off the main square. Pepe's had a reputation for good food and excellent service. The fifteen tables were neatly decorated with maroon tablecloths and white napkins placed in wineglasses. Only eight of the tables were occupied. Julie and Terry were shown to a table halfway down the narrow restaurant, Julie facing the entrance, Terry looking towards the rear of the restaurant. Both ordered fresh prawns with avocado. Julie followed with grilled sole. Terry had the chef's special, veal chop. Both took the waiter's advice and had a bottle of Spanish wine, Estola 1981.

Though the conversation was intense, Julie realised that Terry's eyes were drifting past her to someone behind. Ten minutes passed before her curiosity got the better of her. She turned and looked and was surprised to see a young couple sitting two tables away. The young couple only had eyes for each over. She was blonde with high cheekbones and very beautiful, but the surprise was the young man who had the same features as Terry. She had never seen Terry as a young man, but looking at the man behind her she could visualise Terry looking the same twenty-five years earlier.

The evening passed with the odd glance from both Terry and Julie. Neither of them mentioned the subject for it was surely just a coincidence. They left Pepe's and finished the evening in the Red Lion public house. The place was alive with music and dancing. The jukebox kept the soldiers and sailors from the Rock's garrison entertained.

A goodnight kiss on the cheek and a polite thank you outside her bedroom door confused Julie—she had convinced herself she didn't fancy him. The meal in a romantic restaurant and a few drinks made her feel good and suddenly she wanted more from this handsome man. She put her hands around his neck and kissed him passionately, her tongue searching for his. "Terry…I want you," she said in a low sexy voice.

Terry was uncomfortable with the situation and pulled away. "Julie, I think you've had too much drink." He smiled, holding her at arms length. "I think we both might regret it in the morning. I think we should wait till we're both sober, don't you?"

Embarrassed, she felt like a silly schoolgirl and opened her bedroom door. She went in and closed it before Terry could say anything. She undressed, put on her nightdress and went to bed. She fell asleep hoping in spite of herself that Terry would come to her and make mad passionate love.

The next morning she woke to the sound of Terry's voice.

"Can I come in? I have a cup of tea for you!"

Julie sat up in bed, straightened her nightdress and remembered the previous night, blushing with embarrassment. "Yes, of course," she said self-consciously.

Terry entered the room and placed the cup and saucer on the bedside cabinet. "Did you sleep well?" he said, looking in admiration at her.

"Oh, yes, thank you—like a log." She hoped he wouldn't mention the night before. It was the first time she had seen him in the morning with no clothes on. He looked good with just his towel wrapped around his waist. As he reached the door, he turned.

"I'm setting up for breakfast on the terrace—corn flakes, fresh fruit, toast and coffee. Okay with you?"

She took the cup and saucer from the bedside cabinet and looked up. "That sounds great. What's the time?" She held the cup using her thumb and forefinger.

"8:45," he said looking at his watch.

"I can't believe it's as late as that," she said with genuine concern.

Terry smiled as he left the room and closed the door.

She realised what a gentleman he was. She finished her tea, then showered and dressed in a white tee-shirt and white shorts. She looked into the mirror behind the bedroom door and was pleased with what she saw. She wondered what Terry thought of her body. He was beginning to get to her, she admitted. She wanted him to like her body—and she wanted him to make love to her.

"We're not going to have enough milk for the cornflakes," Terry announced through the closed door. "I'm just going to pop out and get some."

"Okay," she called back to him.

She heard the flat door open and close and his footsteps on the stairs. Her taste buds had woken up and she opened the bedroom door and rushed to the flat door. As she opened the door the front door to the square closed. She really fancied some honey on her cornflakes. As she made her way down the stairs she was startled by the sound of fireworks outside. She opened the front door. Terry was ten feet away and she only had eyes for him. "Terry!" she called out to him. The noise from the square made her disorientated and she couldn't grasp what was happening—the fireworks were going off everywhere. She watched as Terry ran towards her and hurled his body on top of her. Before his weight forced her to the ground the first bullet hit her in the eye. The second bullet ricocheted off the wall into the back of her head.

She died before they both hit the ground. Terry had been unable to shield her from the terrorists' bullets.

CHAPTER 29

Terry 1985

Terry closed the door to his luxury apartment and dropped his keys through the letterbox of his neighbour's apartment. He looked at his watch—5:35 a.m. Willow trees surrounded the mews of eight flats. The whole setting looked beautiful: the cloudless sky and the June morning sun gave everything long shadows. He looked for a few seconds to take everything in. He felt proud of himself. He had left school at fifteen with little education; with hard work and determination life had been good to him. He wondered whether it was the hard work, or was it fate? Strange—he had never felt this way before. Do you make your own destiny, or does fate take a hand and you have no control?

He walked to the communal car park and unlocked his Ford Capri, placed his suitcase in the boot and sat behind the steering wheel. He opened the glove compartment and took out the piece of paper. Julie's address and instructions on how to get there were written in neat handwriting. Twenty-five minutes later he passed South Ruislip Tube Station. At the next turning on the left he turned the three-litre Capri into Gosport Drive. Number 22 was the number he was looking for. One hundred yards on the left the number 22 stood out, the six-inch high letters fixed to the wall beside the front door. Julie's instructions were spot on! He rang the bell and she appeared in the small hallway. She reached up to release the top bolt and the brown silk shirt she wore over her fawn tight fitting trousers rose up to reveal her white silky skin. Her belly button was prominent. The way she had stretched up her arm caused her breasts to be pressed against the clear glass. Terry thought the whole movement was very agreeable.

She released the Yale lock and greeted Terry with a smile and a kiss on the cheek.

It was not until they were shown their seats on the aircraft—that's when Terry realised how embarrassed Julie must feel being seen with a work colleague old enough to be her father, and he told her so. He felt a lot better when she took his hand and said in her normal voice: "Terry, there's quite a few ladies in the company who would love to be in my shoes, so lets have a good time and sod them all."

Looking at the flat from the outside was a big disappointment to Terry. He wanted to apologise to Julie and take her to a hotel, to save any embarrassment, but he decided to check the inside first.

He climbed the stairs and opened the apartment door to reveal a modern well-equipped luxury flat. The disappointment disappeared.

That evening they made their way to Pepes, a small but nice restaurant recommended to Terry by his friend Tony who owned the flat they occupied.

Terry felt good in the company of such an elegant young woman. They seemed to have so much in common—the conversation never seemed to dry up.

He was suddenly taken back when a young couple came into the restaurant and sat two tables away. The young man looked familiar. It was very difficult to look at Julie with out noticing the young man behind her. It was ten minutes before he realised who the young man reminded him of. He felt ridiculous, for the young man had the same features as Julie—so much so that they could have been brother and sister!

After a very pleasant meal and a stroll through the square the music from the Red Lion public house enticed them in. Soldiers and sailors from the Rock's garrison were in good voice singing along to the latest hits on the pub's jukebox.

It was not until drinking their third vodka and tonic that Terry realized the drink had gone to Julie's head. The wine with the meal and after-dinner brandies had started to take effect on her. Her eyes had begun to glaze, her voice had become slurred. She did not object when Terry suggested they leave.

He enjoyed the walk back, her arms wrapped around his left arm. It was just like a courting couple strolling in the park. She needed a little support from him when climbing the stairs. It made him feel wanted. He unlocked the main door and guided her to her bedroom where she turned and gave him a peck on the cheek. "Thank you for such a lovely evening—I really enjoyed every minute." Terry looked into her eyes and smiled. Unexpectedly she reached up with both hands behind his neck and began to kiss him passionately. He had dreamed of this moment from the very first time they had met. Yet, for the first time in his life, he pulled away! His morals came to the surface—he couldn't bring himself to take advantage of Julie while she was in this condition.

That night he had very little sleep. The whole evening kept coming back to him like a video recording. He knew he had done the right thing. He felt good inside. So why was it the women he loved didn't excite him?

Any woman in the past that had put her tongue down his throat and wrapped her body around him would have given him an erection any man would have been proud of.

At seven the next morning he climbed out of bed, had a shower and sat on the terrace. He opened the book he had brought from the duty-free shop at Heathrow. He liked a good read. He was looking forward to reading Harold Robbins' new book *The Storyteller*. He had read all his previous books.

At 8:40 he made a fresh pot of tea and poured a cup for Julie. He wondered whether she would remember the night before. He decided not to mention anything about it. The sexy voice from the bedroom invited him to come in. He placed the cup and saucer on the side cabinet before he realised he was only wearing a towel. For some strange reason he felt embarrassed. He looked at her—fresh and lovely, smiling sweetly, sitting up in bed. After some small talk about breakfast he hurried from the room.

It took him only three minutes to dress, donning a pair of briefs and white shorts, a blue and white shirt and white trainers.

He cut up two bananas, an apple and a grapefruit, and set the coffee percolator going, then filled two dishes with Cornflakes. But he soon realised the half-pint of milk they had bought the day before was hardly going to be enough for breakfast, so he grabbed his wallet and shouted through Julie's bedroom door that he was popping out for more milk. He opened the door to the flat and started to descend the stairs. The noise of a motorcar's tyres skidding to a halt made him stop and wait for the bang that never came. Instead there was the sound of gunfire. It took a few seconds trying to make sense of this—what was gunfire doing in the main square of Gibraltar? He made his way to the front door. He still didn't realise the danger. He opened the door and closed it behind him as he entered the square.

Amongst all the carnage he noticed the young man from the restaurant standing ten yards to his left. Terry started to make his way towards him, but before he could ask him what was going on two things happened simultaneously: stray bullets had hit the young man and the door to the flat opened with Julie calling his name. The danger registered in a flash and he ran towards her, throwing himself on top of her. The tremendous pain in his head made him black out.

It would be weeks before he would regain consciousness.

CHAPTER 30

Paul Quinley 1985

Paul squeezed the trigger to the Browning automatic pistol until the magazine was empty. He had been in the army for seventeen years and this was the first time he had killed anybody. Strange—he had always expected it to happen on the battlefield, not in the main square of Gibraltar.

The feeling was one of excitement—a job well done, just like a tradesman showing off his latest creation. He felt no guilt; in fact, he was proud of his actions.

He stood with legs apart; both hands outstretched, leaning on the Mercedes for support. To an outsider it looked like something from an American gangster movie. Suddenly the pain in his wrist was unbearable, then the sharp pain on the back of the head was so severe he passed out.

He woke three hours later. He had slight concussion from the blow he had received on his head. The lack of sleep over the last few days contributed to the three hours he lay unconscious.

It took him several minutes to pull himself together. At first he thought everything had been a dream and he was in his bedroom at his parent's farm.

He swung his legs off the small bed and just sat there taking everything in. The room was obviously a cell of some kind, about 10ft by

15ft. The walls were green with no windows. The floor tiles were dark grey. Facing the small cot bed was a steel toilet with matching washbasin suspended on the wall. The door was at the far end of the oblong room, while next to the door was an ordinary doorbell button. He stood up and his whole body felt as if he was sickening for a bad dose of 'flu. Of course—it was the after-effects of the concussion. He pressed the button next to the door—no bell, no gong, in fact, nothing. He returned to the bed and sat down. It seemed an age that he sat there, going over everything that had happened to him in the past ten days. His thoughts went to Pickle and Kevin. Had they survived the tremendous amount of ammunition that had entered their bodies? He knew it would be a miracle for one or the other to pull through.

Five minutes passed before he heard the sound of a door opening and closing in the distance. Footsteps got louder until they stopped outside his cell door. The small grill in the door opened and a face appeared—then disappeared as the grill shut with an echoing bang. Then there was the sound of keys turning in the cell door lock. The door opened to reveal a policeman.

From where he was sitting the man looked as if he worked out in the gym or his uniform was a size too small. He stood six foot tall and had a round red face. His fair hair was styled into a crewcut. All this made him look older then his thirty-five years.

He entered the cell looking at Paul with contempt, placing Paul's bag on the bed. "Right you, I don't know who you have for friends, but you're to be ready in fifteen minutes. You're going on a little trip." The policeman turned and disappeared from the cell. To Paul's relief he had left the cell door open.

It was no time at all before the same policeman returned. "Follow me," he said with a look on his face that showed he didn't relish the idea of letting Paul go. He conducted him along the corridor and through the door at the end that led to an office. Two men stood in the middle of the room. Paul didn't like the look of either of them.

The shorter of the two stepped forward and held out his hand. "Hi, my name's Glen—this is Steve," he said, pointing to his companion. "We've been sent to escort you back to the UK. Are you ready to go?" Paul wondered what part of the establishment they where from. They didn't look like SAS—more like MI5 or MI6, the way they acted and dressed. The casual designer clothes they wore were impressive.

All three left the police station. Paul wasn't handcuffed to them yet felt as if he were their prisoner, they kept that close to him. The chauffeur-driven unmarked police car took them directly to the Gibraltar's airstrip. There they boarded an RAF DC 10 on a scheduled flight to Brize Norton. The foreign office had arranged for the three men to fly as part of the crew.

During the flight Paul's escorts said nothing. His questions fell on deaf ears. His two escorts were either not in the mood for talking or under orders not to talk.

His thoughts of being a hero and collecting a medal from the Queen were fast evaporating. He began to worry—his escorts where so intimidating, though they hadn't said half a dozen words between them. An air of brutality surrounded them. He was more frightened of them than he had been in the gunfight. He decided to sit back in his seat and see how things developed.

The plane landed just after 4.p.m. on Monday 9th June. Paul had never been to Brize Norton before. The only knowledge he had of the military airport had been watching the news bulletins on the television three years earlier, about the wounded servicemen returning from the Falklands campaign.

He wondered whether he would have to go through customs and immigration. His thoughts where soon answered when the plane came to a halt and the side door was opened by the cabin crew steward. Parked at the bottom of the gangway, just two yards away, was a top-of-the-range black chauffeur-driven Jaguar car. Within minutes they were speeding on the M40 to London. Even with the heavy

Monday afternoon traffic, the car arrived at the embankment building just an hour later.

The car was checked by a civilian security guard and allowed to drive through the large wrought-iron gates. The driver skilfully manoeuvred the Jaguar to the underground car park. Paul's escorts took his arms and guided him to the automatic lift. At the fifth floor the doors opened. Again, his escorts guided him out of the lift. They could have turned left or right, but it was the corridor facing them that Glen indicated.

Paul noticed all the doors were on the right-hand side—500, then 501, 502...Glen stopped at the next door. The clear sign in black with gold lettering read INTERVIEW ROOM. Glen didn't bother to knock, just opened the door and indicated for Paul to go in. Glen stood in the door, his partner behind him. "Wait there—someone will be with you in a moment." He closed the door. Paul was relieved they hadn't locked him in.

The room was not large or small—about 20ft square with wall-to-wall green cord carpet. The only furniture was a desk and a swivel armchair at the far end and four metal tubular chairs with plastic seats against the wall.

The only thing on the desk was a tape recorder.

The room looked bigger than it actually was due to the large mirror on the far wall. His thoughts went to the James Bond and Harry Palmer spy movies from the Ipcress files—surly it wasn't a two-way mirror! He decided not to take chances: he took a tubular chair and sat facing the desk.

It seemed an age before anything happened, though in reality it was no more than ten minutes. The door opened, admitting a sprightly man wearing grey trousers supported with bracers, his white shirt undone at the collier and his tie hanging loose. He stood 5ft 11ins tall with his greasy ginger hair brushed back. His ginger eyebrows were darker and bushy and made a prominent feature above his pale blue eyes.

As he walked past Paul, Paul caught the smell of body odour and aftershave—the combination of the two made him feel sick. The man walked behind the desk, placed a file on the desk, looked at Paul and smiled. "It seems we owe you a thank you." He held out his hand. "My name is Ryder. I work for MI5. Nice to meet you, Paul."

Paul stood up and walked a couple of paces forward and shook his hand. The door to the office closed. Ryder pulled his hand away and looked over Paul's shoulder.

"Er...this is my secretary, Miss Bennett."

Paul turned to see a large good-looking lady in her thirties; she was so pretty she might have been a model except for the four and half stone surplus weight she was carrying.

The man from special branch sat behind the desk. "Paul, bring your chair closer and I'll tell you how we're going to do this. This is a debriefing, not an interrogation. I'm going to put the tape on and I want you to tell me everything that happened from the time Captain Brown recruited you until the Gibraltar police sergeant knocked you out with his truncheon. Is that okay with you?"

For the first time since the Gibraltar police cell Paul began to relax. "Well, yes—but there are a few questions I would like to ask." He spoke with confidence.

Ryder looked directly into Paul's eyes. "All in good time. If I'm able to answer them I will. But first let's get you on tape. Oh yes...every so often I'll indicate to Miss Bennett to make notes. Are you ready? Let's get underway."

At seven fifty that evening Ryder and Miss Bennett left the room, the debriefing finished for the time being. Paul sat there ready for a drink. An idea came to him: he stood in front of the mirror, held out his hand as if he had a glass in it and waved his hand. Within minuets Miss Bennett entered the room.

"Mr Quinley," she said with authority, "Mr Ryder has informed me to tell you he needs to speak to you tomorrow. He would like you to stay in one of our guestrooms this evening."

Paul wasn't surprised. He decided to find out his exact position. "Do I have a choice?"

Miss Bennett looked at him with sad eyes. "I'm afraid not, but you'll find the room as good as any hotel in the country; you'll have your own bar, TV and radio." She flashed a smile as if he had just won a prize.

The next morning Paul woke nursing a slight hangover. The three-course steak meal, served with a bottle of red wine followed by French brandy, was everything Miss Bennett had promised.

A woman in her fifties dressed in a white overall delivered the breakfast trolley to his room at 8 a.m. Fresh grapefruit and toast washed down with coffee was all Paul could face.

Just after nine the door opened and Glen stood in the doorway.

"You might have knocked," Paul said, hoping not to upset the gruesome figure of Glen.

"I'm a sergeant, I don't knock on corporal's doors," Glen said in a voice that was soft but menacing. He did not move from the doorway. "Are you ready?" He continued without waiting for a reply: "You don't have to take everything—you'll be back." He stood and waited.

Paul grabbed his jacket. "Where are you taking me?" he said, closing the door behind him. He followed Glen to the end of the corridor where they entered a waiting lift. Glen looked into the mirror and brushed his long brown curly hair back with his hand. "Mr Ryder hasn't finished with you yet." When the lift stopped they were back on the fifth floor. Glen led Paul back to the interview room. This time Glen knocked and opened the door to the reply from inside. He indicated for Paul to enter. As soon as Paul was in the room Glen closed the door from the outside and disappeared.

Ryder sat at his desk; a familiar face sat on his left. "Paul, you know Captain Brown?"

Captain Brown stood up and held out his hand. "Well done, Paul—you did an outstanding job."

Paul reddened.

"Please be seated," Ryder said and all three sat down at the same time. Both men had not taken their eyes off Paul.

Ryder broke the silence. "Sorry Paul, but I need you to go through your story again for Captain Brown."

Paul repeated his story, trying not to forget anything.

When he had finished there were a few seconds silence. Captain Brown was the first to speak. "Is there anything you want to ask me?"

"Well, yes," Paul replied, not expecting this luxury. "Did either of your men survive?"

"I'm a afraid not; both men will be buried in the cemetery at Hereford with full military honours."

Paul wasn't surprised. "Was the operation a success?"

Captain Brown pulled a face of disappointment. "Well, we got rid of an IRA unit consisting of two known killers and an Argentine anti-Falklands terrorist. However, in the process two civilians where killed and another is in intensive care." Captain Brown noticed the concern on Paul's face. "You'll be happy to know all your bullets were accounted for. They were in the Argentine terrorist."

Ryder informed Paul he would be a guest of the establishment until investigation by Captain Brown and himself was finalised. Every day he had gone to the interview room answering question after question and hadn't a clue what they were after. Friday morning he made his way to the interview room once again. There was a change this time: Miss Bennett had replaced Captain Brown and was sitting next to Ryder. Ryder was in his normal seat. Ryder pointed to the chair in front of the desk and Paul sat down. Ryder was putting his signature to several foolscap papers. When he had finished he looked at Paul. "You will be glad to know your debriefing is over. Now I want you to listen to me very carefully. Everything I say I want you to take seriously."

Paul realised Ryder was wearing a jacket for the first time. Ryder put his elbows on the table. "This is the situation. We believe your life could now be in danger. As far as we know, there are only seven people who know you were in Gibraltar and why. If the IRA get wind of you, we're sure you'll be on their hit list." Ryder looked back down at the desk. Paul's records were in front of him. "You've signed up for twenty years and you have three years to serve." He looked up at Paul.

"Yes sir," Paul replied.

Ryder took a deep breath. "What we're going to do is pension you off, backdated to the first of June. You'll receive three hundred and eighty pounds a month; in addition, I have a cheque here for fifty thousand pounds, tax-free. One small point—I need you to sign the Official Secrets Acts."

Paul left the building and made his way to the nearest pub. He ordered a pint of bitter and drank a toast to Kevin and Pickle.

Life was going to change for Paul Quinley.

CHAPTER 31

Sean O' Donald 1985

In the town of Ballygowen, twenty miles south of Belfast, unemployed Sean sat at the small kitchen table. The back sports page of the *Daily Mirror* was full of cricket; he would never understand the game of cricket as long as he lived. He turned to the racing page and studied the horses on today's cards. The large mug of tea was lukewarm; he couldn't be bothered to make a fresh mug.

The music on the radio stopped. After a few seconds' silence the voice of a woman with an Irish accent spoke. "This is Radio Belfast, and this is the eleven o' clock news for Monday the 9th of June." There was a short pause. "News has just come in from Gibraltar." Sean put down the paper and turned the sound up. "An army unit believed to be from the SAS were involved in a shootout with members of the IRA this morning. We believe there have been fatalities." There was another short pause. "The shooting took place in the main square on the Rock of Gibraltar. As more news comes in, we will keep our listeners updated. Meanwhile here is the remainder of the news." Before she could carry on Sean turned the radio off, picked up the telephone receiver and waited for the dial tone, then dialed.

Peter Driscal's soft voice answered with a simple "Hello?"

"It's me—Sean. I must see you," he said with excitement in his voice.

"Can it wait till this evening?"

Sean thought for a moment. It would give him more time to gather more information. "Yeah—that'll be fine."

Peter took the excitement in Sean's voice as good news. "The Harp and Angel at seven this evening," he said quickly. Peter hung up leaving Sean with no chance to reply. Sean replaced the receiver.

Within seconds the telephone was ringing. Fifteen minutes later he replaced the receiver. The call intrigued him; another plan was fermenting in his brain.

That evening at seven he entered the back room of the Harp and Angel. Peter sat behind the table smiling. He opened a fresh bottle of Jamison's Irish whiskey and poured out large measures into two tumblers. "Congratulations, Sean—I never thought your plan would work so well."

Sean was disappointed. He had hoped to give the news first hand. "So you've heard all the details then?" He felt such a fool—of course the whole world knew of the killings by now.

Peter, still smiling, took a large gulp from the tumbler, sat back in the chair and put his feet up on the table. "I listened to the BBC. They had nothing but praise for the SAS. If only they knew we felt the same! I drink to the SAS who did our dirty work for us—executed two of our traitors, and without orders from us, killed two English civilians." Peter's tone was mocking and his smile turned to a laugh. "The whole world has condemned the British government and the SAS assassins." Peter took his feet from the table, stood up and raised his glass. "I drink to you, Sean, and your brilliant plan."

Sean raised his glass in return. The news of civilians killed had been broadcast on the 2 o'clock news. He sat down and put his tumbler on the wooden table. "It's a pity they were English. If they had been American or Israelis there would have been a bigger outrage."

Peter poured two more large whiskies. "Sean, we got what we wanted. Let's not be greedy." He smiled. "Any news of the SAS soldiers?"

Sean shook his head. "All I could find out was they were spirited away within minutes. You know what the SAS are like. They would not admit to anybody dying unless it was to discredit the IRA."

Peter held out a packet of cigarettes. Sean took one and waited for a light that came from Peter's American zip lighter.

Peter returned to the chair and replaced his feet on the table. "Have you got any new plans in the pipeline?" His smile turned to a grin.

"I'm working on a plan now," Sean said with pride.

Peter's face registered interest. "Well, out with it."

Sean loved it when Peter relied on his brain. "I had a phone call this morning from a sleeper on the mainland. He works as a cleaner in an animal research centre in Oxfordshire. Our man has been able to obtain a test tube from the laboratory. It contains the virus that spreads Foot and Mouth disease amongst animals."

Peter looked confused. "What good is that to us?" His eyes were beginning to get heavy with the drink.

Sean continued. "The disease spreads like wildfire. If we contaminated two or three farms on the English mainland, then it would only be a matter of time before thousands of farms would have problems from the disease. This would then affect the farming business. Farms would be put out of business. Not only would there be millions of animals destroyed, unable to be used for human consumption, but the snowball effect would cause economic chaos in the country—the government would be in turmoil. It may topple the government."

Peter wasn't impressed. He looked at Sean and his smile disappeared.

"Sean, do you realise in a few years' time, people from both sides of the border are going to get fed up with the killings and bombings?

They are going to want peace talks. I for one will never accept anything but a united Catholic Ireland. Everybody knows that will never happen. That's when we will need to change tactics and become devious. That will be the time when we can let you loose with your foot and mouth test tube."

Sean could see the logic in what Peter was saying. He would telephone his contact in the morning and see if the test tube could be put on hold for a few years.

Peter grabbed the Jamison bottle again, this time spilling the whiskey on the table as he topped up the tumblers. He had been drinking since lunchtime and his co-ordination and speech had started to suffer. "Sean, what we need at the moment is to carry on the bandwagon. I reckon you should be planning a nice big bomb—something important, somewhere in the City of London or that new building down by the London docks, what's it called—Canary Wharf?"

CHAPTER 32

Carol 1985

The sun had risen enough for its rays to penetrate the front bedroom window of the small cottage. The sleeping tablets Carol had taken the night before had done their job, though they had not stopped her nightmares. She lay there thinking. At least the weather forecast had been correct. It was a fine sunny Monday. She thought of Julie and her advice—"Mother, you must start getting out by yourself." She knew she was right, but it wasn't easy.

The idea came to her in a flash. A day shopping in Guildford would do her a power of good.

A cup of strong tea and a soak in the bath gave her the courage she needed.

She sat in front of her dressing table, carefully applying her makeup. She felt the strain of Albert's death, the guilt of being left behind—why him and not her? Is it life's destiny or is it just fate? She never realised just how much she loved him. It was hard to believe she would never wake up next to him again.

The shock and trauma had affected her eating routine. She had hardly eaten at all since his death and had lost ten pounds in weight. Losing the weight, however, had given her a figure any women of sixty-six years of age would be proud of.

She stood up and made her way to the tall mirror on a stand in the corner of the room, her dressing gown dropping to the floor. She looked at her body and felt proud. She was 5ft 4ins tall and weighed just under nine stone. Her breasts were not large but they held firm. Her legs had always been her best assets. She would never cover them in tights but always with the best nylon stockings, and today was no exception. She picked out a slightly tight-fitting light blue skirt from the wardrobe and a white blouse from the matching set of drawers; again, she looked into the mirror. The effect was pleasing. She wondered whether people would look at her and think she was mutton dressed as lamb? She selected a pair of white high-heel shoes and straightened the seam to her stockings. “Sod them all,” she said aloud. She knew Albert would have approved.

She made her way downstairs and into the lounge. The old family clock had started to chime. It was 9 o’clock. She suddenly thought of Julie enjoying herself in Gibraltar. It would be 10 o’clock there. She couldn’t help hoping this new man in Julie’s life was the right man. She really would like to see her married and settled with children.

She locked the front door. Her Ford Fiesta was where she had left it, parked at the front of the house, and she made herself comfortable behind the steering wheel. She placed the key in the ignition and started the car. Before she could put the car into gear a sharp pain shot through her head, so great it paralysed all movement to the body. She just sat there. The pain was terrific—it started in her eyes then moved to the top of her head. For a full three minutes she sat there in pain, which disappeared as quickly as it had come. Her first thought was she had a stroke.

She wiped away the sweat from her forehead, reached up and pulled down the sun visor, checking her face in the mirror. A little face powder and a touch of lipstick brought back the colour to her face. She sat there wondering what was wrong. A few more minutes passed and she felt fine, thinking she must go and have a check up.

The car's engine was still running. She engaged first gear and drove off.

She arrived home just after 7 o'clock that evening, tired but pleased with her day. She had spent two hours shopping, mostly for clothes for Julie and herself. She had a ploughman's lunch at the Jolly Farmer in the centre of Guildford, on the south bank of the river Wey. It always amazed Carol how this particular part of Guildford reminded her of a picture postcard scene. She sat on the pub's veranda overlooking the river. The river was a picture, but the green Surrey backdrop made it impossible to believe that a hundred yards behind her was Guildford's busy shopping centre.

On the way home she felt lonely. She needed to talk to somebody. Though she tried to get it into her mind that Albert had released her, she knew she couldn't get on with her life just like that. She had lived with the man half her life—she couldn't simply cut him out.

She spent the rest of the sunny afternoon walking the grounds of Brookwoods Gardens of Remembrance. After telling Albert off for leaving her she sat on one of the garden benches and had a good cry. She was then able to sit down and tell him all her troubles, all the fears she had for the future. After that she left the Gardens feeling much better. The peace and tranquillity in the gardens gave her peace of mind. She now knew it was a place to come for comfort and reassurance, perhaps guidance.

The excitement of shopping had worn off by the time she had got indoors. She placed the shopping bags in Julie's room. She would wait for Julie's next visit—then they would unpack together. It would be like Christmas.

The gin and tonic she poured herself tasted good. She made herself comfortable in her armchair and used the remote control to switch the television on. The music from Coronation Street was playing—she was just in time for the beginning. By the time the program was over she was fast asleep.

The chimes from the family clock woke her at midnight. She couldn't be bothered with a shower so undressed and went straight to bed.

The next morning she was awake at seven. After a strong cup of tea she dusted and hoovered. She even did the small amount of ironing that had accumulated over the weekend. After the warm refreshing shower she dressed in yellow shorts and a cream polo shirt, having decided to spend the day in the garden and make the most of the lovely weather. The thinly spread marmite on two pieces of toast and a cup of instant coffee went down a treat. She sat on the small patio and looked in admiration at the small cottage garden with all its flowers in bloom. The array of colour would please any gardener. Albert would have been pleased.

The sharp ring of the doorbell interrupted her thoughts. As she walked through the hallway to the front door the lounge clock chimed once—10:30. She wasn't expecting anybody.

She opened the door, making sure the safety chain was in place, and peered through the three-inch gap. A young lady in her late twenties or early thirties stood looking at Carol through the gap. Before Carol had a chance to ask the young lady any questions, she spoke in a quiet but authoritative voice: "Mrs Lyons?"

"Yes, what can I do for you?" Carol said with suspicion.

"Mrs Lyons, I'm Sergeant Helen Thomas—I work for the foreign office." She held out a wallet that revealed an identity card. The name and the young lady's photograph were clear to see. Written across the top of the card were the words *Warrant Card*. Carol couldn't think why this young lady wanted to speak to her.

"What can I do for you?" Carol said, puzzled.

Sergeant Thomas looked uncomfortable. "I have some…some distressing news for you. May I come in?"

Carol undid the chain and opened the door, thinking what could be more distressing then Albert dying. She indicated to Helen to enter, and then closed the door. "Come through to the patio—it will be more pleasant. I'm just having coffee—would you like a cup?" She guided Helen through the hall to the back patio.

"Coffee would be nice—white, no sugar; thank you." Helen selected a chair and sat down. She realised from the moment the door had opened this lady hadn't a clue what was going on. It was going to be more difficult then she expected.

Carol collected her dirty cup and plate, then made her way back to the kitchen. Five minutes later she returned with a pot of coffee and a plate of tea biscuits. She placed the tray on the table, poured the coffee and added the milk. "Help yourself to biscuits."

She sat down and looked at Helen. The young lady was about the same height as herself, her short blonde hair making her chubby round face boy-like. She lacked makeup, though her natural red cheeks glowed. She wore a grey trouser suit with a dark red shirt. Carol liked the combination that suited the slightly overweight young lady.

"Well Miss…" Carol realised she had forgotten the young lady's name. "Sorry, I've forgotten your name."

"That's okay—Helen, Helen Thomas."

"Well, Miss Thomas, what can I do for you?"

"Mrs Lyons—have you been updated with the news since yesterday morning?"

Carol thought for a couple of seconds. "Come to think of it I haven't seen or heard the news since Sunday evening."

Helen placed her half-empty cup in the saucer. "Do you know where your daughter is at the moment, Mrs Lyons?"

"Yes—she's in Gibraltar on holiday."

Helen leaned foreword and took hold of Carol's hand.

"There's no easy way of telling you bad news. I'm afraid to inform you that between nine and nine-thirty yesterday morning your daughter was involved in a fatal accident on the Rock of Gibraltar."

Two lights came on in the cabin indicating passengers were to fasten their safety belts and extinguish their cigarettes. Carol looked at Helen and gave a nervous smile.

Carol knew it must be a case of misidentification. Daughters do *not* die before their mothers. The authorities had it all wrong. The quicker she got there, the quicker she could clear this mess up.

When she saw Julie and told her about this dreadful identification mistake, they would all sit down and have a good laugh.

She was so glad the plane was on time.

Helen had helped Carol pack, then had escorted her to Heathrow Airport where the Foreign office had reserved two seats on the afternoon flight to Gibraltar. Helen had collected the tickets from the Airline desk and within minutes they had boarded the Boeing 737. Ten minutes later the aircraft was climbing to thirty thousand feet. Two hours later it started its descent.

Once the plane came to a halt Brigadier Baxter's staff car drove to the waiting gangway. Major David Oakley greeted the two ladies and escorted them to the Military hospital.

Major Kenneth Kyle sat at his desk. He wasn't looking forward to the meeting with Mrs Lyons, the mother of the pretty lady lying in the mortuary.

There was a knock on his door. He tried to call out for them to come in, but his mouth had dried and nothing came out. Before he had a chance to do anything the door opened and Major Oakley Smith stood to one side "Please, this way, ladies," he said as if he were an usher at a church wedding. "This is Major Kyle, the doctor in charge of proceedings at the hospital."

He stood at the door while both ladies entered the room and shook hands with the doctor. "I'll leave you in the capable hands of Major Kyle. If there's anything I can assist you with, do not hesitate to call me. Bye for now." He walked from the room and closed the door.

"Please be seated." Two chairs were placed in front of his desk. Each Lady selected a chair and sat down. Major Kyle returned to his seat behind the desk.

Before he had a chance to say anything Carol spoke. "Could we get this over with as soon as possible? Because it's obviously a big mistake."

Helen took Carol's hand. "Major Kyle, my name is Sergeant Thomas. I'm with the foreign office. I've been with Mrs Lyons all day. She's convinced the lady you have is not her daughter."

Major Kyle removed his reading glasses. He looked at Carol, the sadness on his face hard to hide.

"Mrs Lyons, I'm afraid there's very little doubt the young lady in the mortuary is your daughter. We just need you to formally identify her."

Carol's scream filled the room followed by her shouts of "*No, no, no!*"

An hour later Carol had composed herself enough to look at her daughter. She did not have a chance to say yes it was she. Her legs turned to jelly and she passed out. The doctor had her sedated, then admitted her to a private room on the first floor.

The next day Carol made a full recovery physically. It would be the mental scars she'd never get rid of—scars that would stay with her for the rest of her life.

She felt well enough to ask Major Kyle for the events that led to Julie's death. He could only tell her the details of the shootings in the square. The SAS covert operation that preceded the shooting was only known to MI5. He did not have all the details.

He also omitted to tell her about the blood tests that had been carried out.

Carol was wearing her dressing gown, sitting up in bed, the white pillows supporting her back against the headboard. She heard every word the doctor told her. Not once did she look at him, staring out to sea through the large bay windows. Helen was sitting next to the bed holding Carol's left hand.

When the Major finished there were several minutes of dreadful silence. Carol looked away from the window, then at Major Kyle. She was the first to speak. "Is it possible to meet my daughter's work colleague and thank him for trying to save my daughters life?" Major Kyle was pleased with her response.

"I had to stabilise him before I could operate. I removed the bullet from his skull last night. At this moment in time he's still in intensive care. I've no idea when he will regain consciousness, if he ever does."

Carol needed to see the man who had been so brave. She wanted to thank him, whether he could hear her or not. "Is it possible to see him?"

"I'll ring through and get you a wheelchair," he said, reaching for the telephone beside the bed.

Carol pulled her hand away from Helen and swung her legs to the side of the bed. "I'd sooner walk, if it's all the same with you."

Major Kyle encouraged her with a smile. "It will do you good." He took both her hands and helped her to her feet. Helen moved from the side of the bed and helped Carol with her slippers.

A few moments later, with the help from Helen and the Major, Carol entered the intensive care unit. There were several rooms, each with a large observation window. She looked through the window of the first room they came to.

The whole room was visible. A man lay on the bed, his head bandaged, a tube coming from his mouth. Two wires plastered to his chest led to a monitor at the side of the bed. The bleep of the monitor was loud and constant. Carol could hear it from were she stood.

The Major entered the room and she followed, Helen remaining outside. She moved close to the bed and looked down at the man. Her heart lurched.

The young boy she once knew had grown into a man. She was looking at the unmistakable face of Terry Gibbons, Julie's father.

Her legs turned to jelly as she passed out.

CHAPTER 33

Diane

Diane closed the *Daily Mail* newspaper and placed it on the seat next to her. She turned and looked out the window. The Hampshire countryside with its many shades of green reminded her of New Zealand.

The Bournemouth express train had left Waterloo on time and was scheduled to arrive at Southampton in thirty-five minutes' time. The eighty-five miles-an-hour the express train was travelling seemed to hypnotise her.

Her mind drifted back over the events that had happened in the last two weeks.

It had been sixteen days since the tragic death of her brother David. The news had stunned the whole family and everybody was still in the state of shock. Her mother Ruth had obviously taken it the hardest. She was still sedated and being looked after by Kate and Tina. Both worked shift work that enabled them to share the work-load. The Hospital had advised Ruth not to travel to the funeral.

Kate and Tina had decided they were unable to deal with the stress of the funeral. They shut their minds off to reality. As far as they were concerned, their brother David was still on his ship sailing the high seas. It was their way of dealing with his death.

David's grandparents were staying with Brenda, helping Brenda to cope with the last few weeks of her second pregnancy. The news of David's death shook Brenda so much she went into labour and within the hour had given birth to a baby girl, four weeks premature.

Keith and Rita became the backbone of the family. Though they loved David like a son their wise old heads seemed to click into action; their comfort and organisation kept the family from running around like headless chickens.

Keith had stepped in and communicated with Barbara. This kept the family updated with news in England. Rita stepped in and became housekeeper and nanny.

At the family meeting, Keith suggested that Diane should be the sole representative of the family at the funeral.

Keith was pleased that Barbara had offered David's ashes to the family. Diane would bring the ashes home with her to New Zealand and to the family plot after the funeral service.

Diane stood and stretched her legs. She was glad the twelve-seater carriage was empty. Her poise and figure made her dark blue leisure suit look more like a suit one would wear to a wedding.

She sat down again and crossed her legs, then opened her white handbag. Tears came to her eyes.

She removed three identical envelopes, all addressed to her. Two were handwritten, the other typed. She had received the letters six days previously. She had read them repeatedly, each time with tears in her eyes. She selected an envelope, removed the foolscap page and read the letter again.

Kevin Bonnie
Hereford

5th June 1985

My Darling Diana

This letter is difficult to write owing to the circumstances. When you receive this letter you will know the worst has happened to me.

You knew I was an orphan, but I never told you what I did for a living. Until I met you the army had been my life.

When I left the orphanage it just seemed natural to join the Army. For the last three years I have served with a special unit mostly on covert duty. I never expected to find life outside of the Army, until I met you.

From the first moment we met I fell madly in love with you. Beyond my wildest dreams, you responded to me. The thoughts of you and our lovemaking are never out of my mind.

I know it's too late now, but I had plans to resign from the unit, then buy myself out of the Army. Then I was going to ask you to marry me, and if you had said yes I would have joined you in New Zealand. All I can do now is help you the best way I can. I have informed the Adjutant we were engaged and you are my sole benefactor.

Diane My Love, just remember—I love you so very much.

Since you returned to New Zealand there has not been a single moment when you have not been in my thoughts. If it is in my power, you will have me as a guardian angle for the rest of your life.

Diane I am so sorry for the way things have turned out.

Please forgive me.

I LOVE YOU SO VERY MUCH

Kevin
xxxxxxxxx

Diane reached into her handbag for a tissue and wiped away the tears from her cheeks. She replaced the letter into its envelope. The second letter, also handwritten, was from Major Evans, the Adjutant to Kevin's regiment. She didn't bother to read the brief but informal letter.

It had stated, simply, that Kevin had died on duty while serving the Queen and country, and that the regiment would make the funeral arrangements, and that the regiment's solicitor would be writing to her regarding Kevin's will.

The third letter was from the solicitors.

Foster, Bush and Foster
SOLICITORS
12-14 High Street,
Hereford.

Dear Miss Maddock,

My associates and I are acting on behalf of the deceased, Sergeant Kevin Bonnie.

His last Will and testament has made you the sole beneficiary of his estate.

As you were not actually married to Sergeant Bonnie, you would not be entitled to an army pension. The Army have informed me to offer you a compensation payment of twenty five thousand pounds. (I do recommend accepting this generous offer; if you take it further you could end up with nothing.)

I have enclosed a statement. We would like to hear from you or your solicitor as soon as possible.

We would like to take this opportunity to send you our condolences and wish you well for the future.

Yours faithfully

Andy Foster

Statement:—Personnel bank account	£32,231,27pence
Insurance policy	£20,000,
Army compensation	£25,000,00
Total	£77,231,27pence

Diane couldn't believe what had happened. Her brother's death followed my Kevin's death—all within seven days of each over. She hadn't had time to take it all in.

She hadn't realised the secrecy that surrounded Kevin's death had caused the government to step in and make the compensation offer. The whole affair had been a big embarrassment to the government. The quicker the whole incident was swept under the diplomatic carpet the better.

Unknown to her, the foreign office and MI6 did not want any awkward questions or legal battles concerning the army compensation. As far as they were concerned the incident on the Rock of Gibraltar did not happen. Diane didn't realise they would have gone as high as fifty thousand pounds had she started to make waves and ask questions.

Because of the sparse information she had concerning Kevin's death, she still didn't connect the two deaths. It would be some time and before she found out that David and Kevin died in the same place by the same gun.

The train arrived at Southampton two minutes late. She managed to pull her suitcase free from the carriage without difficulties and stood on the platform and waited.

"Diane." The unmistakable voice of Barbara made her turn her head. Barbara stood a few yards away.

Diane caught her breath. Barbara looked terrible and her high cheekbones had disappeared. Her skin was pale and lifeless and she had tied her blonde hair into a bun that made her look a lot older. Blue denim jeans and a sloppy tee-shirt didn't do a lot for her either. As Barbara came closer Diane realised the cheekbones were still there but hidden behind a pale and gaunt face. Both ladies placed their arms around each other and cried.

Other then the normal greetings, no words were spoken. Diane placed her case onto the baggage trolley Barbara had ready.

They walked in silence to the car park. Between them they placed the case into the boot. Barbara got to the driver's side, leaned across the seats and released the doorknob. Diane opened the door and slid into the passenger seat. Barbara put the key into the ignition but before turning the key she turned to face Diane.

"Do you know I was there—I was there when it happened? If I had not gone into the chemist shop I would have died with him. Why him? Why not me? Why not both of us?"

Her hands were holding the steering wheel and she placed her head between them and cried. Diane put her right arm around Barbara. "I didn't know you were there. It must have been terrible."

Before she had a chance to ask any questions Barbara pulled away, brushed away the tears and held back her sobbing. "I was only in the shop a couple of minutes. I came out and David was nowhere! I heard the noise from a firework, you know—like a cracker." She paused and Diane nodded her head. "There was a passageway that led to the square and I followed the noise. David was just standing there! The crackers started again and his white shirt became red and wet. He fell to the ground! I ran to him, cradled his head but he was already dead. Diane, it was my fault!" The tears began to stream down her face. "Please forgive me, it was my fault! If I had not gone into the chemist shop he would still be alive."

Diane looked into Barbara's eyes. "Listen to me, it wasn't your fault! You mustn't blame yourself. It was fate. You were both in the wrong place at the wrong time."

CHAPTER 34

Gibraltar

Brigadier Robin Baxter sat at his desk pleased with the fact that MI6 and the foreign office had taken over the investigations and the cover up regarding the shootings that happened fourteen days earlier.

He only had six months to go before retiring and he did not want any blots on his good army record. He had his pension to consider. Being the arrogant man he was it was more important to him that his reputation was kept intact.

He had always regretted he had missed a good war. He had dreamed of being a hero, leaving the army with all the glory and praise like that which surrounded the man he worshipped and tried to emulate in his own life—the second war hero Field Marshall Montgomery.

His thoughts were interrupted by a knock at the door. "Come in!" The door opened to admit Major Kenneth Kyle. The Brigadier closed the pages of *The Times* and placed it in the top drawer of his desk.

"Well doctor, please sit down. You wanted to see me?"

Major Kyle sensed the good mood the Brigadier was in and relaxed. "Yes sir, I have the result back from London regarding the blood test."

The brigadier squinted at the doctor, trying to recollect which results. With the media to deal with and the government in a panic, he had no time to think about anything. He'd forgotten the doctor had connected four of the deaths with the one survivor.

The doctor sat on the chair facing the desk and opened a green file. He extracted a sheet of foolscap paper. "It's been confirmed that Terry Gibbons, the man in intensive care, fathered four of the people who died. First, there was his companion, Julie Lyons. Now this in itself is very strange—for they were travelling together, sharing an apartment, yet when I questioned the MI6 investigating officer he told me her birth certificate showed her father as a Mr Albert Lyons. Then Mrs Lyons came to the Rock to identify her daughter. When she recovered from the shock she wanted to thank Mr Gibbons for trying to save her daughter's life. She took one look at him and fainted. When I questioned her she told me she had never seen him before—but she was clearly lying."

The doctor placed the foolscap paper on the desk. He returned to the folder and took a sheet of paper out.

"The next person was Sergeant Kevin Bonnie from the SAS unit. He was an orphan brought up in an orphanage just outside of Newcastle and spent all his working life in the army."

Again the doctor placed the paper on the desk. Again he went to the folder; this time taking two foolscap pages out and holding one in each hand. He read from the left-hand paper. "David Maddock, a New Zealander from New Plymouth, a radio officer with the British Merchant Navy." With a slight move of his head to the right he read from the paper in his right hand. "Now we have the last but not least—Mr Raul Menzes, an Argentine national travelling on an English Passport under the name of Raymond Miller. Beside that, he had an Irish passport and his own national passport. It seems he was a pilot during the Falklands war and a good one at that. What he was doing with the IRA no one knows. His Machine pistol killed the sergeant and the two civilians and wounded our man in intensive care." The doctor put both papers on to the desk, sat back in the chair and waited for the Brigadier's response.

The Brigadier picked up the four sheets of paper and went through them one by one. He looked up at the doctor. "Does MI6 or the Foreign office know about your findings?"

"No, just yourself, Major Oakley-Smith, and me, of course. Even the lab in London had no names—just the blood samples."

The Brigadier handed the papers back to the Doctor. "Is there any sign of Mr Gibbons coming round?"

The Doctor crossed his legs. "There has been a great improvement over the last few days. We'll just have to wait."

The Brigadier stood up and made his way towards a cocktail cabinet situated a few yards from his desk. He took hold of a Chivers Regal bottle of whisky. "Would you like a drink, doctor?" he said without turning around.

"No thank you," came the reply.

He poured two inches of whisky into a crystal tumbler and returned to his seat. "What do you think we should do with this information, doctor?" he asked, sipping his drink as if it were a hot cup of tea.

"I honestly don't know—I only stumbled onto it by chance," the doctor said, looking wistfully at the whisky glass and wishing he had said yes.

Again, the Brigadier thought of his retirement. He could not see how this complex issue could increase his credibility with the army or government. In fact it could have the opposite effect if the media got hold of it.

"Kenneth, I think we should keep this information to ourselves. It will only bring heartache to the relatives and God knows how our friend Mr Gibbons will react. I cannot see the point of telling him the news that he was the father of four—but sorry, they're all dead!"

The doctor was pleased the Brigadier had taken this line. He felt the same. It would only cause heartache for everyone concerned. "So I'll destroy the paperwork and say nothing? Will you inform Major

Oakley-Smith?" The doctor got to his feet, replacing the papers into the folder.

The Brigadier smiled. "Leave the Adjutant to me. Don't worry—we're doing the right thing."

Major Kenneth Kyle left the Brigadier's office relieved, not worried. If it had gone further he, for one, did not want to be the one to tell Terry Gibbons.

He returned to his own office and placed the folder into his briefcase. He would destroy it later.

The intercom buzzed. Within minutes he was in the operating theatre saving a young soldier's life.

The young soldier had been badly hurt in a motorcycle accident. The four-hour emergency operation cleared the doctor's mind of unwanted files.

The file was destined to remain in his briefcase undetected for some time.

CHAPTER 35

Maria

Maria sat on her terrace looking out over the green fields that lay before her. The winter sun was warm but the wind coming up from the south was cold. The last few days had been bad. The rain and sleet had kept her in the house with the log fire blazing.

It amazed Maria how anybody from the Northern Hemisphere, especially Europe, assumed that Argentine was hot and sunny all year round. The winter months did not seem to last long, but June and July were cold, especially in the south. She looked at the thermometer—50 degrees, slightly above average for June.

Her mind drifted back over the years. She did not remember much as a child, not until her foster parents took her in and gave her a home and their brand of love, yet not the love she craved. Mr and Mrs Weiss were strict but fair, but unfortunately unable to show the tender caring love a child needed—though they must have loved her in some way to have left her the farm.

However, it was Lomas, and his brother Pepe, who had helped her with her ideas that had made the farm the success it was.

Her brains and Lomas' knowledge of horses had made them rich.

Though the last few years had not been kind to Maria, the war with the British had brought about Diago's death. And Raul had become a social misfit, relying on drink to get him through each day.

A white Opal motorcar pulled into the dirt track that led to the house. It was her good friend Antonio Rossi.

The car stopped a few feet from the terrace. Inspector Rossi climbed out of the back seat and made his way up the four steps that led to the terrace. He took Maria's hands and kissed her on both cheeks.

"Antonio, what are you doing here? Your retirement party is not till Saturday." She patted the seat next to her—one of the four wicker chairs around a large matching table. "I was just wondering what I should wear on such an occasion."

He looked at her and smiled. "I'm sure you would look the bell of the ball in whatever you wear."

Her eyebrows rose in surprise. She had known him twenty-seven years and that was the first time he had given her a compliment. She had always respected him; he had a wife and three daughters and lived in the capital Buenos Aries, and occasionally she would invite the family for the weekend. Apart from Lomas' and Pepe's families, she didn't trust anyone. Rossi and his family were the only true friends she had.

Rossi was six feet tall with distinguished grey hair, while his wife Avion was only five feet tall. As a young couple they had looked comical together. Now they had gained so much weight between them Maria felt embarrassed for them.

"Would you like coffee and brandy?" she said, picking up the table bell and ringing for the housemaid.

"I should not really—I've got to think of my blood pressure," he replied, then sighed. "Well, owing to the circumstances, I think I'd better—so yes."

A young girl appeared from nowhere. She was about seventeen dressed in a white overall.

"Ah, there you are, Carmel—could we have a pot of coffee and the brandy decanter please."

"Yes, of course."

Rossi looked at the young girl as if she were on his wanted list. "She sounds common," he said, watching the young girl go through the door to the Kitchen.

"I'm still training her." Her brow furrowed. "What circumstances, Antonio?"

He took a deep breath. "Would you mind if I smoke?" He pulled out a small box of cigars from his jacket pocket.

"Of course not—you know I like the smell of cigars." She felt irritated. Why was he prevaricating about the bad news he clearly had to impart? "What circumstances, Antonio?"

Carmel returned with a tray. The tray held a brandy decanter, a silver pot containing coffee, two small cups and saucers and two-brandy glasses. Maria was surprised the girl had brought the right glasses.

"Thank you, Carmel—you can go," she said, taking hold of the coffeepot and pouring two cups of thick black coffee. She reached for the Waterford Crystal decanter and poured two large brandies. "Are you going to tell me what's wrong?" she asked again, staring straight into Rossi's eyes.

"Its Raul, I'm afraid—he's dead." When she showed no reaction he continued. "He was killed yesterday—on the Rock of Gibraltar. It's a place just at the southern tip of Spain."

"I know where it his," she said with great calm and dignity. "What was he doing there?"

Rossi placed his cup and saucer on the table. "We don't know a lot, but it seems he was involved with a terrorist group called the IRA. A special unit from the British army killed him. I'm afraid that's all we know at the moment."

Maria displayed no emotion. She just sat there looking at the panoramic view of the open plains of the Pampas.

For several minutes she sat in silence, both hands cradling the brandy balloon glass. When she stood up she walked towards the balustrades that surrounded the terrace. She was wearing black tight-fitting ski pants and a thick fluffy white jumper. Her hair was platted and held together with a black ribbon. She leaned against the balustrades and took a sip of brandy. She felt the warmth of the liquid as it went down.

Rossi looked at her. She still had the figure that any woman half her age would have loved. He thought she was even more attractive now than when he first met her all those years ago.

He never dared tell her how much he loved her. He knew if he told her he would lose her friendship.

She looked up from her glass, then into Rossi's eyes. "I've never told you about my sons' father, have I?"

He felt uneasy. There had been many stories that had circulated the upper circles of the Buenos Aries high society.

"No, I just assumed he was a fisherman who fell overboard in the South Atlantic seas without a trace." He took out another cigar. The book of matches was down to its last one. Very carefully he shielded the flame and began to puff. Maria walked back to the chair and sat down.

"That was the story I told everybody. The truth is, their father was a British merchant seaman. Before you condemn me, I was madly in love with him. I thought he would take me back with him. I had nothing here." Antonio tried to hide his shock and disgust. Maria sensed his feelings. "I was young and venerable," she said, trying to make light of the matter.

"Anyway, the boys turned out to be gentlemen, didn't they? Even though some of my so-called friends called them bastards behind my back."

Rossi's face reddened. He had heard the stories that had called Maria a whore and her twins bastards. He had always been too frightened of the Argentine regime to speak up for her. People in high places had it in for her.

The military government they had at the time was corrupt and evil and Rossi knew if anyone spoke out of turn that person would be in danger of being arrested, never to be seen again.

Maria ignored his blushes. She knew what he was thinking,

"My two sons where fathered by a British man and both where killed by the British. Tell me, Antonio, do you think that was fate—or was it their destiny?"

CHAPTER 36

Terry

Terry stood naked looking down on the large double bed. Mrs Loveday lay naked on the black silk sheets. He couldn't take his eyes off her magnificent bronzed body. Her full breasts pointed proudly to the ceiling, her slender waist and rounded, tapering thighs in perfect proportion with the rest of her body. Then there were her shapely long legs that reached to the foot of the bed.

Terry looked at her face, her blonde hair flowing over the black silk pillowcase. Her blue eyes blended with the beauty of her mature face. The sparkle that came from them was an invitation to Terry to come to bed.

He lay down next to her, his lips becoming a magnet to her lips, his tongue penetrated her mouth.

His mind and body, no longer his own, were possessed by her beauty. He moved his lips down to her neck; the heady aroma of her perfume and body excited him. His lips moved further down her body, finally stopping at her left breast. He cupped its liquid fulness with both hands, his mouth gently taking hold of her nipple that peeped through his cupped hands. He sucked at it as if he were a baby and felt it grow hard under his tongue that nibbled and flickered unmercifully. Her heavy breathing changed to whimpers of excitement.

After several minutes he moved to the right breast and applied the same exquisite treatment.

His own erection surprised him—he had never known it as rampant or as stiff as it was at that moment. He felt twenty years younger.

His mouth made its way down her body, his tongue acting like a piston shooting in and out of his mouth, exploring every part of her velvet skin.

The bright morning sun suffused the room, illuminating the silky texture of her pubic hairs as his tongue moved closer to her crotch. She relaxed and opened her legs, the excitement swelling within him as he moved closer to her damp vagina.

The sudden blow to his head stunned him. Three more blows followed and the searing pain was unbearable. He turned his head. Maria was standing next to the bed brandishing a golf club that came down once more with a thud of pain. As she raised the club blood ran down the shaft onto her hands.

"No more!" he cried out. "Don't hit me again!" He raised his arms in an attempt to shield his head from the barrage.

She stopped and looked down at him with contempt and hate. She spat the word out: "Bastard!"

Then suddenly there was another blow to the back of the head, then another and another. He turned to look. At the other side of the bed stood Ruth with a cricket bat in her hands. The blood on the pillow gleamed crimson in the sunlight. She brought the cricket bat down in another blow.

Terry cried out again: "Stop! I've had enough—stop please!" But Maria joined Ruth and started raining blows on him again.

All the same time Carol appeared and grabbed his penis in a desperate bid to yank it off.

Mrs Loveday sat up on the bed, her legs open, pointing and laughing at Terry's penis. It had come off! Carol had it in her left hand and looked down at him. With a laugh she said, "*That* we'll teach you to mess with us girls!"

Terry didn't know what was worse—having no penis or the pain in the back of his head. "Help me—please help me!" he cried out. "Somebody help me!"

"Terry—Terry!" a voice called. "It's all right! You've been having a bad dream. Calm down—it's just a dream."

Terry opened his eyes. The ceiling fan was turning slowly. The white ceiling seemed miles above him.

He became aware of a hand mopping away the sweat from his forehead. His eyes followed the arm that led to the shoulder, then to the face. A plump woman with red cheeks and a nurse's uniform looked down at him and smiled. "It's all right. You were just having a bad dream."

Terry realised he was in a hospital. He couldn't think where and why. "What am I doing here?" he said, grimacing with pain. "The…the pain in the back of my head…it's killing me."

"It nearly did," the nurse said, mopping his forehead again.

Terry looked at her with surprise.

"Don't move…I'll get you the doctor. You've been a very sick man, Terry. You've been unconscious for some time."

Terry stared at her. "How long?"

"Nineteen days." She straightened the sheets and the tucked them under the mattress. "I'll get the doctor." She left the room without saying another word.

Terry tried to gather his thoughts.

The dream he had just had didn't make sense. The four women had not been a part of his life for at least twenty years. What did it all mean?

It was hard for him to imagine being unconscious for nearly three weeks. He tried to remember what happened to bring him there.

The only thing that came to mind was having dinner in a small restaurant. He tried to think with whom. Then there was the face of a young man at the next table. It seemed to be important, but why…?

Julie! He had been with Julie—what had happened to her?

Scattered memories came to him—the scream of brakes from a motor vehicle—then guns firing. What did it mean? What happened?

Oh, the pain in the back of the head! So many things started to rush through his brain. His memory was returning. The memory was returning so quickly his brain had gone into overdrive.

A man appeared in the large window that faced the bottom of his bed. It was like a large cinema screen—but he was the star.

The man wore a white overall and a stethoscope around his neck. Terry hoped he was his doctor. He wanted someone or something to stop the pain. The man moved to the right and opened the door and entered the room. The nurse followed a few seconds later.

"Well, well, well, Mr Gibbons—you've finally decided to join us." The doctor approached the bed. He held Terry's wrist checking his pulse. "You had us worried. We thought we were going to lose you at one point." The doctor took the medical chart from the nurse. Who had taken it from its position at the bottom of the bed?

"My name his Doctor Kyle," the doctor went on. "I'm a Major with the Royal Army Medical Corp. You're in the Military wing of the Gibraltar hospital." He put a thermometer into Terry's mouth. "This is Sister Miller, also with the Royal Army Medical Corp. She tells me you woke up from a bad dream."

"You could say that," Terry mumbled through the side of his mouth, thinking about his penis in Carol's hand.

After a full examination the doctor prescribed painkillers for the head wound.

"Well, Mr Gibbons, I think you're well on the way to recovery. You've been a very lucky man. The bullet that entered your head just missed the brain. It was so close to the brain I was worried about brain damage. It seems you've recovered well. How is your memory?"

"Fine...I think. It took several minutes to focus in on the past, but it's there. The trouble is I'm having a problem with the day of the shooting—and the day before. Everything comes in flashes. How is my friend Julie taking all this?"

The doctor and nurse looked at each over. Terry had been unconscious for nineteen days. Everybody assumed he knew she had been killed.

The news was a complete surprise and shock to Terry. The doctor prescribed a sedative and within twenty minutes he was back in deep sleep.

Ten days later Terry sat in the garden of the hospital. Doctor Kyle had just given him a clean bill of health, but advised him to stay another week to convalesce. Terry surprised himself by agreeing. But he couldn't face his friends or colleague at that moment. He looked out to sea. The Straight of Gibraltar looked a picture in the midday sun. He couldn't help thinking of Julie. Guilt ate away at him. If he hadn't asked her to accompany him to Gibraltar she would still be alive.

He knew one day he would have to face up to his responsibility and meet Julie's mother to apologise. He wondered what she was like.

He stood up and started to walk back to his private room. Not once did he think about who was paying for all the special treatment.

It would be a year before he found out the truth.

He lay on the bed and thought about his life. Forty-eight years of age, unmarried and no children.

What would his life have been like if he had been a father?

He laughed aloud. "I'm not cut out to have children. That's not my fate, or my destiny."

Epilogue

From the first day each one of us is born, no one of us knows what life will bring.

Could it be fate that guides us through life? Or perhaps our lives are planned from that first moment—in which case our lives are shaped by destiny. Or is life a matter of luck that takes us from day to day? Some people believe life is what you make it.

In the next book Terry will find out and may be able to answer the question: "Is life luck—or is life what you make it?"

About the Author

The Author Tony Filler (pen name A.J Bushy) was born in 1945. He left school at fourteen and joined the Merchant Navy. After fifteen years he became a publican in the West End of London. Several years later he sought the quiet life of Hampshire and a country pub. In 1990, shortly after the Lockerbie tragedy, he joined BAA security at Heathrow.

In 2000, shortly after his wife died of cancer, he took early retirement and moved to Spain where he started and finished his first book.

0-595-24653-2

Printed in the United Kingdom
by Lightning Source UK Ltd.
93163